GRIT

G

R

GILLIAN FRENCH

I

HARPER TEEN
An Imprint of HarperCollins*Publishers*

T

HarperTeen is an imprint of HarperCollins Publishers.

Grit

ISBN 978-0-06-264255-4

Typography by Erin Fitzsimmons
17 18 19 20 21   PC/LSCH   10 9 8 7 6 5 4 3 2 1
❖
First Edition

For Darren, who never gave up on the dream

O N E

I SWORE I wouldn't come back here this summer, not to Mrs. Wardwell's foghorn voice and blisters the size of nickels. But when I went down to Gaudreau's Take-Out on the last day of school and asked for an application, you know what Mr. Gaudreau said? "Sorry, honey pie, this is a family business." Honey pie? Hell, I could sling Rocky Road faster than his girls, and I'd always offer jimmies. They're wicked tight with jimmies at Gaudreau's.

Anyway, it's Friday, July 28, opening day of wild blueberry season all across eastern Maine, and my sister Mags and I are back in the barrens for the harvest. The sun looks swollen and hazy, but I'll be all right as long as I've got my straw cowgirl hat and my SPF 50.

I'm raking circles around Mags. I've filled thirty-two boxes of berries and we've only been at it since seven a.m. I meet her eyes and grin. She scratches her cheek with her middle finger, slow. Pretending I want a drink of water from our gallon jug, I walk by and goose her, making her gasp, "Darcy Prentiss! God!"

Our cousin Nell is raking way over by the stone wall, but she knows what happened and her giggles echo across the fields. Soon Nell will start singing, which she does day in, day out, all season long, driving most of us crazy by quitting time. Still, Nell's special, so when she bursts into "Go Tell It on the Mountain," nobody tells her to shut up.

Raking goes like this: you bend at the knees and sweep a two-handled rake across the low bushes, filling the tines with berries. When your rake's full, you dump it into a big plastic box stamped *E. F. Danforth & Son*. When the box is full, you open another one.

I don't notice Nell racing across the rocky field toward me until she's by my side, breathless. "He's here. That Jesse Bouchard." As we watch the pickup rumbling up the dirt road, she adds, "He's late." Even though she's eighteen, in a lot of ways, Nell's like a kid; I guess you could call her a little slow. As my aunt Libby likes to say to Mom, "At least I don't got to worry about what *my* girl's been up to." Then she looks straight at me.

Jesse Bouchard parks his truck, and he and his buddies take their sweet time climbing out. Mr. Bob Wardwell, who's field boss, goes over to bawl Jesse out, but before you know it, they're laughing and shooting the shit like old buddies. Jesse's gaze finds me and I look away, putting a hand to my hat even though there's no wind today.

"Let's move before he tries talking to us." Nell tugs my arm.

I shake her off. "Get back in your row or I'll tell your mom you were slacking."

Jesse makes his way over, wearing worn-out jeans and a white T-shirt, putting me in mind of that old picture of Bruce Springsteen on the cover of Mom's vintage vinyl album. You know, with those dark curls and that sexy stare? All he says to me now is, "Nice to see ya," while giving me the slow once-over, reminding me of all the places where my tank top is clinging with sweat.

His buddy Mason Howe follows—a big, blond, slow-moving guy who always seems to have his hands in his pockets—and behind him is the one person I was hoping to dodge for the rest of the summer. Shea Gaines flicks the brim of his ball cap, one corner of his mouth quirking up like somebody just told a dirty joke and the punch line was me. "Look who's here," is all he says.

His anger shifts under that sure-footed cocky act of his, and I breathe out, holding his gaze as he passes on by. Mags and Nell move in on my left and right until we form a wall. Mags wipes her sweaty brow and says, "What's up his butt?"

I shrug. "Tell you later."

I fill ten more boxes before Mr. Wardwell blasts his truck horn three times, signaling all one hundred and fifty or so of us rakers to come up to headquarters (where the Porta-Johns are) for an earful. Mags and Nell and I sit in the grass together, scarfing down our lunches, chugging water, and baking in the noonday heat as we get ready for Mrs. Evelyn Wardwell's Jackassing-Around speech.

She squats in her camping chair, a two-liter of diet soda at her feet, eyeballing us. She's huge, 275 easy, and the sleeveless flowered shirt she wears looks like it could cover a love seat and leave a few yards to spare. Her husband kind of fades into the background as she heaves herself up and stands with her head thrust forward, fists on hips.

"Listen up. We got a lotta berries out there this year." It's true; it was a rainy spring and now the barrens are green and fit to burst. "Next two weeks, I wanna see asses and elbows, everybody showing up on time"—her gaze finds Jesse, Shea, and Mason—"nobody cutting out early. No jackassing around. We don't pay you to jackass around. I catch you at it, you're outta here. I know plenty of folks who want to make some money. And don't come to me saying so-and-so is paying more in their fields than we do. You get two-fifty a box here and that's it."

I sneak a look at Jesse. He sits with his forearms resting on his bent knees, and my gaze follows the line of his muscles all the way down to his wrists. You get ripped like that from tossing bales into a hay truck and thrashing down weeds to clear pasture, which he's been doing over at his uncle's place since he graduated in May, so I heard.

Shea catches me looking. He leans over and whispers something to Jesse, then smiles at me, hard and scalding. He's not just mad at me; he's ready to draw blood, and I turn away, a flush rising in my face as Mrs. Wardwell keeps going.

"This ain't gonna be like last year. None of that foolishness is gonna happen again. Understand me?" We all stop fidgeting. "Nobody's allowed on this property after quitting time except me, Bob, and the migrants staying in the cabins. I'll be here to see that the rest of you clear out. Get a ride or hoof it into town, I don't care which. I can't be responsible for what goes on after hours, got it?"

Everybody nods, us locals giving the migrant workers the once-over and the migrants looking right back to show they've got nothing to hide. Got to give the Wardwells credit: one of the posters, tattered and faded, is still taped to their camper door. Even twelve months later, the word *Missing* stands out.

"Awright. Finish up eating and get back to work." She

drops into her chair, which is right outside the camper doorway so she can sit in the shade of the awning and prop an electric fan on the steps.

We get back to raking, but Mags and I don't joke around like before, and Nell's soft, flat crooning blends with the droning bugs and the sound of distant traffic from Route 15. Clouds move in. Rain's coming.

After I load my last box of berries onto Mr. Wardwell's flatbed, he walks around the tailgate, smacking his gloves together. He's about half the size of his wife, with a thick head of white hair and skin so weathered it looks like old saddle leather. "You're Sarah Prentiss's girls, ain't ya?" We all nod; Nell's close enough to a sister. He grunts, scratching his stubble. "You heard what Evelyn said about being careful?"

I don't remember her saying that, exactly, but Mags nods. "It's okay. We stick together."

"Good deal." He heads for the truck. People are worried these days. Worried the ground's going to open up and swallow another Sasanoa girl.

Exhausted and aching, the three of us walk down the road to Mags's beat-to-hell Mazda. A group of guys hang around Jesse's truck, talking trash. As we pass, Shea calls, "See ya at the quarry tonight, Darcy?" to big laughs.

I don't stop or turn around, but once we're in the car, I kick the dash so hard it sends the little hula girl into fits. Mags wears her know-it-all look, and the only reason she bites her tongue is because Nell's in the backseat. But this time, Mags doesn't know it all. She doesn't know a damn thing.

Mags shifts hard into drive and we raise a rooster tail of dust behind us. Overhead, the sky looks ready to open up any second.

T
W
O

AFTER MY DAD, smoking is Mom's second true love. Dad died eleven years ago, so Kools are all she has left. She practices her skills every night, blowing rings or letting smoke trickle out her nostrils so slowly it hurts to watch. Sometimes I think she smokes so she won't have to talk to us. Can't really blame her when Aunt Libby is around, which is always, because her trailer sits on the edge of our property.

"You're out of milk here, Sarah." Libby sticks her head into our Frigidaire so that her rear end blocks my way, like she didn't know I needed to get by. I have to climb over a chair to get back out to the porch. "This orange juice is expired. You know that?" She holds up the carton and

sloshes it around to get Mom's attention. "You're gonna need
bread. I'll make French bread, how about that?" She searches
the cupboard and sighs, flopping her arms down. "You're out
of flour."

Mags and I trade looks and go back to our game of Hearts
with Nell. We play cards on the porch all the time, betting change while Mom sits in a wicker chair with her feet
propped on the railing, puffing and staring down to where
Old County Road connects with 15. Tonight, us girls all have
wet hair from showering, and moan and groan about our
aching muscles whenever we shift around on the big faded
area rug. Still, it's worth it: by the end of harvest, I should
have enough money saved for new school clothes and one of
those clunkers down to Gary's Salvage, which is where Mags
bought her car last fall. You won't catch me tossing coins for
shotgun again.

Nell is eating pretzels. She considers each one before she
puts it in her mouth, like she's expecting to come across one
shaped like Abe Lincoln or the Blessed Virgin. "I liked the
movie on Saturday, but it wasn't my favorite." She's been
saying that since we got back from the Sasanoa Drive-In last
weekend. The first movie of the double feature is always a
Hollywood classic, and Nell lives for it.

Mags rolls her eyes behind her dark-framed glasses. "Go
on, tell us what you thought of the kiss." She picks up the
first trick and leads with spades.

"Wellll"—Nell flops back on her elbows and walks her toes up the railing—"the boy was attractive. . . ." That's her new thing: guys aren't hot, they're attractive. Marlon Brando's all I remember from the movie, too, because I was half-gone on rum and Cherry Coke that my friend Kat brought in a thermos. "And he kissed like he meant it"—she makes a big smooching sound, and Mags and I crack up—"but he was too rough with that girl. Kisses are supposed to be soft. That's how every kiss should be."

Mom speaks in her low smoker's voice, holding her cigarette out to smolder in the muggy air. "And who're you planning on kissing?" When you look at Mom, you can see what Mags and I will look like in twenty years or so: sandy blond hair, wide-spaced blue eyes that tilt up at the corners like a cat's, short nose, pointed chin.

My gaze slides to Nell, but she doesn't miss a beat. "None of those blueberry rakers, that's for sure. They're not gentlemanly." We crack up again. "Well, they're not."

"What're you talking about, Nellie Rose?" Libby leans in the doorway. She thinks Nell gets this stuff from *The Young and the Restless.* "You better watch yourself."

"How can I watch myself? I don't have eyes in the back of my head." Nell laughs and laughs like it's the best joke ever, which gets Mags and me going again.

Libby puts her hands in the pockets of her denim jumper. That's how she dresses, like a Pentecostal, even though we're all lapsed Catholics: long hems and long braids and granny specs perched on the end of her nose. "Somebody mind telling me how I'm supposed to fix a celebration supper if I got nothing to work with?" She gives us a sly look as we turn to stare at her.

Mom grinds out her cigarette in a coffee cup. "You finally going to tell them?"

"What? Who?" Nell sits up. "Me?"

"You made it, baby." Libby smiles. "Got the call today. You're gonna be a Princess."

Nell shoots up off the floor, shrieking and hugging her mom, jumping around to bring the porch down, which wouldn't take much. I scoop up the cards and shuffle, since you can't play Hearts with two people and Nell's going to be over the moon for the rest of the night. She's only wanted to be a Bay Festival Princess since forever, and here's one thing I haven't told you yet about Nell: she's beautiful. Not beautiful like a Victoria's Secret model, but pure, untouched gorgeous, the kind that scares most guys away. Skin like china, wavy Black Irish hair she got from her dad (wherever he is), dark blue eyes all starry and full of little-kid innocence.

Mom clears her throat. "That ain't all the news, Lib." Libby hugs Nell to her and lifts her chin stubbornly, saying nothing. Mom looks at me, and I stop in mid-cut. "Lady from the Festival Committee left you a message, too, Darce. You were nominated."

Mags's mouth drops open, and then she falls over laughing. I stare at Mom, waiting for her to crack up, but when I see how sour Libby looks, I know it's no joke. I burst out, "By who?"

Mom shrugs. "You know that's kept secret. Guess you got a fan." And that's all I'll get out of her tonight.

Nell screams again and pulls me into a hug that makes my spine pop, jerking me up and down. Meanwhile, my darling sister gasps and takes her glasses off to wipe her eyes. "Oh my God . . .wow . . ."

For supper, we eat spaghetti and a pound cake Mom's been hiding in the freezer behind last summer's zucchini. I stab my fork into my plate harder than I need to, refusing to look at anyone, waiting for the world to come back into focus. Every time Nell shakes my arm and says, "Isn't it awesome? We get to do it together!" Libby adds something like, "Lots of girls make the first round, you know," or "Winning Queen is about more than just looks," until I spill my iced tea accidentally-on-purpose to give her something else to bitch about.

I look at Mom as Libby fusses with paper towels. "Can I go?"

Mom waves her hand. I go upstairs, touching the framed picture of Dad hanging on the wall above the newel post; there could be bombs dropping on the house and I'd still remember to do that every night. In the picture, I'm two years old and Mags is three and a half. He's holding us in each arm like we weigh nothing, a grin on his face, leaning back against whatever hot rod he was tinkering with at the time.

The night air is thick, still waiting for the rain that's been promised since this afternoon. Mags, Nell, and I sit where the roof flattens outside Mags's bedroom window. We have to be careful because the shingles are crumbling, like the rest of the house. If we knock chunks down onto the porch, we could wake up Mom. Nobody knows we come out here at night, and we like it that way.

"You know what got you the vote." Mags grins at me. "Those Daisy Dukes of yours. They scream Sasanoa's Finest." She leans back against her window. "I can see you up onstage now. Tiara, sash, and a bottle of Colt 45."

I tug at my cutoffs. "They're not Daisy Dukes. If the hem's longer than the pockets, they're not Daisy Dukes."

"That's the rule, huh?"

I want to whomp the hell out of her, but ever since we were kids, we've tried to go easy on each other when Nell's around; she hates fighting. Nell holds her second piece of pound cake in a napkin and picks at it, watching me close. "Are you mad about the pageant?" The way she sounds, you'd think I wanted to cancel Christmas.

How can I explain to her that this is somebody's screwed-up idea of a joke? Darcy Prentiss, White Trash Princess.

Whoever they are, they must be laughing their asses off. I just don't know who'd go to all this trouble. I've heard Libby say plenty of times that to make it onto the ballot, it takes one nomination from somebody in the community and then a Festival Committee member to second it. She nominated Nell herself. Doesn't matter; no way am I making a fool of myself up on that stage come August 19.

"She's just trying to decide what color corsage to wear, that's all," Mags says, patting Nell's knee.

"Oh, Darcy, you can't know that until you find your dress."

I start to say something I'll regret, but then the rain comes down, taking our breath away. Nell scrambles for the edge of the roof, feeling for the living room window casing with her toes before using it as a step to drop into the flower bed. If Libby ever did any weeding—she grows the flowers, Mom grows the veggies—she'd find bare footprints sunk deep into the soil. Waving to us, Nell runs for the trailer, taking bites of cake as she goes.

"One of these days she's going to Pollyanna herself right off this roof," Mags says, once we've crawled back inside her dim bedroom.

"And land on her feet." I wipe rain off my face. "Nell's got luck like most people got zits." I catch Mags studying me and stop. "What?"

"I didn't forget about Shea." She sits on her bed. "What

happened between you two?"

I turn away, touching the ballerina jewelry box that she's had as long as I can remember. The porcelain dancer's arm is so thin I could snap it between my fingers. "Nothing special."

"Was it him, on the Fourth? Was that why you were acting so weird that night?" She waits. "Really, Darcy? Shea Gaines?"

At once I'm so tired I can barely stand it. I point to the open window. "Rain's getting in," and leave her sitting there in the dark.

T H R E E

THE NEXT DAY is Saturday. I come downstairs around six a.m. to the sound of an ax thunking into the stump outside. I fix toast—nothing left but the heels, which Mom and Mags won't touch; to me, it's all bread—and look out the window to see Hunt Chapman splitting wood for us.

I step outside in the big T-shirt I wear to bed and call, "She's not gonna like that."

He stops, lowers the ax, and glances back at me. "Morning." He stands the log on its end again and splits it in half, then tosses the stove lengths into the pile he's been working on since probably five a.m. Hunt's our landlord. He's also one of Mom's managers at E. F. Danforth & Son, the blueberry packaging plant in Blue Hill. Hunt's a tall drink of water, broad-shouldered and not bad-looking for an old guy, if you like the silent type, which I usually don't.

"I'll tell her you're here." I find Mom already in the kitchen, knotting her robe around her waist as she peers through the curtains, her hair a little crazy. That robe is the only pretty thing she owns, a threadbare red silk kimono Dad gave her for her birthday a long time ago.

"What is he doing?" she says under her breath.

"Keeping us from freezing to death in August."

She takes one look at me and gives me a stinging swat on the thigh. "Get upstairs and put on some pants." I eat my toast instead, following her as far as the doorway. She goes out onto the porch and stands with her arms crossed. "Hunt Chapman, tell me you didn't buy us firewood."

He splits two pieces before he answers her, chewing over his thoughts like Big Chief tobacco. "Apple tree blew down in my north field last night. Wood's dry enough. Shouldn't smoke up on you too bad this fall."

"Tell me what I owe you." In the quiet, Mom jerks her chin. "Give me a figure, Hunt."

He stops, taking a breath before bringing the ax down and twisting it out of the stump with a one-handed motion. "Just being neighborly."

"You live halfway to Brewer." Hunt seems to have run out of words, and Mom sighs, stepping back. "Let me fix you

17

breakfast, at least. Coffee while you wait?"

He looks at her for the first time, with a hint of a smile. I think Hunt smiles mostly on the inside; it kind of warms up his features without changing them much. "That'd be fine, Sarah." Sweat glistens along his hairline, where threads of gray are coming in with the chestnut brown.

I hear Mags's heavy footsteps overhead and hustle upstairs to the bathroom to get ready before she can beat me to it. No point in showering before raking, but after I brush my teeth, I look back at the mirror for a second and dab on a little waterproof mascara and some tinted lip gloss. Never know.

By the time we're ready to go, Hunt is standing outside with Mom, sipping from one of our heavy white china mugs. Nell comes tearing around the house with our lunch bag banging against her leg, scared she's late, one hand to the blue bandanna she ties over her hair while she's raking. She calls to us, "I got meat-loaf sandwiches and Swiss rolls."

Mags makes me pay her gas money every week, since I failed my driver's test four times and Mom says I can't try again until I get more practice, but Nell's saving for cosmetology school—pretty funny for a girl who isn't allowed to wear makeup—so Mags has her fix our lunch for us instead.

My sister respects saving up for school. She's been building her college fund since she was twelve. She's going to UMaine–Orono in the spring, after she earns money for books and stuff this fall. Most of her friends are starting in

August or September. She broke up with her boyfriend, Will, back in May, right around their one-year anniversary; she says she wants to be "free" when she goes away. I think she's nuts. Will was a dork, but he was real sweet. One time he had roses delivered to her in study hall.

Libby brings up the rear on her morning trek to talk Mom's ear off, and her eyes narrow behind her glasses at the sight of Hunt. Without even a hello, she says, "She tell you about that light switch in the living room?" I don't know how he manages to keep his face so still, but he doesn't even flinch at how god-awful rude she sounds. "Makes a crunching sound like peanut shells when you flip it. Wiring's gone bad."

"I'll take a look."

Libby's always carping about how our old farmhouse and the trailer are falling apart and how Hunt would rather repair than replace things. But I know for a fact that Hunt gave Mom a break on the rent after Dad died so we could keep living here and not have to move in with Gramma Nan, who lives way the hell up in Aroostook County and keeps pigs. The way I see it, we owe him big. I think Libby's sour on all men because Nell's dad took off even though they were engaged and she was seven months along with Nell.

As we pile into the car, I roll down the window and call, "Bye, Hunt."

He flicks us a salute. Little stuff like that is how we know he likes us even though he doesn't talk much.

As we pull out, Libby's on her way inside to help herself to Mom's coffeepot. I bet she'll find a way to cadge some of Hunt's bacon and eggs, too.

Jesse Bouchard has the darkest eyes I've ever seen, and I stare into them as he puts ice cubes in my hand and closes my fingers over them. The shock of cold on my fresh blisters makes me catch my breath, but I don't look away. He's got a chipped canine tooth you only notice when he smiles. "There. Bet that feels better."

I nod. The ice came from Jesse's water jug; he fished it out and brought it over to me when he saw me stop raking to blow on my burning palms. "Guess I lost my gloves somewhere," I say. "Pretty stupid, huh?" I can feel it there, that pull when we lock eyes that makes my stomach twist in the best way. I've been crushing on him hard since last harvest, when some part of me woke up and really saw him for the first time.

"No. But you better borrow a pair or you'll be a hurting unit tomorrow." He sits back on his heels and grins. "And how're you gonna make top harvester with jacked-up hands?"

I duck my head and laugh. Top harvester always ends up being one of the migrants, usually some Honduran guy in his twenties who travels cross-country, living crop to crop, somebody with endurance and a system to their harvesting. Being a raker isn't the same as being a harvester; harvester's a title you've got to earn. At the end of each season, the Wardwells pay out seven hundred dollars to whoever brought in the most pounds of berries, giving everybody a good reason to bust their butts. Shea might give everyone a run for their money this year; seems like every time I look up, he's filled another box.

Jesse has a dancing light in his eyes—devilish, you could say—and I'm thinking he looks good enough to eat, when a fight breaks out over by the big cluster of boulders. It's migrants against locals, and surprise, surprise, look who's in the middle of it: Shea. He's got a handful of another guy's shirt, trying to drive him back against the rocks; the guy boxes him twice in the ear, and they fall down together in a tangle.

"Hey!" Duke McCutcheon, Mr. Wardwell's strong right hand, is coming, but then Mason wades in, grabbing Shea under the arms and lifting him almost off his feet. Shea's tall but wiry, lean everywhere Mason's broad, and you can see it takes everything Shea's got to twist out of Mason's hands. The other guys clear out, making themselves scarce as Mr. Wardwell gets there. Migrants can't afford to get canned. Most of them don't have any money to speak of except what these berries put in their pocket week to week, and if they lose out on raking, they'll go hungry until the potato harvest starts up north.

"What's going on here?" Mr. Wardwell looks from brown face to white, but nobody's talking. Mason's hands go into his pockets. Everybody knows that somebody—Shea—must've brought up Rhiannon Foss, last summer, and the rumor that it was a migrant who did it. Not that Shea and Rhiannon were friends. Far as I know, he never had much use for her at all.

"This happens again, you're both done. Got it?" Mr. Wardwell waits until they nod, then stalks off to his truck. Mrs. Wardwell hollers, "What happened? Bob?" from her roost outside the camper.

Shea swears, picks up his cap, and smacks it against his thigh before putting it on. He sees Jesse standing with me and stares a long time before turning away, shoulders stiff. Duke says something sharply and cuffs him on the back of the head. Duke is his family, an uncle or a cousin.

After we've all gone back to raking, Mags sighs, her long blond ponytail spilling over her shoulder as she dumps a rakeful into a box. "You sure know how to pick 'em."

"I don't *like* Shea."

"Who would?" She glances at him. "But talking looks-only here . . . he is kind of sexy."

"Don't you mean attractive?" She snorts, and I'm over being annoyed with her for nagging me last night about what happened on the Fourth. Shea's got eyes the color of sunlight through brown sea glass, and his hair's maybe three shades darker, a little long on top so that it falls over his brow when he isn't wearing a hat, which isn't often. Today he's wearing a washed-out denim shirt with the sleeves ripped off and a pair of dark Wranglers, and if it weren't for the fact that I know he's got a personality to match one of those black pincher bugs that crawl out from under our back steps, I could almost forgive myself for the mistake I made on the Fourth of July.

Nobody has extra gloves. I suck it up and keep raking, but I'm losing ground to Mags, and that stings worse than the blisters on my palms. My hands will callus and toughen up eventually, but not before quitting time tonight, and that means money slipping through my fingers. Mags fills her fifty-third box and starts on the next. I haven't filled forty yet.

Jesse blows out early, getting the okay from Mr. Wardwell with that wicked charm of his. At five o'clock quitting time, we girls are getting ready to leave when who should come barreling up the road in his truck but Jesse. Boy's got balls coming back here when he's supposed to be at the doctor's or wherever. Mrs. Wardwell stares at him like she'd like to drag him around by his ear, but it's quitting time, so there isn't much she can do but bark at her husband to start loading up.

Jesse idles in front of us and rolls down his window. "Here." He tosses something out the window to me. It's a pair of yellow work gloves; they're beat-up and too big, but I grip them to my chest like they were made of spun gold. "Knew I had an extra pair at home somewhere." He nods at me and drives up to get Shea and Mason before I can thank him.

None of us speak as we get into Mags's car, and the silence is heavy. I want to gush about Jesse Bouchard, how everybody has him all wrong, but Nell speaks first. "Those things aren't even new."

"God, Nell." I jerk around and give her a between-us look that makes her shrink back against the seat. "Don't be rude."

Mags turns right onto 15, heading toward the east side of Sasanoa and home. "Listen to you. 'Don't be rude.' Didn't know I had the Queen of England riding shotgun."

Heat comes into my face. Sometimes Mags is so much like Mom it makes me crazy; they both have a way of cutting through bullshit. A natural-born bullshitter like me doesn't stand a chance in this family.

Nell and I sulk as we cruise down Main Street, passing the post office, Gaudreau's Take-Out, the Irving gas station, the Hannaford supermarket, and a dozen quiet streets where little kids have marked up sidewalks with pastel chalk and dogs snooze in porch shadows. Sasanoa's sleepy, all right. Sometimes you want to check to make sure it's still breathing.

Running parallel to Main Street is the wild and woolly

Penobscot River, and the Penobscot Narrows Bridge span-
ning it. Of the thousand or so construction workers who
built that thing, our dad was the only one who died, all
because of fifty dollars and a tinsel Christmas star. Hardly a
place in town you can't see the bridge from, sunlight gleam-
ing off the concrete support posts during the day, red safety
lights blinking at night.

Tom Prentiss was a crazy man, though; wasn't a chance
that he wouldn't take, Mom says. Which, Libby always adds,
is why he didn't live to see forty. If you want to get Mom
talking, ask her about Dad. Ask her about midnight rides on
his old Indian motorcycle when he was three sheets to the
wind, or brawling at the Bay Festival truck pulls, him bleeding at the mouth, spinning one guy around by his shirt collar
with another locked under his arm, laughing all the while.

Mags turns up Second Street. She doesn't say a word; she
doesn't have to. I start grinning. Nell leans between us, real-
izes where we're going, and whoops right in my ear. "Last
one in the water buys at Gaudreau's!" She drags her shirt off
over her head, hardly noticing when a guy on a bike sees her
and almost takes a spill into a blue hydrangea.

F
O
U
R

THE QUARRY ROAD is dirt, winding up through the woods until you reach a cable blocking the way with a sign reading *Prvt Prop*. Ours is the only car, so we race out into the clearing, stripping off our clothes.

Mags and Nell stop at their bras and underwear, but I take it all off, ignoring their catcalls as I scramble down the granite ledges to the dark, oily water and cannonball right in. It is *cold*—kids like to say the Sasanoa Quarry has no bottom—and I keep my eyes squeezed shut until I surface, gasping and pushing my hair back.

The girls follow me, and for a while all we do is swim and splash and sigh as the sweat and field grit rinses away. It's like floating in a deep bowl down here, listening to birdcalls echo off the rock walls and shouting, "Hell-o," just to hear your voice bounce around. Even though the sign says private property, lots of us party here, lighting bonfires and daring each other to jump from the highest ledge.

Nell climbs out first, wringing her hair and picking her way along the ledges as Mags and I tread water. "Are you going to keep those gloves?" She watches her feet as she walks, arms out for balance. Her underwear is sensible, her bra white cotton with a tiny rosette like you'd see on a little girl's undershirt. Anybody who was opening the front clasp would have to touch that tight satin swirl, have a second to think about what they were doing, and then keep right on digging. I swallow bitterness and tell myself I won't think about that. I promised myself I never would.

"Yeah," I say. She purses her lips and shakes her head, saying *mm-mm-mm*. "What's your problem? Jesse's never done anything to you."

"He's nasty."

"He is not. Name one nasty thing you've seen him do."

"I don't mean he picks his nose. He's not good enough for you." She keeps her gaze down, like she knows that if she looks at me, she'll have to remember our secret, and realize that she's got no place tearing the wings off what I got going with Jesse.

"Half the girls in school could tell you if he's a boxers or briefs man," Mags says.

I mull it over. "Jockey shorts."

"Forget it, Nellie." Mags climbs out of the water. "She won't be happy until she's felt him all over to make sure he isn't missing any parts, and then she'll ask us why we didn't try to talk her out of it." I'd never say this out loud, but Mags is built like Libby: five foot ten and full-bodied, her breasts and hips straining against her sports bra and boy shorts. I'm smaller and curvy like Mom, but I'm strong.

Nell walks in a careful line, swinging one arm at her side. She stops, positions herself, and says, "I want to thank you all so much," in a big, clear voice.

Mags grins and heads up to the car to grab something for us to dry off with. I swim to the ledge and fold my arms on it, playing my part as I pretend to talk into a microphone. "How does it feel to be up here in front of all these people, Miss Michaud?"

"Like I'm with my friends. I can't say how much your votes mean to me. I promise to do all I can to make my town proud."

"And how do you plan to use your scholarship money?"

"It's my lifelong dream to learn the art of cosmetology at Pauline's School of Beauty in Bangor." Nell pauses. "And if I ever open my own shop, I promise it will be here in Sasanoa." She bows so deeply her hair brushes granite, and I clap. Breathless, she gives a little skip and drops into a crouch beside me. "So we need to be over at the town hall tomorrow by two o'clock."

"What for?"

"Darcy! Didn't you call the festival lady back? We have to register for the pageant and get a packet about what we need to do and everything."

I didn't call the festival lady back, and I look to Mags for help. She's brought a blanket from the backseat, and she gives me a heavy look as she dries off and hands it to me. She's made up her mind that this is one of those Things We Do for Nell. I groan. "Look, I don't . . ." My cousin's eyes are so blue and serious that I can't finish the sentence. "Okay. Fine. Why not."

I wrap the blanket around myself as we climb back up to the grassy clearing. For a second I don't see my clothes, but then I spot my tank top off to the far left. I'm half-dressed when Nell says, "Somebody moved our stuff."

"Huh?"

"We didn't leave our clothes back here. Mags and I were over there when we took them off. Now they're almost in the bushes."

I look down at my shorts and underwear and pull them on, fast.

An engine starts in the trees. Tires crunch over dirt, and we run to the trailhead, only to get there too late. Nothing left but some tire tracks in the mud.

★   ★   ★

Gaudreau's is packed, the line reaching back to the picnic tables on the pavement. It isn't full dusk yet, but the strings of twinkle lights are on and the fluorescent sign is buzzing. I expect everybody to point and laugh at us, but if the person who got an eyeful up at the quarry is here, they must've kept it to themselves so far.

Mags treats. She and Nell order sundaes, I order a Moxie and fries, and then we scoot off to a picnic table with a red-and-white-checked umbrella to wait for our number to crackle over the loudspeaker. "I don't get why whoever it was didn't come down and swim, too," I say for the second time. "If they're so scared of some half-naked girls that they have to lay a patch getting out of there, they got issues."

"Well, in your case, it was the full monty. I was scared, too." Mags dodges the straw wrapper I throw at her.

Nell cups her elbows. "He touched our clothes."

Mags sighs. "You're imagining things."

When our order is called, Mags and I go to the pickup window, where one of those sleepy-eyed Gaudreau girls asks if we want ketchup and salt. Mr. Gaudreau is supervising, and he comes over, his potbelly straining against his powder-blue polo shirt. He leans on the sill and grins at me. "Well, hello there, Miss Thing." The light catches one of his metal fillings. "You know, I was hoping you'd come back around. No hard feelings about us not having an opening for you this season?"

"Nope." Behind him, I watch a Gaudreau girl making a

cone like she's got arthritis in both wrists.

"Sometimes it's tough being the one who does the hirin' and firin' around this place."

"Uh-huh."

"My Fern's going to be staying in Boston next summer. Maybe I can get you behind the counter then." He winks and slides the tray over. "Sweets for the sweet."

I dump vinegar on my fries. "Bye."

As we walk away, Mags says, "Maybe it was him."

"Who was watching us swim?"

She laughs. "Who nominated you as Princess."

"Oh." I glance back, but he's already gone from the window. "I dunno. If it was, I don't think he could keep his mouth shut about it for this long."

Back at our table, we dig in. Lots of familiar faces from school at Gaudreau's tonight, and one of them belongs to Mason Howe. He's eating burgers with his mom. Mason's knees press against the underside of the picnic table, and he has to hunch under the umbrella as he crams his food down. I don't know if I've ever seen him without Shea or Jesse outside of class. His fair hair shags into his eyes, and the back of his neck is halfway between deep sunburn and mahogany tan.

One of the *Missing* posters clings to the telephone pole nearest our table. The evening breeze flutters a loose corner, and slowly we stop chitchatting and look at it, listening to the classic country drifting from Gaudreau's speakers.

"Were Shea and that guy fighting today because of

Rhiannon?" Nell looks at us. She has a little dab of hot fudge in the corner of her mouth.

Mags wipes it quickly with her thumb, saying, "Shea's a hothead and a bully. Rhiannon was just an excuse to mix it up."

Nell's quiet for a second. "She's dead, isn't she?" She looks at our careful expressions. "Well, it seems like she would've come home by now, if she wasn't."

My stomach does a slow roll. My fries already seem soggy, thick with grease. I push the cardboard dish away. "Nobody knows for sure."

I remember looking out the window of Mom's car last fall on our way to Ellsworth and seeing Mr. Wardwell driving his tractor across his west field with an oil burner dragging behind, blowing flames across the berry bushes, tossing up thick black smoke. The fields have to be burned or mowed flat every other year to grow a good crop, but it felt like more than that. Felt like Sasanoa burning a wound clean, scorching the place where Rhiannon Foss was last seen so we could forget about her and move on. And sometimes you can forget—for weeks—but then you see one of the posters and it all comes back, the wondering and the not-knowing, and you have to turn to somebody and dig it up again.

We may not have been friends anymore, but Rhiannon was my age, sixteen last summer, and one way or another, she never came home again.

F
I
V
E

LIBBY GIVES US a ride to the town hall on the way to her Sunday shift at Rite Aid. She wears that blue smock with pride, let me tell you.

Unlike Mom, her hair has gone mousy over the years, and she doesn't even touch it up with Clairol.

She smooths wisps back into her french braid as she lectures Nell. "Now, you listen real close to everything they tell you. And don't forget your packet. We're gonna need that."

"I *know*, Mom." I used to think it was cute when Nell got sick of Libby's nagging, but then I realized how hard it's going to be for her to cut her mom loose after we graduate. Libby's always been right there, treating her like a baby and pushing her in this direction or that, and I know that Nell's going to keep living at home while she's in beauty school next fall.

What Libby doesn't know is that getting out of Sasanoa would be the best thing for Nell. Never mind that she's almost nineteen, going into her senior year like me because she had to repeat first grade. The bad stuff has already gotten to Nell, the stuff that Libby thinks only happens *out there*— anywhere that isn't in spitting distance of her doorstep. Nell and I, we've got secrets even Mags doesn't know. The sooner Nell learns to stand on her own, the better, because I won't be hanging around Sasanoa forever, playing guardian angel. Don't ask me what I'll be doing, but I won't be doing it here.

Libby lets us out at the hall. "I'll be parked right over here when you get out, Nellie." Libby and I don't say good-bye to each other; I'm not exactly sure when we stopped talking. Maybe it was when I figured out that she was talking trash about me behind my back, repeating town gossip to Mom and painting me as the black sheep. Or maybe it was when I started picking up on all her little put-downs and snipes that Mom doesn't even seem to notice. Libby doesn't try it with Mags. Just me.

There's a paper sign taped to the door saying that the Bay Festival Princess Welcome Meeting is in the main hall, so we go in. It's shadowy inside and smells like floor wax, old carpeting, and dusty radiators. Takes me back to all the holiday concerts we put on here in elementary school, roasting alive in ruffled dresses and sweater tights.

The main hall is full. I count fifteen girls, most of them from Sasanoa, most of them sitting with their moms. Even though I went out of my way to dress lazy—holey jeans, halter top, wedge flip-flops—I knot up inside when their eyes find me. Alexis Johnson's mouth falls open, and she whispers to Bella Peront, who, shocker, also got nominated. Bella: living proof that beauty doesn't come from within. She was voted Homecoming Queen last fall, which isn't even supposed to happen. A senior always wins, since it's their last year and everything. When Bella and I make eye contact, all the anger I felt January of sophomore year comes rushing back, making me strong, and I stare at her until she wrinkles her nose and turns away with a swish of her flat-ironed hair.

In study hall sophomore year, I overheard Bella making fun of Nell for taking special classes with Mrs. Hanscom and Mr. Ellis in the resource room, so I lit into her with a three-subject notebook. Nell does the same work as everybody else, but she needs more time and help understanding the directions. That notebook was the closest thing handy, but the spiral binding scratched Bella's cheek and earned me a three-day vacation from Sasanoa Area High School. Mom didn't even want to hear why I did it. She made me clean the house from attic to laundry room and shovel paths to the shed and back steps so Hunt wouldn't have to do it. Then it snowed again and he came over on Sunday and did it anyway, which figures.

As far as Nell's concerned, the only important people in the room are us and the lady running things. "Hi," Nell says, giving her a thousand-watt smile, and pulls me into a seat next to her.

"Okay. We can probably get started now," the lady says, shuffling her armload of photocopied packets. Guess they were waiting on us. She's short and round and fortyish, with a fluffy sprayed hairdo straight from the Great Lengths salon on Main Street. She wears full makeup, and pinned to her short-sleeved cardigan is a button from last year's festival with the slogan *A Real Maine Agricultural Fair! 50 Years and Counting.* "For anybody who doesn't know, I'm Melissa Hartwell, treasurer of the Bay Festival Committee. Now, the competition for Queen is very dear to me, and I'm so glad to meet all of you ladies and be here to answer any questions you might have." Bella's already got her hand up. "Yes?"

Bella folds her arms. "I heard that if the committee doesn't like your dress, you have to buy a new one."

I say in Nell's ear, "How is that a question?" She grins and puts a finger to her lips.

"We-e-ll, it's more like they might ask you to tone down your look a little." Mrs. Hartwell's voice perks up. "This is a family event, after all. You don't want to be flashing cleavage at your grandmothers. And you'll each need to find a local business to sponsor you for the pageant. They'll be the ones supplying the funds to buy your dress and flowers. There's more information on that in the packet. Now, we want to include a photo and a short bio of each of you in the Festival brochure, so people know who's in the running. Email me those by Wednesday, please, and we'll get them off to the printer's."

A bio? Darcy Celeste Prentiss. Lives in the ass-end of nowhere. Rakes berries. Flunks algebra. The end.

Mrs. Hartwell goes on to tell us that rehearsals for the Queen's coronation, which happens on the first night of the festival, will start Wednesday evening. At least it sounds like we just have to walk onstage, stand there, and answer a few questions from the panel of judges; nobody expects me to flip batons or make up a dance routine or anything.

"So, I brought this along today as a little treat." She picks up a white box that looks like the kind pastries come in. "Most people never get this close, but I think it really says something that you've been nominated as Princesses. Your town chose you. Remember that." She opens the lid and folds back tissue paper to bring out a crown.

It's actually sort of beautiful. Made of some kind of thin metal, it's all twisted and swirled, set with glass stones ranging from sky-blue to jade-green. Nell grabs my hand and squeezes tight.

★   ★   ★

The drive-in screen finally flickers to life, and I whoop, honking the horn along with a dozen other yahoos. Mags pushes my hand away. "Easy, killer."

The Sasanoa Drive-In is like most Maine outdoor theaters, a clearing in the woods with mounds for cars to drive up onto. They tore out the speaker posts a long time ago, and now you listen to the movie by tuning to 89.3 FM on your radio, starting your engine every now and then to keep the car battery from dying. Some of the migrants are here with their kids, watching them run around and throw Frisbees and holler. Whole families roll into Sasanoa in July for the harvest, driving RVs and rusted-out vans from as far away as California or Florida; I've seen a kid no more than four years old working right next to his dad with a child-size rake, until the sun got to be too much for him.

I reach back through the seats. "Moxie."

Nell digs around. She's got blankets, pillows, popcorn, and enough soda to guarantee that we'll spend half the night making bathroom trips. Everybody except her is here to see the second movie, some new action flick, so people are out of their cars, leaning in friends' windows or walking to the snack shack during the first show, some classic called *East of Eden*.

The word *Overture* appears on the screen across a shot of waves crashing on rocks, and people boo. I prop my feet on the dashboard, ready for boredom—but you know what?

The movie's actually good. It's about a boy named Cal (Mags says the blond guy playing him is James Dean), whose mom took off and left him and whose dad is super strict and thinks Cal is no good. His brother Aron is the favorite, and he has a girlfriend named Abra, who Cal wants really bad. At one point, I reach back for popcorn and see Nell hugging her pillow, eyes wide, drinking in every detail on the screen.

Things heat up between Cal and Abra, and by the time they're sitting at the top of the Ferris wheel together, we're all holding our breath. Cal leans in for the kiss.

"Hey," a lazy voice says right in my ear, and I jump.

A flashlight clicks on and off under a thin face. Kat Levesque leans into the car. "S'up, girly. I been looking for you."

"*Shhh*," Nell says. Mags doesn't say anything, because she hates Kat and likes to pretend that she doesn't exist.

I angle toward the window. "What's going on?"

"Not much. Got some Captain's, some joysticks, back of my truck. Wanna come?"

"*Shhh!*"

"All *right*. Jesus." I push the door open, and Nell reaches for me.

"No, don't. Stay with us."

"Yeah." Mags means it. "Stay here."

I wave them off. "Be right back." Maybe. Anything can happen with Kat.

"Early start tomorrow," Mags calls as I follow Kat into the dark, and I raise a hand even though she can't see me.

Kat's little white pickup is parked way back by the trees, where you can do anything and not get busted. The smell of weed is a sticky-sweet cloud as we climb into the truck bed. In the backlight from the screen, I can see only shadows and cigarette cherries floating in air. I jostle somebody and laugh. "Who's that?"

"Guess." He tickles me and I shriek, falling into his lap. Kat's twin brother Kenyon is the only person who tickles me every time I see him, and I recognize his Old Spice body spray, so I snuggle in and take the plastic cup Kat hands me. It's not Captain Morgan's and Coke. It's Blue Raspberry Pucker, and I almost gag.

"Want me to pour it out?" There's a smile in Kat's voice. I knock it back and toss the cup in her direction. She cackles. "That's my girl."

"How do you drink that crap?"

"As fast as possible." Kat burps.

"Sexy," Kenyon says.

She's back on her feet. "I want nachos. Darcy, come on."

As I stand up, the car next to us starts its engine, and the headlights fall on a girl sitting on the wheel well across from me, a drink in her hand. For a second, I swear it's Rhiannon Foss. In the time it takes for a cold shock to run through my body, I see it's just that sophomore, Sophia-something, who has shoulder-length red hair like Rhiannon did. Other than that, she doesn't look anything like her. A year ago, it would've been Rhiannon sitting there; she and Kat hung out sometimes, and this is the kind of place I'd run into her. Then we'd ignore each other.

I slide off the open tailgate and follow Kat, but somebody claps their hand over my mouth, grabs me around the waist, and slings me in a circle so hard that I scream for real this time, almost losing one of my flip-flops.

Everybody's laughing. Kat's flashlight beam lands on us. Shea's holding me, and I see other boys sitting in the grass with their backs against the truck, sharing a joint.

I drive my elbow into Shea's ribs. "Stop it!" He lets me twist for a second just to prove I can't hurt him, then lets go. I turn, take two steps, and shove him as hard as I can. "Real funny, asshole."

His eyes are lionlike and intense in the half-light. "What? Too rough for you, Darce?"

The way the other guys laugh, I can guess what he's told them. I turn my back and walk away, wiping furiously at my mouth, not stopping until I reach the snack shack take-out window, where I realize I'm shaking all over. Kat comes up behind me, and I turn on her. "Why didn't you tell me he was over there?"

Kat blinks, her big brown eyes heavy-lidded and smudged with kohl liner, her dyed-black hair chopped in super-short bangs. She's stoned pretty much all the time, but there's no way she forgot what happened on the Fourth between me and Shea. She was there that night; she saw how drunk I was. "I didn't think it was a big deal."

"Well, it is! He hates my guts now." Something clicks. "Did he send you over to get me?"

"No. Swear to God." She catches my arm when I turn away. "I didn't know he was gonna do that, honest. Look, you can have my nachos, okay? I don't even want them, I was just bored. Stay."

I stand with my arms crossed while she orders, and then we sit together in the grass, looking up at the screen. I've missed a lot of *East of Eden*; Aron's leaving town on a train, and things seem pretty grim. Nell will tell me the whole plot tomorrow anyway, scene by scene, whether I want to listen or not. My heartbeat's back to normal, and I dig a huge glob of melty cheese out of the dish. "I wouldn't have freaked out so bad if I hadn't been thinking about Rhiannon's spooky missing ass. Shea scared the crap out of me."

"He's a tool." Kat nudges me with something. I reach down and it's her flask, the one with the Misfits logo on it. I laugh and take a sip. Captain's. "Wanna get out of here? Some people partying at the quarry tonight. Could be fun. No d-bags allowed. Promise."

I don't even think about it. "Cool."

There's a high-pitched whizzing sound, and sparks

explode off to our left where the migrant families are parked. Firecrackers. There's yelling and confusion, and shadows pelt past us, whooping and beating it out of there before the usher shows.

When the firecrackers are spent, there's smoke in the air and the sound of more than one little kid crying. A lady gets out of one of the vans and rocks from side to side, bouncing on the balls of her feet. It takes me a second to realize she's soothing a tiny baby, whose cry is so small it sounds like the creak of a gate in need of oil.

S
I
X

"DARCY PRENTISS." MOM'S talking from someplace far away. I roll over. Sleep's better. She jerks the bedsheet back. "Get up."

Through the fog of whatever I drank last night, I see her standing over me, looking about thirty feet tall. A rectangle of morning sunlight stretches across my ceiling, tossing rainbows through the crack in the windowpane. I sit up—the piano that lands on my head makes me wish I hadn't—and see that my alarm clock reads 7:15. Oh, crap.

"The girls left." Mom's dressed for work, a seersucker blouse and jeans she'll wear under her clean-suit cover-up and hairnet. She doesn't have many wrinkles for a mom, but when she frowns like that, the lines between her eye-brows turn into a deep V and she reminds me of Gramma Nan when one of the pigs gets out and trucks off to visit the neighbors. Mom turns and leaves, kicking my dirty clothes from yesterday out of her way. "Go shower. You smell like booze."

I jump under the cool spray, then whip my wet hair into a ponytail, swallow a couple aspirin, and head downstairs, where Libby sits at the table stirring sugar into her coffee and pretending to read the paper. She watches me over the top of her glasses; figures she'd be smug as a cat on a sparrow, seeing me get in trouble. Holding her gaze, I swallow handfuls of dry cereal to put something into my stomach before I throw up (I've got half a memory of doing it last night, too) and think of all the things I'd love to say to her.

Mom comes in and gets her keys, purse, and the fleece jacket she brings to work because it's so cold in the E. F. Danforth refrigeration plant. She's actually come home with frostbite on her fingers before. Got it right through her gloves.

Crunching Froot Loops, I mutter, "Can't believe they just left."

She stares at me like she's considering giving me my first thrashing since grade school. "I told them to leave. Your sister knocked on your door for about five minutes. Nell wanted to go in and shake you."

She goes outside and I follow her, but she stops me on the porch. "Uh-uh. Forget it. You're not making me late for work."

"It's on your way!"

Mom shrugs. "Guess you shouldn't have missed your ride." She opens her car door, then stands there for a second, almost like she's looking through me, or seeing somebody else. She exhales and shakes her head. "I hope you know enough not to get yourself pregnant."

She leaves me standing there with the wind knocked out of me.

I go inside to find Libby leaning back in her chair, taking the world's longest sip of coffee, tilted at the perfect angle to watch Mom and me out the front window.

Now that it's just the two of us, the tension is electric. I scowl at her as I stuff my feet into sneakers, and she lowers her chair to the floor, hitching her big boobs up onto her folded arms and giving me a look like *I know you, little girl.* As if she's got the slightest clue. I could cut her so deep with the truth. I'd make her bleed, if it wouldn't mean doing the same to Nell. I open the door, say, "Don't you have anything better to do than eavesdrop?" and bang out before she can answer.

It's hot. I'm about four miles into the walk down 15, and I can see the barrens over the next rise. Sweat rolls down my back. Serve Mom right if I keel over. Death from dehydration.

46

They'll find me in the ditch with crows picking at me, and the cops will bring her up on child abuse charges, and I'll laugh. Laugh from my ditch.

A car slows behind me, but that's been happening all morning and nobody's stopped yet, so I don't even turn around. A maroon truck crosses the line and pulls into the breakdown lane in front of me. I recognize the toolbox in the bed and jog over.

"Thanks." Inside the cab, Hunt's got the air-conditioning cranked and I sigh, closing my eyes for a second as it blows over me. Stars burst against the back of my lids. "Really. I almost died."

He checks the rearview mirror. "Hot day for a walk."

"You're telling me." I crane my neck to look at the oncoming lane. "You're good." I flop back. Classic rock plays softly on the radio. I wonder if Mom knew Hunt would probably come along on his way to work and get me, or if she even cared. I know better than to tell him what happened—Mom will kick my butt if I air dirty family laundry—so I leave it alone.

He's wearing his work duds, which are almost exactly the same as his handyman duds: chambray shirt, fat carpenter pencil in the chest pocket, Dickies pants, boots. He sees me looking and gives me one of those Hunt smiles, humor showing only in his eyes and playing around his mouth. "Good year for berries?"

"Oh, yeah, they're all over the place. We're killing ourselves." My stomach does a dipsy-doo all of a sudden and I sit up straight. Swallow. Ugh. Tastes sour. Hunt's watching me. "Uh . . . I think . . . maybe . . ."

He pulls over again, quick. Thank God I make it onto the shoulder before I heave up the aspirin and cereal and whatever else is left in my poor stomach.

I stand there, hands on my thighs, head hanging. Broken Bud glass glints in the dirt. I'm so embarrassed that I think about making a run for the woods, but then he'd think I was crazy on top of not being able to hold my liquor. I can't look at him as I get back in the truck. "Sorry."

He puts a thermos cup in my hand. It's iced black coffee that smells like it could peel paint. I drink, making a face. "Better eat some of this. Take it slow." He's unwrapped half a bologna-and-cheese sandwich—he's giving me his whole lunch here—and I start to argue, but his expression is so serious that I do what he says, fighting it down until my stomach settles. Finally, he says, "Long night, huh."

I laugh weakly. "Oh, yeah."

"Maybe I ought to take you home."

"Nah, I'll be okay. I've raked more hungover than this." He doesn't move. "Seriously. And I need the money." I guess he knows it's true, because he shifts into first and we go.

He drops me off at the top of the barrens road and I wave. I don't have to worry about him telling Mom anything; I know our ride is between us. And Mom's so closemouthed that she'll never ask if he saw me, anyway. Those two could split one word down the middle and make it last the whole day.

Mags straightens up at the sound of Hunt's truck leaving, but Mrs. Wardwell gets to me first. "Look what the cat drug in." She eyes me from her lawn chair, fanning herself slowly with a Hannaford flyer. The chalkboard where she keeps track of who's in the running for top harvester leans against the camper; Shea's name is number six. The rest are all migrants, names I don't know. "Your sister said you were sick, missy."

"I was." I duck into Mags's car to get my gloves and cowgirl hat. "Now I'm better."

She grunts. I hear her sipping soda as she watches me walk into the field, those hawk eyes of hers burning a couple dime-size holes into my back. The thing is, I really hate being late. I hate looking like a bad worker. But I don't think anybody would believe that on my best day.

Mags says to me as we rake, "You call Hunt for a ride?"

"No. I was walking and he picked me up."

She's quiet. "You could've told us you were going to the quarry last night. We waited for you." I don't answer. I didn't tell them because I knew they'd try to talk me out of it. "Let me guess. Kat set 'em up and you knocked 'em back until you couldn't see straight again."

Color creeps into my cheeks. "I drank what I wanted. It's not her job to stop me."

"She thinks it's funny when you're drunk, Darcy. She wants you to make an ass of yourself."

"I can do that without her help."

"Mom fell asleep on the couch waiting up for you."

I stop, not realizing how out of breath and dizzy I am until I almost lose my balance. I must've walked right past Mom in the dark last night after Kat dropped me off. Was she awake, the throw pillow under her head, watching me do a careful drunk step through the living room and up the stairs? Things have changed since Rhiannon, and I know it. Moms' minds go straight to murder when their kids come home late. I look at the ground. Mags doesn't have to say anything more.

I focus on work until I have to stop and take a long drink from Mags's water jug, scanning the rows to our right and left. Today, the sight of Jesse makes me feel like I bit into a lemon. He's sexy as hell, shirt off, tanned so deep that he doesn't have to worry about burning anymore. Shea tosses something at him—a garter snake—and Jesse jerks away, laughing and cussing him out. Mason checks the snake over and then sets it on a rock, out of reach. I remember last night at the quarry and turn away.

Jesse was there, with his hands all over Emma Bowen. Hanging his arm over Maddie Clark's shoulder. Grab-assing with Kat, who most guys stay away from because Kenyon's always around, even though Kenyon doesn't care. I was probably the only girl Jesse didn't touch last night. In fact, he didn't talk to me at all except to say hi. And here I was, panting for him, getting all giddy over a pair of old gloves. Wow.

At quitting time, I go up to headquarters to get our paychecks. Duke McCutcheon's cinching the straps on a truckload of boxes bound for Danforth's. Shea's hanging off the other side, holding them taut. If I squint, I can see the family resemblance between him and Duke; add thirty pounds, a handlebar mustache, and a Harley-Davidson T-shirt, and you've got it. Duke climbs down from the flatbed and swings into the driver's seat. Funny to think that after those berries go through the winnower at Danforth's, Mom will be sorting through them, fingers freezing through her gloves, picking out anything squished or white.

The guy in front of me in line for checks is a migrant, a short, muscular guy with skin the color of rosewood. I wonder what it feels like to be that dark. He speaks with a pretty thick accent when he tells Mrs. Wardwell his name. "Say again?" She squints up at him.

He repeats himself. There's grumbling from people behind me, and I hear somebody say, "Don't sound like English to me."

The guy's back has gone rigid, and he says his name a

third time, slowly: "Al-e-jan-dro Sán-chez. Do you want me to spell it?"

More muttering. "Awright, shut up back there." Mrs. Wardwell finds the check and gives it to him. He gets out of there pretty fast. I wonder what they're saying about us locals up there in the cabins. Can't really blame them for not wanting to mix with us, considering the way people treat them now. You can't help but wonder if the ugliness was always there, though. I don't think this much hate grows overnight, just because of Rhiannon. "You"—Wardwell crams all three of our checks into my hand—"keep the line movin.'"

As I leave, I hear somebody say, "Ale-who?" to a couple of snickers.

Mags and Nell are already walking to the car, Nell looking back with her hand cupped over her eyes to make sure I'm coming. I stoop to grab our water jug when somebody comes up behind me and slides their hand into the front pocket of my shirt, tucking in a bundle of buttercups. It's Jesse, so close that I smell his fresh sweat and sports stick. He smiles, showing the chipped tooth that makes him look a little off center, a little wild. "There." He walks backward, framing me with his hands. "Perfect."

Speechless, I touch the flowers and watch him go.

SEVEN

MOM TAPS OUT a Kool, sweat glistening along her hairline as she fishes in her pocket for a lighter. It's too hot to eat, too hot to move, and the girls are already out on the porch squabbling over a game of Crazy Eights, but she raises her eyebrows at me when I push back from the supper table. "Hold it. You're on dish duty."

"For how long?"

"Until I say." She sparks the lighter three times, then pulls her mouth to the side, touching the tip of the cigarette to the flame. I run water into the sink, watching her, remembering how hard Mags tried to get her to quit those things a few years ago. Hardly anybody's parents smoke; you just don't see it. Mags used to hide Mom's packs behind the couch or up in the attic, and then she'd leave printouts from the American Lung Association site on Mom's nightstand. I took a look at some of those, and it made me notice little things about Mom, like the stains on her fingertips where she holds her smokes, and the faint yellowish tint to her skin. Finally, when my sister put a *No Puffin* sticker on the fridge smack-dab in the middle of all the clippings from Nell's plays, Mom said, "Margaret, enough," in the tone that brings things to a full stop in our house.

Mags stared back at her, her hands in fists. "They're *killing* you. Don't you care?"

Mom blinked—maybe winced—then turned away, smacking the top of the Kools carton. "I find any more of these missing, they're coming out of your savings account."

I sweat while I scrub and rinse. A June bug bangs off the window screen above the sink. I watch it, thinking. "Has Hunt ever been married?"

Behind me, Mom coughs. "What brought that on?" I've surprised her out of being mad at me. I'm glad Libby's at work and not here to remind her.

"Just wondering."

She's quiet for a second or two. When I glance back, she's letting smoke trickle out her nose, watching it waft onto the sticky evening air like moth wings. "He was. Before we knew him."

"What happened?"

She shrugs. Her collarbones are sharp against her old wash-worn sleeveless blouse. "Didn't work out. You don't ask somebody for details about their ex."

Which meant they'd talked about it. I slide a dripping plate into the dish rack. "Well, she must've been an idiot to let go of Hunt."

"You think so, huh." Her tone reminds me that she has a few opinions about idiots herself. I'm not off the hook with her.

"Yeah. Seriously, Hunt's awesome. He's never a jerk and he knows how to fix stuff and he makes pretty good money at Danforth's, right? And he's cute, for an old guy." My words land hard when I remember what she said about me getting pregnant this morning. That's right. I'm supposed to be mad at her, too.

Mom inclines her head. "Hunt fixed up this house with his wife. Put that trailer out back so his mother could live close. Planned to build a barn, too, so his wife could have horses." The Kool grinds into the cut-glass ashtray, and then she's crinkling the pack for another. She still wears her wedding ring, the one Dad bought at a pawnshop with his whole week's paycheck. It's engraved with some other couple's names inside, but Mom didn't care; it was a joke between them, calling each other Wendy and Greg, signing cards to each other that way sometimes. "Marriage went south before they had more than the foundation laid. Hunt filled it with dirt so one of you kids wouldn't fall in and break your neck when you were out running around in the woods."

"I didn't know that." She lifts a shoulder. "Wait. Is that where all the lupines grow?"

"Mm-hmm. He seeded it."

I haven't been that far out back for a while, but I can picture it, a field of white, pink, and purple, shifting in the breeze. However things went down with his wife, Hunt couldn't be too bitter if he planted those flowers where their life was supposed to happen. "What happened to his mom?"

"She got Alzheimer's and ended up in a home," Mom said, considering the tip of her cigarette. "Believe she's dead now."

As I dry our big salad bowl, I wander over to the front doorway and watch Mags and Nell play cards through the screen door. "Nellie," I say, "what happened in the movie yesterday? I missed most of it."

She claps her hand to her chest and flops back onto the floor. "Oh!"

"Nooo." Mags holds her head, but it's too late. Nell's off.

She runs through the entire plot, backtracking a lot to fill in stuff she forgot to mention, doing impressions that get me laughing. Mags shoots me a dirty look. "Thanks. It's all she's talked about since we got home last night."

"I don't care. I loved it sooo much." Nell's cheeks flush. She's dreaming about a Technicolor James Dean, all lit up and beautiful and bigger than life. "My favorite part was when Cal and Abra finally kiss on the Ferris wheel, right at the top"—she sighs—"and it was perfect. They have the whole town around them, but they're still all alone. That's how it should be." She has her eyes closed, and at once I wish she'd stop talking, wish I'd never brought the subject up. She puts her hand to her chest like somebody moving in their sleep. "It's best when nobody knows. When your love lives in your two hearts, and nobody else matters."

Mags stares at her, then at me. I say, "Only in the movies, right, Nellie girl?"

She looks at me, eyes damp. "Uh-huh. Only in the movies." She lies back, puts her hands behind her head, and starts to hum.

I didn't really forget about sending a photo and a bio to Melissa Hartwell, but I pretend I did when Nell reminds me. I've actually been worrying about it ever since the welcome meeting. Once the booklets are out there, everybody will know. *Darcy Prentiss is on the ballot? How the hell did that happen?* I read through the Princess packet; Queen wins about $1,700 in scholarships, and second runner-up and Miss Congeniality get $100. I'll be happy if I get out of this thing without a bucket of pig's blood dumped on my head.

I have no idea what to say in my bio. I feel silly even writing it.

"How can I write a biography if I don't have a life?" I push the laptop across Mags's bedspread to Nell. "You think of something."

She pushes it back. "It's about *you*. I can't write it." She wrote hers in ten seconds. Easy; she's been practicing her acceptance speech since the fourth grade. She also has the business she wants to sponsor her all picked out: Weaver's Flowers & Gifts. "They sponsor a girl every year," she said. "Plus everybody gets their bouquets there anyway, so it'll be one-stop shopping." I tried not to laugh at how matter-of-fact she sounded, paging through one of my *Seventeen*s. "You should ask Hannaford. The twins work there, so you know somebody. That helps."

"Give it to me." Mags reads aloud as she types: "Darcy is an upcoming senior at Sasanoa Area High School. Her interests are . . ." She snaps her fingers at me. "Quick. Make something up. G-rated."

I throw her stuffed rabbit at her. "I'm gonna gut Mr. Buns while you sleep." I take the laptop back, feeling a brain cramp coming on as I stare at the blinking cursor in the email. Finally, I type *Darcy plans to travel after graduation*, then hurry downstairs to get the camera and put on some makeup before I can change my mind.

Don't ask me where that came from, traveling. The farthest

I've ever been was the Maine Mall in Portland back in seventh grade. I went with Rhiannon; her mom drove us and took us out for lunch. I remember Rhiannon and I bought necklaces at Claire's, hemp chokers with little clay beads and half a heart charm each. Rhiannon got the one that said *Best*.

I know Nell and Mags must've read what I wrote, but they don't tease me about it when I come back. "Stand here." Mags guides Nell back against the paisley throw with a picture of Janis Joplin on it tacked to the wall.

All it takes is one click. We look at the preview and Nell is gorgeous. She never looks self-conscious in pictures, just beaming and natural and completely herself. One of her curls spirals off at an angle from her widow's peak, but it looks right, somehow.

Next, I stand in the same spot. "You know, everybody else is going to use their senior pictures, I bet." I run my hands through my hair and fluff it out, which is impossible since it grows straight as a stick. "Bella probably went to Trask Studios and ordered the princess package or something."

"Darce." Mags raises the camera. "Shut up."

After five retakes, I can live with the last one. I look kind of tired, but not too bad, considering how the day started. I'm not smiling, but like Nell's crazy curl, it looks right.

After Nell's gone home to bed, I lie out on the roof, slowly turning the buttercups between my thumb and forefinger.

I just fished them out of the pocket of my work shorts, so they're a little crushed and wilted, but I think I might hang them from the curtain rod in my room and let them dry.

Mags crawls out, and we sit together, watching the lights blink on the Narrows bridge. Libby's car turns into the driveway. We stay quiet as she gets out, grabs her big patch-work shoulder bag, and goes into the trailer. She's got this self-righteous swish to her walk, head held high, like the world owes her because she got left at the altar (almost) by some dude none of us know anything about, least of all Nell. I say, "I yelled at her for eavesdropping on me and Mom this morning." Mags laughs. "I'm just so sick of her."

"I know."

"Wish she'd get her own place and move out of here. Nell could stay with us." I pause. "She hates me. Libby."

"I don't think so."

"You sure? She's been running her mouth to Mom behind my back, repeating stuff. I don't even know how she finds half of it out."

"All she has to do is ask Nell. You know she won't lie."

I let that one slide, swearing and crossing my legs at the ankle. "Nobody's business what I'm doing." I chew my lip, remembering Mom this morning. "Don't you think it's weird that Mom never talked to us about sex at all?"

"Probably would've been weirder if she had."

"But isn't that what a mom's supposed to do? Tell her

daughters about getting their periods and sex and every-thing?"

"Maybe on TV."

"No. Real moms do it. Kat's mom took her to family planning and got her on the pill when she turned thirteen."

"Ha. That's because she knew if she didn't she'd be raising another pair of bouncing baby hellions on top of the ones she's already got. You remember a time when Kat's mom *didn't* have gray hair?" I shake my head. "Exactly." We sit there awhile. She looks at the buttercups. "Pretty." I nod. "Listen. I'm not trying to boss you here, but . . . on the Fourth, when you and Shea . . . were you safe?"

I lower my eyelids, turning the bridge lights into fuzzy bursts of red, then darkness, then red. You could see the fire-works from the quarry that night. That's what it was like, colored bursts in the sky and bonfire smoke, the sound of people laughing from the other side of the pit. Him kissing me in the dark and me letting him, my back pressed against a tree, then the two of us going down into the grass together. "You don't have to worry."

She nods. The silence stretches out, awkward because I won't say more. "Night, then."

She climbs back into her bedroom. I hear the sound of her mattress creaking, then the rush as she turns the box fan on. I'm so tired I feel drugged, and I actually slip under for a few minutes before I jerk awake on the roof, tingling with the knowledge of how close the edge is, that I could've gone over.

I tiptoe through Mags's dark room, into the hallway of our sleeping house. In my room, I tie the buttercups to the crystal hanging in the window. That's when the headlights come on.

The car's parked maybe forty yards down from our house. They must've been sitting there for a long time; nobody turned down our road while we were on the roof. They idle for a minute or two, then pull into the road and drive slowly past our house.

I wait for the sound of the engine to fade away, but instead, it comes back. They must've turned around on the old logging road a quarter mile down from our house. They tap their brakes at the stop sign where Old County Road meets 15, and like that, they're gone.

EIGHT

THE NEXT DAY, fog rolls off the river, spreading white fingers as far inland as the barrens. It's the coolest day we've had so far, but everybody's sticky with humidity and hoping we'll get rained out. Can't rake berries in a downpour.

We've cleared the whole south field, so we spread out over the rise. I end up a few rows away from Shea. I catch myself trying to match his pace, raking so fast I'm breathless.

Shea's flying. How did I miss this last summer? One minute he's at the start of a new row, and the next he's halfway down, doing these loose jabs like he's shoveling snow. Leaves and sticks are scattering everywhere. He's filled another three boxes when I finally can't keep my mouth shut anymore.

"You clearing those bushes?" My voice is low.

At first, it seems like he's going to ignore me. Then: "You quality control?"

"You're fast, that's all."

"Didn't think you liked it any other way."

A muscle jumps in my jaw, but that's it. "Bob gets a look at the leaves and crap in your boxes, you're gonna get busted."

"Worried about me?" He turns, taking me in. His voice is different, stiff, when he asks, "That's really all you've got to say?"

I keep my eyes on my work, my skin burning, praying he'll let the moment pass. He snorts, and says something under his breath that I don't quite catch.

We both get back to it. I rake so hard that my arms feel like they want to come off at the shoulders, and when everybody breaks for lunch, I'm only two boxes behind him.

Around a mouthful I say, "This is amazing."

Nell nods, picking her sandwich apart into small pieces. "I made the bread."

"Holy crap, really? It's awesome."

Mags brushes off her hands. "Beats the stuff Mom buys."

"Hell yeah." I drink some water, catching a glint of silver at Nell's collar. Christ. She's wearing the necklace again. She's tucked it into her shirt, but I can see the bump of the little comedy and tragedy masks underneath. It's a pin, really—everybody who was in the one-act play two years ago got one—but she threaded an old chain through it like it's special, like it was given just to her. I told her last summer that if I ever caught her wearing it again, I'd rip it off her neck, and now she knows I've seen it. She flinches and looks down.

Then Jesse's between us, close enough that our arms touch. He nods at Mags and Nell. "Ladies." His shirt's open.

Mags scoots over. "Hello." I wish she wouldn't sound so bitchy.

He plucks a piece of grass and rolls it between his palms, blowing through a gap to make a buzzing sound like a kazoo. "Gross day, huh. Ten bucks they call it by two o'clock."

Nell's staring at his hands. "How'd you do that?"

"This?" He makes the sound again, then flicks the blade away. "Whistle grass."

Nell looks like somebody just told her that down is up and the stars are alien lightbulbs, sort of in on the joke but wanting to believe anyway. "He's messing with you," Mags says shortly. "There's no such thing as whistle grass."

"Sure there is." Jesse smiles at Nell, and I can see the exact moment when he charms her. So much for Jesse Bouchard not being good enough. The girl needs sandbags tied around her waist to keep her from getting swept away by the slightest breeze. "Got to have a sharp eye to see it, though. Maybe every sixteenth piece of grass, you'll find some."

She leans down, smiling. "Where? They all look the same."

"It's a real dark green. Like that." Nell picks it, rolls it between her hands, and blows. No sound. "Shoot. Well, keep hunting. They're out there." He finally looks at me. "You gonna be around this weekend?"

"Around where?"

"You know. Quarry. Drive-in. Kat's house."

I feel warm all over, but Mags's stare reminds me not to act the fool, either. "Could be." I don't say anything else, and he starts to get up. "Best way to make sure of that would be to bring me yourself." I lean back on my elbows. "Just saying."

Tires crunch on gravel, and we look up to see a Sasanoa police cruiser coming up the road. Jesse's grin fades.

Everybody watches the car park and the officers' fresh-shined shoes touch gravel. Hard to believe that it was this time last year that I was sitting in a chair down at the station, staring back at an officer named Edgecombe as he asked, *You a part of what went on out there last night?* No, I said. *But you have been in the past.* Not telling, I thought. *What happened to Rhiannon?* Why ask me? I said.

Mrs. Wardwell is on her feet, hobbling to reach the officers before they get within earshot of us. The cops are both pretty young, with sunglasses and sunburned crew cuts. They stand with hands on hips, checking out us rakers.

Knowing we're being watched makes me realize how weird we must look, segregated even at lunchtime: migrants grouped off to the left, locals to the right. A couple migrant women in sweat-stained ball caps whisper to each other and turn their backs on us. It's not just a race thing; there're plenty of migrants cut from the same white bread as us. The difference is in how they hold themselves, how they move around the fields like they understand them, like they've done it all before because they have, except maybe the crop was celery in California or apples in Massachusetts. How they got no intention of putting down roots in a dusty little speck like Sasanoa or anywhere else, and that makes them foreigners to townies like us.

Mr. Wardwell shows up, pulling off his work gloves as he joins his wife. Cops talk, Wardwells listen. I hear Mrs. Wardwell say, "Oh, sweet Jesus." Her hands rise up to her face, then drop as the cops go on.

"They found her." Mags's voice is low. "Must've."

We owe Jesse ten bucks. Rain comes down and we're sent home. Usually Mrs. Wardwell leaves us out there until we're drowned kittens, but today Bob blasts his truck horn three times and yells, "Bright and early tomorrow." The migrants grab their lunch pails and head up the hill to the cabins. One guy has his little girl riding on his hip, her sandaled feet dangling down.

On 15, local and state cop cars are parked along the breakdown lane where the barrens turn to woods. As we pass, I see cops in rain gear and reflective vests milling around in the trees before my breath fogs the glass and erases them.

"She can't be out there," Nell says softly. "We looked. We looked through the whole *woods*."

The search party combed the barrens and woods all the way over to Great Pond. Turned up plenty of old Winchester shells and beer cans, I bet. I don't know for sure because I didn't help search.

Back at the house, I take the first shower while Mags disappears into her room to check for news online. I'm in the kitchen getting a drink when Nell comes back from the trailer, her dark hair wet and combed straight back from her brow. It's pretty rare for us to have a minute to ourselves, so I stop her on the porch, hooking my finger under her necklace. "What's this?"

She cups her hand over it, flashing me a wounded look. "Nothing."

"Don't give me that. You promised." She looks at her feet. "Nell. You *swore*. Take it off."

Whispering: "No."

I grab at the chain. With a soft sound, she darts around me into the kitchen. I jerk her back by the elbow, then stop cold when I see Mags standing on the stairs.

My fingers loosen, my face softens, and I'm hoping it

looks like we were just horsing around, just play-fighting. Nell doesn't help me, either; she goes into the living room without a word, leaving me there with my sister. I don't know how much Mags heard, but I'm guessing not much. After a beat, I say, "Find anything out?"

"The news isn't even running the story yet."

I pick up my glass from the table. "You really think they found her?"

"Maybe." She keeps looking, probably for signs that I'm finally going to crack and bawl for my old bestie, but she should know better. I didn't cry that Saturday morning last summer when Rhiannon's mom called me. She must've been at the bottom of her list of names, calling the girl who didn't come around anymore. *Did Rhiannon sleep over last night?* No. *Have you seen her? Was there a party?* My mouth too cottony from sleep to speak. *I can't find her. I can't find her anywhere.*

I didn't cry at the assembly on the first day of school, when they asked anybody with information to come forward. Half the people who did cry didn't even know her. I knew her once. Back when she had braces and a pageboy haircut she was always pushing back behind her ears, and her wardrobe was made up of Camp Mekwi Teen Counselor or anime T-shirts. I didn't cry during the dedication at the end-of-school slide show, a parade of pictures of Rhiannon, starting when we were in sixth grade and dissected fluke worms. Rhiannon in shop class, smiling behind plastic safety glasses. Changing with each year. Growing her hair long, parting it on the side, learning how to wear makeup, how much was too much, changing her style, changing who she was, changing even her smile at the camera until it was a thin hint, a sly joke on us.

While Nell and I watch daytime TV like we'll turn to stone if we look at each other, Mags brings the laptop downstairs and keeps going to the *Ellsworth American* and WABI-TV sites, checking for updates. Mom's late getting home. She's almost never late. I keep glancing out the window, hoping to see her pull into the driveway.

Around five forty-five, the front door opens and Libby comes into the kitchen, probably surprised not to find supper ready and her place set at the table. She looks through the living room doorway at us. "Where is she?"

Mags doesn't turn. "Late."

That's when Hunt's truck pulls into the driveway. We all go into the kitchen and watch Mom get out of the passenger side.

"Where's your car?" Libby's on her as soon as she opens the screen door.

"Sitting in Danforth's parking lot. Hunt thinks it's the starter." Mom sets her scuffed leather purse on the counter and sighs, pushing her hands against her lower back, which has pained her ever since she got in that motorcycle accident with Dad before we were born. Mom ended up in the hospital, and Dad's Indian went to Gary's Salvage, where it probably still sits, buried in junk. Right now, it's hard to think of Mom at twenty, hugging Dad around the waist as they took tight corners too fast; she always looks so washed-out when she gets home from work, like a photo of herself left too long in the sun.

I hear the truck engine start outside. "He's leaving? Didn't you ask him to stay for supper?" Mom opens her mouth, and I say, "I'll get him," running down the steps into the rain, waving my arms. "Hey!"

He tries to beg off, but I won't let him, steering him inside and pushing the extra chair up to the table. Hunt's wearing a dusty orange Husqvarna ball cap, and he takes it off, squeezing the brim in his hands as he watches Mom. He has dark spots of rain on his short-sleeved dress shirt and glistening in the hair on his arms.

"Hope you don't mind waiting." Mom wipes her hands on her jeans, looking as flustered as she ever does. "I'm not sure what we'll have—"

"We'll figure it out." Mags opens the fridge. "Corn on the cob? Darce, go pick some. Nell, make some burgers, you're good at it."

Our corn is pretty small this year, and when I shuck the ears, I have to evict a couple fat borers, but nobody will be able to tell the difference once they're boiled. Nell, Mags, and I split the work, while Libby brews coffee and drops ice cubes into it, watching Hunt through the steam.

Mom's fixed Hunt a meal at our place here and there, but this is the first time he's ever stayed for supper. He looks kind of uncomfortable sitting there with his forearms resting on the vinyl place mat. Maybe it's because that chair's too short for him. I switch the radio on; the hourly news starts, and, remembering Rhiannon, I shut it off. I don't want her at our table.

Meat sizzles in the skillet. Mom fills a mug for herself and Hunt and sits, clearing her throat. "I should probably call Gary now."

Hunt nods. "Beat the rush."

Mom laughs—everybody knows Gary usually sits outside the office in a cane-bottom chair, spitting dip into a soda bottle and swapping stories with his mechanic—and that's the Hunt factor, actually getting my mother laughing, putting color back in her cheeks.

"So you two are going to ride together until the Subaru's fixed?" Libby smiles in a way that doesn't touch her eyes. "Cozy." I set the ketchup and mustard down so hard that the napkin holder jumps. Libby says to him, "Did you ever get an estimate on how much it'll cost to put a new coat of paint on this place?"

"I did." He lets her wait a second. "Too much. I'll do it myself."

"When?"

"Next week, if you like."

"I would like." Her smile is a mean little bow, and I imagine punching it off her face, sending her over backward in her chair, her glasses landing splat in the butter dish. She'd be out on her ass if it wasn't for Hunt and Mom; she couldn't afford a two-bedroom trailer on her Rite Aid paycheck without Mom chipping in and Hunt charging next to nothing. He holds my gaze for a second, and I get the feeling he almost read my mind, because he keeps his mug up high like he needs it to hide his mouth.

"Well, there's no hurry, Lib." Mom's got that V between her brows again. "It's paint. He can start whenever he's got time." She turns her back on Libby as Mags sets the food on the table. "I'm guessing they let you girls out early?"

We nod. Nell says, "The cops came." Her eyes widen when she notices me and Mags staring at her. "Well . . . they did."

"What did they want?"

Nell glances at us, then blurts, "They talked to the Wardwells. Mrs. Wardwell said, 'Oh, Jesus.'" She purses her lips, but the rest of the words bloop out like sour candy: "Cops were looking around in the woods, too."

You could hear a grain of salt fall. Mom turns to me. "They give you any trouble?" I was the only raker who was questioned twice last year, because they didn't believe my answers. I shake my head.

"Could be they found her." Libby butters her corn.

"Animals might've dug something up."

"I can't see the cops and the search party missing something so close to where they turned up signs of that fire." Hunt uses the ketchup. "That was about all they had to work with for evidence, paper said."

A scorch mark in a nest of boulders, like someone had wanted to hide the firelight from the road. A blackened forty-ounce bottle and some crushed beer cans. And Rhiannon's messenger bag that had once been army green before it was fed to the fire, with a few smart-ass buttons pinned to it. You could still read one shaped like two cherries on a stem that said *Eat Me.*

Berry bushes around the rocks had caught, smoldered, and gone out in the early-morning drizzle. The Wardwells could've lost half their harvest if it wasn't for the rain. I saw the scene myself, me and the other rakers who were working that section of the field the morning after Rhiannon disappeared. Her mom must've called the Wardwells that morning, too, because when Bob saw that bag in the ashes, he called the cops.

"I don't know about this, Nellie Rose." Libby shakes her head, and Nell looks up quick. "I told you I didn't want you raking again this year. It's a trashy job, hanging around with a bunch of drifters."

"She doesn't," Mags says. "She works and then she comes home." Maybe I didn't want to rake this season, but Nell did.

This is her only chance to earn money for herself all year, because Libby wants her to focus on her schoolwork the rest of the time. Except for drama, of course. Got to make time for that, it being Nell's passion and all. Nell's tearful and blinking hard now.

"All the same. Everybody knows that Foss girl got mixed up with one of those migrants and got herself killed, and one of these days they'll turn her body up in the Penobscot, just like they did that fella who jumped off the bridge last winter." The river tends to give people back one body part at a time.

I hate the scared *don't say I can't go anymore* look on Nell's face, and I feel like I have to speak up. "That doesn't even make sense. Why would Rhiannon be hooking up with some migrant? She didn't do stuff like that. And a migrant wouldn't start a bonfire down in the field, anyway. They have their own pit up at the cabins."

"Maybe he didn't want anybody knowing he was carrying on with a sixteen-year-old girl. They got laws against these things. Little girls aren't supposed to be out drinking and screwing." Libby gives me a cool stare. "Doesn't stop some people, though, does it?"

My hands slowly curl into fists. Mags and Nell stare at their plates.

Hunt clears his throat. "Now this," he says, taking a bite, "is how you make a burger."

N I N E

FROM THE ROOF, we can hear the argument grow and fade as they move around the kitchen, slamming chairs into the table, scraping plates.

Mom: "Who you were trying to embarrass more, me or him or the girls? Real nice talk, Lib—"

"—think he's always coming around for?"

"He's the landlord, for God's sake—"

"Oh, please. You'd have to be blind . . ."

Nell lies with her head on Mags's lap, staring off at the woods. "I'm sorry I told about the cops."

"It's okay." Mags pets her hair. "It wasn't really a secret. I didn't tell you not to say anything."

"But I should've known. I should've known it would ruin everything." I recognize the clenched, concentrated look on her face; she's angry at herself for always being a half-step behind. I've seen it on and off all year long, whenever she's remembering and the words almost slip out in front of Libby or Mags before she catches herself, probably flashing back to the way I shouted at her that night last August. The way I shook her, and shoved her back against the car door and nearly hit her for the first time in our lives because I was so crazy-mad, aching all over with the truth of what she'd done. "You didn't have to tell Darcy not to say anything."

I hear the faucet go on full blast and dishes clunk into the sink. Mom sent us out of the room after Hunt left, so I guess I have him to thank for getting me out of dish duty tonight. I'd rather be scrubbing than wondering if Hunt will ever speak to any of us again after the world's most awkward meal. "That's sister stuff. Don't you know all sisters are psychic?"

"Quit it," Nell says.

"Swear to God." I look over at Mags. "See? Right now, she's thinking how much she wants to go to Gaudreau's and get me a butterscotch sundae with whipped cream and lots of jimmies just the way I liiike it. . . ." Mags shakes her head. "Then give me your keys and I'll go." She laughs. "Whatever. Wait till this fall. I'll get my license."

"Yeah, you and that three-legged dog hangs around the dump," Mags says.

Nell's smiling again, which means we've done our job. I sit back, feeling the grit of the shingles against my elbows and palms. Below, voices rise. Libby: "You going to play blind with your own daughter? Everybody knows, Sarah. Everybody sees." I run my fingertips over the grit, grinding it into my skin. "How long are you gonna let it go on? Till she winds up like that Foss girl?"

"All right, stop it."

"It could happen. She's asking for it. Every time she walks out that door in those skimpy little shorts with her shirt cut way down to here, she's asking for it. It scares me knowing that my baby's out there with her sometimes, running with God knows who. It's not the same world it was when you and Tommy used to go out raising hell, you know. You better get your house in order and fast, or—"

"*Stop telling me my business.*" Mom's voice is ferocious, making all of us jump. Nothing but shocked silence from the kitchen. "I don't need you telling me my business."

We sit, staring at each other, waiting. The next sound is the screen door banging as Libby walks out.

They found Rhiannon's car.

When I come downstairs the next morning, our daily *American* is already lying on the kitchen table. That's the front-page story: *Missing Sasanoa Teen's Car Found in Woods.* There's a photo of a silver Honda Fit being towed out of the trees. It's funny; I expect it to be rusty or covered in mud or something, but it just looks like a car, and it's only been missing a year, anyway. I look for the sticker in the back window, some manga creature from one of those graphic novels she loved, and find it, sure enough.

Mom walks in and sees me standing at the table. We don't speak as she reads over my shoulder. Smelling the simple powder scent of her, I remember how she shut Libby down last night. Over me. It doesn't seem quite right to say thanks, and it sure as hell would be the wrong thing to tell her that we were listening in, so I stay quiet. She grazes my shoulder with her hand as she moves to the bread box. "You eaten yet?"

"No." I watch as she pops two extra slices into the toaster.

Mags comes downstairs. She stops when I show her the article. "Somebody called in an anonymous tip." I lay the paper facedown so I won't have to look at the Fit anymore. "Paper says her car looks like it's only been in the woods for a few weeks."

"Makes sense." Mom pushes the toaster lever down. "Hate to think that the search party missed a whole car."

"It's creepy. Where's it been all this time?" I push the paper away. "Why'd somebody want it found now?" My skin prickles at the thought of it: Rhiannon's little silver car moving through the night while Sasanoa slept. Tires rolling down into pine needles and dead leaves. A door shutting. Footsteps fading away.

It reminds me of the headlights I saw in the darkness from my bedroom window, but that was days ago, not weeks. "I don't even get what this means. Did a migrant do it or not?" I try to put a familiar face on the night driver in my imagination, but the features swim and blur.

"Could be." Mom brings her breakfast to the table and sits, reaching for her Kools and the ashtray. "If he came back to rake for the Wardwells again this year, he could've moved the car from wherever he hid it last summer." She exhales through her nose. "Wanted to scare everybody all over again."

"Nell's gonna freak." Mags puts on her sneakers. "That's the part of the woods her group searched."

Nell really wanted to help find Rhiannon, like she owed her or something. They weren't friends, and I'm pretty sure that Rhiannon thought she was weird, even if she never said so. Rhiannon was a Gemini through and through; you never knew what kind of mood you'd find her in, but you lived for her good days, because she was bubbly and so much fun when she wanted to be. Whenever Rhiannon came over to our house, Nell would hang out, too, as usual. One time, when Nell was in the bathroom, Rhiannon whispered to me, "Isn't she in special ed?"

I said yes. Rhiannon didn't bring it up again. After a

while, we started spending more and more time at her house without ever talking about why. But in the back of my mind, I knew. And I hate that I never called her out. I hate that I wanted her friendship more than I wanted to stand up for Nell.

Now Nell comes to the door, opening it a couple inches and peering at Mom like she's nitro in a bottle. I guarantee she's been listening to her mom gripe about her aunt Sarah all morning. "Hi," Mom says without looking up, and Nell's shoulders relax. She isn't wearing the necklace anymore. Thank God.

As we head out the door, I glance at the trailer. No Libby walking over this morning with her mug in hand. The windows of the trailer are dark as we drive away.

The day flies by, with me keeping track of Shea from the corner of my eye all the time, working hard to match him if I can't beat him. He knows what I'm doing, I think, and pushes harder.

I bump into Mason at one point while I'm rushing around, stacking boxes. We've been working side by side for hours. "Sorry," he says right away, keeping his eyes down.

"My fault." I watch him dump his rake into a now-full box, stack it on top of four others, and walk off to grab more boxes from the pile that Mr. Wardwell and Duke dropped off the last time they drove through. I wonder if Mason hates me because of lies—or maybe truths—that Shea's told him. Or maybe he's somebody who makes up his own mind about people. Either way, it's a distraction I don't need, so I train my eyes back on raking.

I walk over to headquarters during lunch, standing in front of Mrs. Wardwell with my hands in my back pockets. She squints at me. She looks bad, pale, with bags under her eyes, like she was up half the night. "Yeah, missy?"

My gaze goes to the green chalkboard, smeared from being erased and rewritten every evening at quitting time. The name *Gaines* has been bumped up to the seventh slot, with 6,675 pounds raked in three and a half days. "Has a girl ever made top harvester?"

"You gonna throw in?" She gives a lopsided grin. "You know you can't keep up with them boys, right? Just talking facts." She gives her grunty laugh. "Like to see 'em last through a thirty-hour labor, though, huh?" She seems to remember that I've never been through labor, either, except as the one being pushed out, and gets moody again, chewing her lip. Never thought about her and Bob having kids. They must be all grown up, probably living as far away from Sasanoa as possible.

I step back, glancing toward the woods where Rhiannon's car was found. I feel like we've all been trying not to look there today, like it's an open grave or something, but everybody's whispering about it. I want to say something to

Mrs. Wardwell, like maybe that it sucks, them getting pulled into this again, all because Rhiannon decided she wanted to prove something by working in the fields one summer, but the words won't come, so I step away.

"Prentiss." I turn back and she's studying me. "No. A girl's never made it."

We stop to gas up at the Irving station after work, along with half the other rakers from town. While people pile out to make Gatorade and jerky runs, I see a black pickup pull into the lot behind us, bass cranked so high I can feel it through my sneakers. I grab Mags's shoulder before she opens her door. "I'll pump."

"Go for it. You're paying."

I round the bumper, looking straight into Jesse's windshield as he pulls up to the pump behind me, revving the engine twice before cutting it.

He gets out, hooking his shades into his collar. "Hey."

I feed a twenty into the machine and pull the nozzle free, glancing back at his truck. "Where's the wolf pack?"

"Riding with Duke." He locks the nozzle, letting it fill while he turns to face me. "You got plans?"

"Not really."

"Want some?"

I bite my lip so he won't see the smile creeping across my face. "I thought you meant this weekend."

He grins. "I can't wait that long."

His pump shuts itself off; he couldn't have been more than a couple gallons low. I focus on the digits scrolling by in front of me, then screw the gas cap on tight, making him wait. "Hold on." I poke my head in Mags's window. "I'm going with Jesse."

"Uh, aren't you grounded?"

"Mom never said I was. Just tell her I'll be home by ten. She won't care."

"Yes, she will," Nell says quietly.

"Not if you guys sell it." I hold up my hands, backing away from the window. "Counting on you."

Without another word, Mags guns out of the lot while Nell watches me through the back window, never looking away as long as I can see them down Main Street. Meeting Jesse's gaze, I open the passenger door of his truck and climb in.

He looks in at me. "They mad?"

"Nah." We stare at each other for a second. "Are we going or what?"

He thumps his hand on the frame and climbs in beside me, smelling like sweat and heat and boy and making my whole body wake up and say yes, please. I hang my arm out the window as we take off, raking my fingers through the wind.

★   ★   ★

Jesse drives too fast down back roads, passing on curves, trying to get a rise out of me. I just smile. I've played this game
before.

I sit with my knee bent, heel propped on the dash, never
reaching for the oh-shit bar. He jerks the wheel, stomps the
brake. I twirl the end of my ponytail around my finger. He
works up a sweat. I wish I'd brought lip gloss.

The next thing I know, we're hanging a left onto a long
dirt driveway that stretches arrow-straight to a farmhouse in
the distance. Dust billows on both sides of us. Faster, faster.
At the last second, when it seems like we're either going to
spin out or crash straight through into the living room, I
lurch forward for the door handle—

Jesse whips us to the right and we bump down a pot-
holed drive you'd never know was there, hidden by the low
branches of an oak. There's a corrugated steel barn up ahead,
a chicken house, and fields of blossoming potato plants on all
sides as far as I can see.

Jesse parks in a bald patch by the barn and cuts the engine,
looking at me. A smile like that should be against the law.
"Doing all right?"

"Uh-huh."

"Looking a little peaked over there."

I give in and laugh, punching his arm. "Ass."

Knowing he won this round, he surprises me by opening my door for me. I step out, pushing my hat back and

looking around. "Whose place is this?"

"My uncle Caleb's."

"Nice."

"You want to see nice." He goes through the open barn doors. A couple minutes later, he rides out on a dappled gray horse, bareback, no bridle or reins or anything. I step back fast. I went on pony rides at the Bay Festival when I was a kid, but never on an animal as big as this one. Jesse holds a handful of the horse's mane as he leans down and thumps her side. "Climb on."

"Um . . ." I step forward, then back. "How?"

"Not a horse person?"

"I like them. I've just never . . ." If this is another test, I'm going to ace it. I set my shoulders. "What do I do?"

I end up standing on a stump so I can grab her mane, swing my leg over her back, and sit in front of Jesse. His arms are snug around me as he nudges her ribs with his heels to get her moving down a rutted tractor path. We're up high and swaying, and I'm glad that we take this ride slow.

Jesse guides us out into the acreage, beyond the crops to the hay field. Giant bales are spaced evenly across the clearing. It's quiet out here, no sound but insects buzzing, and the breeze moves the grasses in the distance like a wave. Pretty as hell. He gives me a hand as we slide down. The horse wanders off to graze. I brush her hair off my shorts and thighs, saying, "I heard you were haying for your uncle."

"Earning my keep and a little extra. I live with him."

"Yeah?"

"My parents gave me the boot junior year. Couldn't make it work." I start to say I'm sorry, but he shrugs to show that it didn't touch him. "Caleb's okay. Pushes pretty hard, but he's trying to make a living from this place. I come out here till sundown most days after we get done raking."

I turn, closing the space between with a slow lean. "You didn't bring me all the way out here to work, did you?"

I kiss him on his smile. He kisses back, hard, stealing my breath. We sink down onto the grass together, and everything goes out of focus except the feeling of his skin on mine, his hands running up and down my back, under my shirt. We taste each other's salt and grit. I pull the elastic from my hair, shake it out, and roll over to straddle him, reaching for the button on his shorts.

I've got his fly open and my fingertips on the fabric of his jockey shorts—knew it—when he makes a sound and pushes me back, laughing, wiping his mouth. "Damn, slow down. You got somewhere to be?"

I stare. Shock makes me flush dark red. I get up, spin around, not sure which direction to go, only knowing that I have to get away from him. He says my name. I ignore him.

"Darcy? What're you doing?"

"Stop laughing at me." My voice sounds awful, croaky, like I'm going to cry when I'm not, never would.

"I'm not laughing"—he's laughing when he says it—"I'm not laughing at you. I just didn't think . . ." He catches my arm and turns me around. I whistle and snap my fingers at the horse, as if I could get up on her by myself and gallop away. She ignores me.

I come back at him, "If all you wanted to do was hold hands, you should've said so."

"Listen. That was . . . awesome." He reaches down and adjusts himself, his eyes never leaving mine. "But we got time. Right? That's all I'm saying." He tilts his head to hold my gaze. "If you want."

I watch him suspiciously, then step back and shrug. "Maybe."

"Cool." We mill around in the awkwardness for a minute or two. Jesse tosses some straw at me. I throw some back, half-hard. The corners of my mouth twitch and my heart settles back into a normal beat.

I guess we're okay.

But we're careful with each other after that. We ride the horse (I find out her name is Stormy) through the tall grass to where fields give way to woods, and follow a path that runs alongside a stream, eventually looping back to the farm. Jesse keeps one hand on my thigh, and I keep expecting him to realize what he passed up and go for it, but he never does. When we get back to the farm, we kiss for a while, and it's good. Better than good.

When he drives me home, Mom's on the porch, smoking, her feet propped on the railing. Feeling her gaze on us, I take a few steps back from the truck and raise a hand to him. "See ya."

Jesse smiles. "Bright and early." He pulls out, spraying a little gravel even though Mom's right there. I watch him go, not really sure what to make of him, or what we didn't do together.

TEN

THE METAL RISERS are set up in the main hall when Nell and I come for Princess rehearsal at six o'clock the next night. We're early, so we stand over by the wall and watch the others wander in.

"How come you won't tell us what happened?" Nell rubs the heel of her Keds against a scuff on the high-polish floor.

"I did tell you. We rode his uncle's horse on some trails."

"Mags says that's only half of it. She says otherwise you wouldn't be so quiet."

"Yeah, well, Mags doesn't always know. Remember that time she couldn't find those earrings she got for her birthday, and she was sure that one of us must've borrowed them without asking and lost them? She wouldn't talk to us for almost a week. Then she found them behind her dresser."

"But that was a long time ago. She's usually right about things now." Nell chews her lip. "Hmm. He just better not have done anything bad."

If I've been quiet today, it's because I've been busy thinking. Jesse and I didn't talk at work, mostly because I was raking like a madwoman, picturing Shea's name on that chalkboard every time my body said quit. My biceps are swollen and sore, and my head swam when I stepped out of Libby's car onto the sidewalk tonight, but I raked about 2,200 pounds today, a new record for me, and there was a bunch of buttercups waiting for me under Mags's windshield wiper at the end of the day.

But about yesterday, with Jesse? It's like having a feather down the back of your shirt, sliding out of reach and then cropping up again, niggling at you. He shot me down. No guy's ever done that before. They've dumped me, ditched me, led me on, and lied to me, but never once have they said no. I don't know how to feel about it, but I know I want it to be just the two of us again real soon.

"Okay, ladies." Mrs. Hartwell steps in front of the risers with her hands clasped. She wears a wedding band attached to a huge diamond engagement ring. Back in the day, I bet her husband was captain of the SAHS football team and she was Festival Queen, with hair big enough for sparrows to nest in. "Tonight, we'll practice our choreography for the coronation ceremony. Now, the stage at the fairgrounds isn't set up yet, but it's about three times the width of these risers and maybe five feet higher, so keep that in mind. Remember, you'll be lifting dress hems and walking in heels, so careful, careful. Nobody wants to trip, but if you do, keep in mind, life goes on. None of us is perfect."

She splits us into two groups, separating me from Nell. Our groups line up on either side of the risers and climb the steps as Mrs. Hartwell claps, keeping pace, calling, "Veronica, continue to the center, and Blair, you walk to meet her, then both face forward. Pretend there's a crowd out there. Beautiful! Follow their lead, everybody, keep walking, keep walking. . . ."

Nell watches her feet and moves her lips, I guess counting how many steps it takes to hit her mark because that's the kind of thing she'd like to know. Bella is two spots behind her, and when the girl between them finally steps on Nell's heel and they stumble together, Bella says, "God!" loud enough for everybody to hear.

I'm ready to teach her how it feels to hit every riser on the way down, but Mrs. Hartwell speaks up: "Girls, the Miss Congeniality title is slipping through your fingers as we speak. Patience and kindness are virtues." I don't know how she gets away with those corny sayings, but they don't sound too bad coming from her. Almost like she means them.

We take it from the top—ten more times, at least. Everybody's sick of stepping and pivoting and smiling and sitting with right leg crossed over left, but by the time seven o'clock rolls around, we're moving like a well-oiled machine. I watch Nell's face when she smiles out at the imaginary crowd. She's seeing something real, and not the folding chairs and bingo tables the rest of us see. You know what? No matter how weird it is for me to be here, I'm glad I'm going to get the chance to see Nell live the dream. She deserves it.

Mrs. Hartwell finally lets us go, reminding us to meet at the fairgrounds on Sunday morning, when we'll add "the next phase" to our routine. Libby's parked outside, reading one of her Amish romances under the dome light. Mom's car is at Gary's and should be back tomorrow, once the new starter comes in. I've got enough sense not to ask Mom how it's been, riding with Hunt, but we all watch out the window as they pull in together at night, watch them linger and talk a minute as the twilight comes down. Libby's been quiet since the big blowout, but she speaks her mind each time by letting the back door slam behind her when she leaves.

We stop off at Hannaford so I can talk to the manager about sponsoring me for the pageant and Libby can pick up a few things for her cupboard. I'm nervous, but Nell isn't. "It's okay," she whispers as we wait at the customer service desk for the manager to answer his page. "People like doing stuff like this. It makes them feel good."

"Giving away money?"

"Helping." She folds her arms. "You'll see."

The manager's a nice-enough-seeming guy in his thirties who says yes pretty much right away. "Got to love the festival. Best part of the summer." He says to come back tomorrow and he'll have a two-hundred-fifty-dollar check ready for me, enough to cover whatever dress and shoes I end up buying and flowers. I'm not sure why I need flowers or what I'm supposed to do with them, but I'm betting Nell does.

Once Libby's loaded up her basket, there's only one register open, and it's Kat's. Kat leans on the counter, but she draws lazily up to her full five foot three when she sees me coming. Her red employee polo shirt tents off her bony shoulders, and her black jeans are so skinny they look airbrushed on. "Supertramp," she greets me. "Shopping with the fam-damily. Love it."

I grin. Libby's grown stiff beside me. "Kenyon working?"

Kat pops her gum. "Called out sick again. Loser." She totals our order and stares at Libby, who swipes her card and gets an error message. "Wrong way." Kat keeps chewing and staring as Libby fumbles the card around and tries again. "Wrong. Way." When Libby finally gets it, her face is brick red. Kat rips the receipt and holds it out to her, smiling with her little sharp teeth.

Libby leaves in a rustle of plastic bags, and Nell, who watched the whole thing with her eyebrows raised, follows, glancing back to make sure I'm coming. I linger for a second, hissing at Kat, "You're gonna get your ass fired. She'll complain to your manager."

"So? That's your aunt, isn't it? You said you hate her."

I hope she didn't see me flinch. "I said she can be a bitch sometimes." Kat rolls her eyes like *same difference.* "I gotta go. Stay out of jail."

She slides back into the position she was in before, fingering through the tabloids. "No promises."

Libby puts the pedal down before I even have the door shut all the way, and I have to buckle up as we drive. The angry flush reaches all the way to the back of her neck, and I can't help feeling another twinge of guilt.

Kat and I first started hanging out the winter of sophomore year, after Rhiannon and I had our big fight and stopped speaking. Until then, I'd always hung out with normal, middle-of-the-road kids, but there I was, between friends and spending a lot of time not liking myself very much. I had Mags and Nell, of course, but family's different. Kat and I worked on a project together in American history and got to talking. She was funny and didn't give a crap what anybody thought, so when she asked me over to her house one Friday, I said okay.

Once we were up in her room with her speakers blasting, she reached under her bed, brought out a shoe box, and said, "Take some." It was full of lipstick, eye shadow, foundation, you name it, all sealed, some with Rite Aid sale stickers on the bottom. Most of them weren't even Kat's shades, just random colors she must've stuffed in her pockets without really looking. Now, if I were Mags, I would've said no. I would've said it was wrong, and told Libby. But since I'm me, I took a bottle of nail polish called Plum Velvet. It's still on my vanity, half-buried in cotton balls and hair elastics.

It's nearly dark when we get home, and the porch light is on. There's a cop car in the driveway. Our headlights flare off the reflective lettering across the door, and my heart rises into my throat.

I'm the last one inside. Mom's sitting at the table. Officer Edgecombe sits across from her. The air is hazy with smoke, looking like a scene from a bad dream, one where I can't move forward or back because I'm rooted to this spot on the peeling linoleum for all time as Mom says, with her face giving nothing away, "Darcy. He's got some questions."

Edgecombe is older than Mom, his face loose and jowly, his gut a heavy sack hanging over his belt, somehow making him look even bigger than he is, which is big. He's as tall as Hunt and must have forty pounds on him. He seems old to still be the kind of cop who has to wear a uniform; I thought the same thing last year when he sat me down at his desk in the corner of a room full of other desks that were empty because most of the force was out looking for Rhiannon.

Now I read his name tag and it says *Corporal,* which I guess means he can boss the younger guys around a little.

"Darcy." Maybe it's the jowls and the hound-dog eyes, but this guy always manages to make me feel like I've disappointed him. "I didn't want to have to make this visit."

I sit at the head of the table with my fists in my lap. Libby and Nell stand at the counter. Everybody seems like they're caught in the same bad dream. Feet too heavy to run, lungs too tight to breathe.

"I'd hoped you were honest with me last time we talked."

"I was." Libby makes a sound, and I hunch my shoulders. "I *was.*"

He takes a shallow breath, making a show of getting out a notebook and clicking open a ballpoint. "Ms. Prentiss, this might be easier if Darcy and I could talk one-on-one."

Mom scrapes her thumbnail across the unlit tip of her next Kool. "Now, that wouldn't be a very good idea." There's a humorless quirk at the corner of her mouth, and in this moment, I'm so, so glad she's my mother.

Edgecombe blinks, says mildly, "This isn't an interrogation. It's a conversation. There's no reason it has to become anything more than that."

"What's wrong?" Nell's voice is high and sharp, her gaze going between Edgecombe and Mom. Libby takes her arm but she pulls away, turning to her mother. "No, why does he want to talk to her?"

"Lib, we'll see you guys tomorrow." Mom doesn't lift her gaze from Edgecombe. It must be killing Libby to miss this, but she takes Nell out. Mom taps her lighter on the tabletop. "So this has to do with the car, right? Everybody knows you found it."

"In part." He looks at me. "Last summer, you said you hadn't been friends with Rhiannon for a long time. That you two didn't talk anymore."

"Yeah."

"What happened?"

I've already answered this, or danced around it, anyway. I fight the need to glance at Mom, to see if she's been wondering the same thing or was just glad when Rhiannon stopped coming around. I always got the feeling that Mom never liked her much. "Nothing. Just grew apart."

"You stopped being friends for no reason?" He waits, using the silence. I know that trick from years of living with Mom, and don't rush to fill it. "I find that very hard to believe. When was the last time you were in Rhiannon's car?"

"Never."

"You never rode with her. Never even sat in it?"

"No. She got it after we stopped hanging out." For a second I panic, remembering all the places in that car that my hands have touched, but I don't think Mom will let him print me.

"When did you last see Rhiannon?"

"You know. That Friday, end of the day raking berries."

"Friday, August twelfth?" I nod. "And she was doing what?"

It's a snapshot in my mind now, a nothing-special moment sharpened with each passing month that she's been gone. Rhiannon knelt about twenty feet away, packing up her bag, pausing to pull a piece of hair from the corner of her mouth when the wind kicked up. She looked over her shoulder and laughed at something one of the boys said to her, but whoever it was didn't make it into the shot.

When it came to Rhiannon, I was used to pretending not to see, not to listen. I was so mad when she showed up that first day of the harvest. She didn't need to work. Her parents gave her everything, most of all a brand-new car as a congrats gift for getting her license. She always used to spend her summers as a volunteer counselor at Camp Mekwi, this day camp in New Hampshire where she'd been going since she was little. She loved it, but I think she loved getting away from her parents more; they're one of those couples who've been divorced for years but still hook up sometimes and make tons of drama. Rhiannon had *camp friends*, which are almost as bad as church friends: strangers who steal your bestie title when you aren't around to fight for it. Whenever she'd tell stories about them all teaching kids how to macramé or put on plays together, I couldn't help feeling jealous, sure they were all cooler or funnier than me. "She was getting ready to leave."

"By herself?"

"I think so. But I didn't stand there and watch her drive away or anything."

"What was the plan for later?" He gestures with his pen when I hesitate. "Was everybody going to meet up at the fields after dark, or did it just turn out that way?"

Now that bugs me, him trying to trap me like that. "I don't know. I didn't go back to the fields that night. I went for a drive with Kat Levesque."

"What if I told you I talked to somebody who says they saw you in the fields?"

The wall clock ticks. Ash drops from Mom's cigarette. Another scar for the tabletop.

"They're lying." I need to clear my throat.

"Why would somebody do that?" Edgecombe watches me. "Hmm?"

"I dunno. To get me in trouble."

"You think somebody would lie to the police, take a risk like that, just to cause trouble for you?" He gives a low whistle. "You must really know how to make enemies."

I look at him, without a clue how to answer. All of a sudden the day's work pulls on me like a weight, and I wish I could drop into my bed with its rumpled sheets and old stuffed dog hidden between the wall and box spring and not wake up until summer's over.

That's when I see Mags. She's sitting on the last stair riser in the near darkness, wearing light-colored shorty pajamas, watching us through the railing. Knowing she's been there the whole time helps me to find the words: "If you tell me who you talked to, then I can tell you why they might lie."

He looks at me steadily, seems to decide something, then clicks his pen and tucks it into his chest pocket. "We'll talk again soon, Darcy." He gathers his notebook, which he didn't write a word in. "In the meantime, think about what's important here. The Fosses are in a lot of pain. We're working hard to give them some answers." He waits. "If you know something, we will find out."

Mom stares at the place mat. Her voice stops him on his way to the door. "My daughter had nothing to do with this." She lifts her gaze. "You go tell your chief that."

Once he's gone, Mom heads out to the porch. I hear Mags's footsteps disappear upstairs, walking on the sides of the risers so they don't creak, our old Nancy Drew trick. I don't know what brings me to the screen door, watching Mom through the mesh. She sits in her usual chair in the far corner. Moths flutter around the overhead light, battering the frosted glass like they think heaven's inside, like they could touch it.

Mom says, "You'd better start telling the truth, little girl. Not a thing in the world I can do to help you until you do."

"I *am* telling the truth." My voice sounds tinny, faraway.

She shakes her head slowly and says nothing. I go upstairs, touching Dad's photo on the way. He was a big guy, a real

bruiser, wearing a plaid work shirt rolled to the elbows, cigarette pack popping his pocket flap open. I study my laughing
face when I was a little kid.

Mags's lamp is on. I know she's waiting up for me, but I
ignore the invitation, go to my room, and shut the door.

I lie there for a long, long time, staring at the dried buttercups hanging in my window. After the house has gone
quiet, a light rain falls. I'm almost lulled to sleep when I sense
a change in the darkness and open my eyes.

Headlights shine through my curtains. They burn in place
for a while, then glide up the wall, across the ceiling, and are
gone.

ELEVEN

NEXT MORNING, JESSE walks his fingers up my spine as he heads past me into the fields, following Shea and Mason. Later, I see him pause to watch me across the rows, but when I wave, he only gives a flick of his hand that somebody could mistake for swatting flies.

I think we're supposed to be a secret.

I don't mind. I've played this game before, too. Don't touch me in front of my buddies, don't smile like we've got something going on. Maybe I didn't expect it from Jesse, but I'll run with it.

I've loaded forty-six boxes by ten thirty, more than I've ever done before lunch break. My heart feels like a bird slamming itself against a cage, and I squat down on my heels to catch my breath when I see Duke's pickup coming up over the rise.

He grabs my boxes, carries them to the bed, then notices me looking at him. "What's up?"

"Who would you say rakes the most in a day?" I straighten up. "I mean, who's had the most boxes this harvest, that you've seen?"

Duke leans on the truck, scratching at his chest. He's hairy like a bear under that Harley shirt, I can testify; on scorchers, he strips right down. "Coupla migrant fellas over toward the south end. But Bob's picking up his share, too, so I don't see everything." He squints at me. "Why?"

I shrug. "Just wondering." He loads our boxes, both mine and Mags's, then drives on.

Mags watches him go. When she turns back, she comes out with the one thing that's been eating at me all morning. "Somebody was parked outside the house last night. Just sitting there."

I pick up my rake. "Probably somebody pulled over to text."

"At two in the morning? On our road?" I don't say anything. "Maybe it was that cop, Darce. You think of that? Maybe he was waiting to see what you'd do after he bluffed you about that witness." She sounds mad, but I know Mags. She's scared and putting up a front. "He was bluffing, right?"

"I wasn't at that party. Kat and I went out driving."

We rake a minute. "You can tell me things, you know."

"I know." The quiet stretches out. I trust Mags. She'd cut her tongue out before she told a secret. But if she thought she was doing the right thing—saving me from myself, using that good head on her shoulders—she'd speak up. And I can't have that. Because in this case, this one time, doing the right thing would be wrong for everybody. It would rip the heart out of who we are, and Nell—our Nellie, who we used to hold in the grass and tickle with dandelions, who helped Mags walk all the way home from Back Ridge Road when she twisted her ankle, who cries over old movies and has enough dreams left in her to love an actor who died before our moms were born—couldn't be who she is anymore. I don't even want to think about who people in this town would make her out to be.

"If you see the car again, tell Mom." Mags sounds stiff. I've hurt her. "And don't say anything to Nell. She'll be seeing kidnappers everywhere."

"No. I won't tell Nell."

An early moon hangs in a still bright-blue sky at five o'clock when I toss my rake into the bin and clap my gloves together, sending tiny green leaves and sticks flying.

Nell comes on the run. "Did you see it?" She waves toward the camper when I stare at her. "On the *board*. Mrs. Wardwell wrote your name."

Mags catches up to us and we go take a look. *D. Prentiss* is scrawled in the last slot, number ten. Three slots below *Gaines.* I'm not the only girl on the board, but I'm the only local one.

I can't help it; I whoop and do a little victory dance, throwing one of those high kicks we learned in cheerleading in sixth grade. Mags laughs, catching my shoulders before I tip over.

Mrs. Wardwell watches from her chair and snorts. "You boys better look out," she calls. "She's comin' to get ya."

She's making fun of me, but I don't care. I never thought I'd make it on to the board this harvest, period, and my tired feet feel a little lighter as we walk to the car.

There's a folded piece of paper waiting for us under the wiper. Mags opens it, reads the message, and sighs, holding it out to me.

In round, messy handwriting that fits Jesse perfectly, it says: *Quarry tomorrow before work be ready 6:00.*

I look around, but he and Shea and Mason are already gone. Nice how he doesn't wait to see if I want to go or anything, just assumes the answer is yes. Which it is.

"Oh no," Nell says, and we follow her gaze. Two cop cruisers are coming up the barrens road. "Darcy, they're not here for you, are they?"

Maybe Edgecombe's behind one of those tinted windshields. Maybe he really wasn't bluffing last night about the witness, the person who said they'd seen me in the barrens. It's not until the cruisers pass by that I can breathe again. "Don't be crazy." But my voice doesn't sound quite right.

Everybody in the field watches the cops continue on to the cabins. "Wonder what they're going up there for," Mags says.

Nobody has an answer.

I try to stay up late that night to see if the car comes back, but sleep wins out. The next thing I know, my alarm is going off at five thirty a.m. and my whole body is crying *nooo.*

What the crap was I thinking? I can barely get myself out of bed in time for work, and that's an extra half hour of sleep on top of this. I tiptoe into the shower and shave everything that needs it, then put on my hot-pink bikini under a white mesh cover-up.

By the time I'm at the kitchen table, I remember to be nervous, and can't eat more than a couple bites of breakfast. I scribble a note for Mom—*Gone swimming*—then sit on the porch steps with my tote, hoping Jesse has the sense not to rev his engine when he gets here and wake everybody up.

He doesn't try anything fancy, just idles and waits for me to climb in. He's shirtless, wearing an unzipped hoodie over baggy surf shorts and sandals; he looks as tired as I do, and we don't say much more than hey before he pulls a U-ie and drives toward the quarry.

Downtown is hushed and empty, only a few employee cars parked at the Irving station and Hannaford. We park in the usual place in the woods and make our way down the cliff to the water. The sun hasn't been up long, and there are still some streaks of orange reflecting off the water, which is black and flat as a stone otherwise. The thought of swimming here alone at this quiet time adds to the chill of the water. I slide in and kick my way deeper, taking measured breaths.

Jesse and I swim around each other, just swim, like we're here for the exercise. He's as strong a swimmer as I am, which is saying something, but he can't lap me as we follow the curve of the quarry wall. Big rocks jut out of the water here and there like dinosaur backs, and I dodge them before climbing onto one of the ledges to catch my breath, grinning as he swims up.

He pulls himself up next to me, streaming water. "Hungry?"

"Starved." I watch as he follows the path up to the truck and comes back a couple minutes later with a plastic bag. He's got muffins and little bottles of orange juice. I've never known a boy to think of bringing food anywhere; I blink, taking a muffin. "Did you make these?"

"Yeah. Started baking around three this morning." He breaks up laughing at my expression. "Bought them yesterday." He takes a bite. "Still good, though."

We eat for a minute, looking at the water. I give a shudder.

"Almost looks dead, doesn't it?" I giggle awkwardly. "Sorry. Don't know why I said that."

"No, I know what you mean. Something weird about water that doesn't move. Give me the ocean any day, some-place with a tide." He swallows. "Think of all the junk that's ended up down there on the bottom over the years. Like that quarry in Hallowell. You read about that?" I shake my head. "Some company drained the Hallowell quarry a few years ago because they decided to start mining the granite again. People had been swimming there for like eighty years, like they have been here. I guess they found a ton of crap on the bottom. Stuff you wouldn't believe. Jewelry, unopened cases of beer, car keys. A safe with a hole blowtorched through the side—"

I laugh. "I believe that."

"So this one guy hears they're draining the pit and gets an idea. Like thirty years before, dude went for a swim and dropped his brand-new school ring into the water. Searched and searched for it, but the quarry was so deep, there was no getting it back. His mom tore him up one side and down the other. That shizz is expensive." Jesse spins his bottle cap on the ground. "You believe that guy climbed in and found that goddamned ring? Covered under dirt and junk, about forty feet straight down from where he was swimming that day."

I feel a different kind of shiver at the thought of the gold ring drifting down, down through the still water, coming to rest on a ledge with a tiny puff of dirt. I look at Jesse and I don't see him the same as I did before. I didn't know he thought about things like this. "That's insane."

"I know, right? Seriously, that ring should've been gone forever. He never should've found it." Jesse shoves his wet hair back from his brow. "I dunno, life's weird. Think something's over, think again, huh?"

"Yeah. True." I hug my knees. The sky is brightening, getting bluer, and the water's surface is getting bluer along with it. "It'd be cool to put something down there on purpose, in case they ever drain this place, you know? Something so people knew we were here."

"Like a time capsule." Jesse smiles. "What would you want them to know about you?"

I glance at him, quick. The question gets my back up. What does he expect me to say? He's prying into places I'm not sure I want him looking, so I strike a bombshell pose, leaning back on my hands. "What do you think?"

He stares for a second, then goes in for a kiss, and pretty soon I've got the granite against my back, towel under my head, his wet warm skin under my fingertips as I pull and stroke the muscles of his shoulders. He kisses down to the hollow of my throat, and I unhook my bikini top and feel his lips slide south.

I close my eyes and it's good, what's happening, but the darkness behind my eyelids reminds me of this same sky at night, with bursts of colored lights against it. Smells of smoke and burnt sugar and weed, sounds of voices, laughter—everybody's right over there, too damn *close* for this—and I stiffen, my thighs tensing in memory. I open my eyes and it's Jesse, the one I want, looking a question at me: *Stop?* I shake my head and kiss him hard to prove I mean it.

Eventually, Jesse ends up being the one to stop us, groaning and sitting back. "We better go. It's almost six-thirty." He stands and stretches, not looking at me as I straighten my suit and put on my cover-up. I tuck my towel into my bag, careful to hide the half box of Trojans I put in there this morning.

He takes me home. Wouldn't want to be seen riding to work together. We don't kiss when we say good-bye, and now he's got a distracted thing going on that I don't understand at all. With a rep like his, you wouldn't think he'd run so hot and cold.

I go inside. Mom and Mags haven't been downstairs yet, so I crumple my note and go to my room to get changed.

"You're up early," Mom says when she comes down and finds me reading the funny papers. She's been short with me since Edgecombe, but at least she's talking to me.

"Yup." I turn the page. Mags makes herself breakfast, resting her head on her fist as she chews. Good ol' Mags. I can trust her not to say a word, most of the time.

TWELVE

I'M ON FIRE. By the end of the day on Friday, I've moved up to the ninth slot on the board, and Mrs. Wardwell's laughing out of the other side of her mouth. I'm feeling pretty good—hell, I'm flying—even though I pulled something in my back today and can't really bend over. That's okay; after tomorrow I'll have Sunday to rest before destroying whoever's in the eighth slot on Monday. Time's running out: only the west field still needs to be raked, and another harvest will be over. Then back to bad ol' SAHS for Nell and me. School's such a crock. Teachers are all burnout cases or worse. I'd drop out if Mags wouldn't skin me alive. I don't think Mom would really care as long as I got a full-time job right quick.

When we get home, there's a ladder leaning against the house. The old yellow paint has been scraped off the clapboards as high as the second-story windows. As Mags parks, Hunt comes around the side of the house, dressed in an old T-shirt and his Husqvarna cap. He raises his hand to us and picks up the ladder, carrying it with him out of sight.

"Your mom must've really got under his skin the other night," Mags says back to Nell, grinning. "He started early."

I walk over to where Hunt set the ladder down, massaging the pain in my back. "Did you actually take a vacation day?"

He scrapes a gnarly old strip of paint that's been on our house as long as I can remember. "Half a day."

"What color's she going to be now?"

"Well. I been thinking on yellow."

I grin and watch him work for a bit, poking at bits of old paint in the grass with my toe. "Listen, we're going to Gaudreau's to pick up supper. You want anything?"

"I'll be gone by the time you get back. Thanks."

"You'll be sorry. Best fried clams in town."

"I thought you didn't eat anything but cereal and Moxie."

"No. I eat fried stuff, too."

Mags and I shower, leave a note for Mom telling her we'll buy her a shrimp basket, and walk to the trailer to get Nell.

We don't come here much anymore, which is kind of sad, considering it's a stone's throw from our back door. We girls used to hang out in the trailer a lot growing up, back when

Libby wore her hair cut short and wasn't so mean. At least I don't remember her being that way. I remember this one time, she let us use this old Snoopy snow cone maker that belonged to her and Mom when they were kids. It leaked sticky red sugar-water all over the place, but Libby just laughed and let us make a mess.

Mags knocks once and lets us in. Everything looks the same: vinyl dinette set in the kitchen, framed JCPenney portrait of baby Nell on the wall, couch covered with a bedsheet to hide the rips that their old cat Tiger left behind. Libby looks up from her knitting, calls, "Nellie," without so much as a hello. She has this mitten obsession; she knits them year-round. I guess it soothes her. We've all got more pairs than we can use, so she ends up donating a bagful to the Coats for Kids drive each December.

Nell's bedroom is at the end of the hall, and she waves us down. It's a crazy mess, as always, makeup and brushes scattered in front of the mirror, dog-eared cosmetology how-to's crammed onto her bookshelf next to her old Baby-Sitters Club and Boxcar Children books. She's still got those pink-and-white tissue-paper flowers she made in sixth grade stapled over her bed. Around them, she's printed out a bunch of James Dean pics and stuck them to her wall in a collage. Some black and white, some color, all different sizes: Jimmy hanging over motorcycle handlebars, walking down a city street in a black overcoat, smirking around a cigarette. I guess

Libby decided it was safe for Nell to have a crush on a dead guy. Not much chance of him crawling through her daughter's window at night.

Nell finishes buttoning a sleeveless pointelle shirt and arches her back, tugging at the fabric. "I got it over to Twice Is Nice. You think it's too tight in the chest?"

"No, it's cute." I reach into the ceramic dish on her dresser and hand her some pearl studs, careful not to touch the comedy-tragedy necklace coiled beside them like an eel. "These. Definitely."

Libby watches us over her glasses as we walk by. "Nell. Bring your phone. And put on a sweater."

"It's hot."

A beat passes. "Go get a sweater." She sets her needles down. "You can borrow my cardigan with the little pearl buttons."

Nell brightens. "Okay." She goes back down the hall while Mags and I stand there, fidgeting. Back when I was eight years old, making jacked-up Snoopy snow cones in the kitchen, I never would've guessed I'd feel this uncomfortable here someday.

Libby's gaze goes to the sitcom on TV. "I want her home by eight thirty."

Eight thirty? Seriously? For a girl who's turning nineteen in November? I picture Libby sleeping down the hall from Nell every night, dreaming sweet, smug dreams without even the slightest clue that her baby's had everything stripped away from her, just everything. It makes me sick, and I snap, "We're getting supper and coming right back."

"I heard that one before. Then the three of you disappear until midnight."

Okay, so that's never happened. At least, not all three of us. Mags sighs, giving Libby her *you bore the crap out of me* attitude.

It feels good to be in Mags's car again with the windows down, free. We pass Mom and honk; her Subaru is back on the road, burning oil and flaking rust. I look in the mirror to watch her pull into the driveway and walk over to see what Hunt's done so far.

Gaudreau's is nuts. People know they're running out of summer. By Labor Day, the shutters will be up on the take-out windows, and the sandwich board will read, *Thanks for Another Great Season!*

The side door opens, and I recognize a migrant guy from the barrens, wearing an apron and lugging a couple bags of trash to the Dumpster. Mr. Gaudreau must pay under the table for kitchen help. Huh. Some family business. "Order for me, okay?" I hand Mags a ten so she won't give me crap about not chipping in.

I sit at the only empty picnic table, watching the migrant sling trash, thinking how much it would suck to rake all day and then slave here until closing, when somebody sits down next to me.

Shea. It's a shock, partly because I'd forgotten what he looks like cleaned up, his hair a little damp from showering, wearing a white polo shirt that's maybe a little nicer than most guys might wear on the average day. That's Shea, though. He's the kind of guy who buys only the right brand of sneakers and spends all his time tricking out his motorcycle, a Kawasaki Ninja 300. He's got me pinned with those lion eyes. "Congrats."

I set my face. "What."

He puts a booklet on the table between us. It's the Bay Festival events brochure, and the high I've been riding since work drops me flat. Mrs. Hartwell must've put in a rush order.

The cover has a swirly font and photos from last year's festival: a Guernsey cow winning a blue ribbon at the livestock judging, a lobster dinner, kids on the Tilt-A-Whirl. You can tell Shea's been rolling the paper, working it in his fist.

"I heard about this. I just didn't believe it." He flips through, holds it open at page twelve.

My face doesn't move, but the shame tastes bitter as I stare at the picture of the unsmiling blond girl with her stupid untrue bio—*Darcy plans to travel*—printed beside her and wish to God I'd quit the pageant when I'd first wanted to. Now everybody knows. Shea knows, and that's the worst.

He moves closer to me. His smell is spicy cool aftershave and peppermint gum, which he must've spit out right before he came over. He acts like he's teasing, like this is some in-joke between us. "I mean, do they know who they're dealing with? You must have a rep clear across Hancock County by now. You oughta hang a sign out in front of that fallen-down old dump you live in."

Shea and his dad and his dad's girlfriend live in a tiny pre-fab house over on Merrill Avenue with one of those corny gazing balls in the front yard, so I don't know what he thinks he's talking about. I fold my arms and look straight ahead.

He's quiet a second. "How come I never heard from you?" I study the flecks in the pavement, the corner of a ketchup packet by the table leg. "Huh? I thought you were going to call."

Normally I'd say, *Phones go both ways*, but it's like the real me has tunneled down somewhere deep and can only send up flares. He reaches out—as if he's actually trying to be tender—and smooths a piece of my hair. I jerk away. He doesn't move, giving me this intense look, trying to see right through me. A muscle jumps in his jaw, then he makes a dis-gusted sound and leans in close to my ear:

"You can get up on that stage and dress all pretty and say your little funny things to try to make people like you. But I'm gonna be out there, knowing I tapped that, and I didn't even have to work for it. Same as a lot of other guys. Nobody's gonna be handing out any crown to some trashy-ass slut who gets so wasted every weekend she doesn't know whose backseat she's been in."

The words sink in. One of the flares finally rises higher than the rest, the light and the hissing growing until it fills me, until I remember who I am and turn and say in his face, "I'm gonna beat your ass in the field on Monday."

Shea sits back, snorts. "What?"

"You heard me. I can rake harder than you, and I'll prove it."

He laughs, but it's okay, because I've got my feet under me again. "You really think you can win top harvester."

"No. Just so long as I beat you."

Nell comes through the crowd toward us, frowning so deeply I hardly recognize her. She takes my arm. "Time to go."

Still kind of laughing, Shea says, "Wait a minute—"

"Don't talk to her." Nell stares at him for a second, her face set hard, like she's daring him to speak. He doesn't. He's still smirking, but I guess having the hot special ed chick yell at him is interesting enough to actually shut his mouth.

She pulls me away, hugging my arm against her ribs. "Are you okay?"

"Yeah. Why wouldn't I be?"

"You didn't look okay. At all. You looked scared."

That spins me out a little, and I shake free. "Where's Mags?"

She's over by the car talking to a couple kids from school,

our greasy take-out bags sitting on the hood. They're all using hushed, excited voices. "You're not gonna believe this," Mags says once we're in the car.

I shrug, not in the mood for gossip.

"The cops got somebody. For Rhiannon." Nell and I stare. "Two different people who live on Church Street saw them take him in, and nobody's seen him come home yet. Been almost two days."

Lots of people live on Church, but there's only one house that I've been to about a hundred times.

"Kenyon Levesque." Mags glances at me. "They put him in the back of a cruiser Thursday night."

I sit back slowly, my breath trickling out of me. As we leave Gaudreau's and pull onto Main Street, I see Shea sitting at a table filled with people I know, including Mason and Jesse. Jesse turns his head to watch us go.

THIRTEEN

KAT'S NOT ANSWERING her phone. I left three messages last night—*I heard about Kenyon. Call me.*—and another one this morning, but still nothing. It's impossible, Kenyon getting arrested, him hurting Rhiannon somehow. He and Rhiannon were friends, or at least friendly; they used to party together, and I remember seeing them sitting on the bleachers during gym once, talking, just the two of them, ignoring Coach Tremblay's whistle. It hits me that Kenyon must've been the one to tell the cops that I was in the barrens the night Rhiannon disappeared. I can't understand it, not at all.

Mags has been nice about it—even though this proves her

right about the Levesque twins—making conversation about other things and not chiming in this morning when the locals knotted together in the barrens before work to kick Kenyon's name around like he's something the dog coughed up. Nell bites her thumbnail and watches me. She's been watching me ever since she yanked me away from Shea. She saw something in my face that I never meant her to, and now I don't know how to make it better. This isn't how it works. I'm the one who takes care of her. I don't like things being backward.

Now, a parade's coming toward me with Shea in the lead, followed by Mason and some other guys. Most of them are grinning, carrying their rakes and water like they're planning on staying awhile.

I fold my arms and meet them. Shea stops short of stepping on my toes. He looks me in the eye but he doesn't talk to me; he talks to the guys, saying in that loud, warm voice, like he's joking around, "Miss America here says she's gonna beat my ass."

Laughter. Only Mason isn't smiling. He watches me closely, grimly, like he's trying to figure something out. I search for Jesse's face but don't find it. "That's right."

Shea throws a look back at his buddies, and they feed him with more laughter and catcalls. "Told you guys." He leans down into my face like I'm a little kid. "Okay, Princess. Don't blame me when you go home crying."

I pick up my rake and turn into the first row of the day. "You still talking?"

And like that, it's on.

I'm not aware of anybody but Shea. There's a powerful wind today, pushing puffy white clouds across the sky and kicking up leaves and dust, making my eyes water. I don't need to see. My body's a machine: rake-rake-rake, dump, rake-rake-rake, dump, close the box, open another. Guy talk and laughter hums in the background like power lines.

Lunchtime. "Darcy, what's going on?" Mags's face hovers in front of me as I shove food down, not wanting to waste a second and lose ground. "Why are you racing Shea? Hey, are you hearing me?"

Maybe I grunt out an answer; I don't know. I churn the afternoon away, then stand, fists on my hips, one knee twitching like a racehorse's as Mrs. Wardwell tallies up the day's haul and writes in the new standings.

Shea's moved up to the sixth slot. I've moved up only one slot to number eight, dogging some migrant named Bankowski.

Can't believe it. I busted my ass today for one stupid slot? Shea's smirking hard enough to give himself a hernia, shaking his head as he gathers his stuff. The other guys are leaving, too, talking about what they're going to do after work, acting like it's over.

Not even close.

★　★　★

Mom's garden is a thing of beauty. Ruler-straight rows, stakes labeling what's what. It puts Libby's neglected jungle of a flower garden to shame, which is why nobody cares that Hunt's poking his ladder holes all through the marigolds and bleeding hearts.

After supper, Mom goes out to weed and pick green beans. I watch her through the window as I wash dishes. She's hunched over, wearing her gardening stuff, old cutoffs and a T-shirt so thin you can see the knobs of her spine through it as she bends forward. It's her day off, and she spends it slaving. Go figure.

I wander outside, standing over her until she looks back, squinting in the fading golden light. We haven't talked about Edgecombe or telling the truth since that night, but I guess she reads something in my face, because she slaps the ground beside her, and I sit.

I tug some weeds, splitting a strand of witch grass down the middle with my fingernails. The wind picks up, making a hollow howl through the moose blowers—tin cans with string threaded across the opening, meant to scare off the crows—and flapping the old shirt hanging from the scarecrow's frame. It's a man's shirt, probably one of Dad's. She's got all his stuff packed in boxes in the attic. Not like a shrine. It's good stuff and we might get some use out of it. There's a big pair of steel-toed boots, a heavy Gore-Tex coat he wore when he worked the tugs out of Belfast, a collection of Clydesdale beer steins.

"What did Gramma and Grampie say when you brought Dad home the first time?" It's an old story, but I love hearing it.

Mom snorts. "You know what they said." A pause. "You know your grandparents are good Catholics."

"Not like us."

"No. If Gramma Nan isn't sitting in her pew Sunday morning, you'll know the Rapture's come. And Grampie can be a hard man to live with." She hands me the colander and gestures for me to start picking. "The first time I saw your dad, he was parked outside a St. Patrick's Day dance they were having at the Elks Lodge. I didn't want to go, but Libby did, so I went along because I'm older and that's what you do. Your dad was sitting outside on his old Indian bike wearing this red-and-black lumber jacket, and he had the best-looking head of hair I'd ever seen."

I smile. "Love at first sight?" Behind the trailer, the clothesline jerks and begins to move on its rusty wheels.

"Close enough. Libby got mad at me over something stupid and left the dance early, so your dad offered me a ride home." I hear a *huh* from the direction of the trailer's back steps, which happens to be within earshot of our conversation. "I took him up on it. When Gramma saw us pull up, she went straight for her rosary beads. Grampie was waiting for us at the door, and the first thing he said was, 'Son, you know that bike ain't inspected?' Your dad said yeah, he knew. 'Well, who the hell do you think you are, driving my daughter around on a piece of junk that ain't road-legal?' And he sent Dad packing."

She always pauses here. I'm grinning as I snap beans off the vine, because I know what comes next.

"Next Saturday, up pulled Tommy Prentiss on the same Indian, but the exhaust was fixed and there was an inspection sticker on the plate. Grampie took one look at him in his jacket and said, 'Son, if you think I'm gonna let my girl go anywhere with you dressed like some kinda bum, you're crazy.' And he kicked him out.

"Saturday after that, Dad showed up wearing some shiny Goodwill suit with a pink handkerchief in the pocket and two-tone wingtips. Came to the door smelling like Aqua Velva, gave me a rose, and asked Grampie's permission to take me out for a nice time. Grampie says, 'Where you planning on going?' And Dad said, 'Demolition derby over to Fort Kent.'"

I laugh. "And he let you go?"

"You know he did. Grampie was speechless. Stayed that way clear through our wedding day."

I trail off to giggles, feeling the day's tension rolling off me. "House is coming along."

"Mm-hmm." Hunt's scraped the clapboards completely

bare on this side. He was here working this morning, gone by the time we got home from the barrens. Looks like he took our trash to the dump and did some weed-whacking around the shed, too.

There's another huff, and then Libby comes around the trailer, lugging a laundry basket. She calls over, "It wasn't stupid, Sarah. I had a perfectly good reason to get mad at you that night."

Mom cranes her neck. "Like what?"

"You blew me off for some fool in a lumber jacket."

I call Kat again. It goes straight to voice mail, same as before. When I turn around, Mags is on the porch, looking in at me through the screen door.

"No luck?" She could care less how Kat's doing, but it's nice that it doesn't stop her from caring about me. I start to ask her something, but she cuts me off. "Lemme guess. You want to go over there. You won't be able to sleep tonight unless you do." She sighs and slides her feet into her flip-flops. "It's going on your tab. Nobody rides for free."

Nell's lying on the porch floor, examining her hand in their game of Spit. Mags tells her where we're going. "Better stay here, hon. Your mom wouldn't like it."

Nell surprises us by saying, "Okay," and climbing up into the swing without any questions. Usually she hates being left behind, especially when it's because Libby wouldn't approve.

Mags tells Mom what's up, and then the two of us drive into town together. I don't try to explain how it is between Kat and me. It's not like we're BFFs or anything, but she was my friend when lots of people at school wouldn't be seen with me on a bet, thanks to Rhiannon's mouth.

Okay, so maybe Rhiannon wasn't the first one to spread the rumors—the seniors we met up with at the soccer fields Halloween night of sophomore year told people, too, I'm sure—but she said enough. Even now, my face gets hot remembering a girl's voice, maybe Georgia Cyr's, drifting into the bathroom stall where I sat, trying not to breathe: *said he almost asked Darcy Prentiss. I don't get it. She's not even that pretty.* Rhiannon, with this dry little laugh: *Don't worry about it. He just wanted to get some.*

And I remember how much I still hate her for that.

Mags says, "So spill. Why are you racing Shea at work?"

"Because he's a jerk."

"Well, yeah. You must have a better reason than that."

I scan through radio stations. "He gave me a bunch of crap about the Princess thing, so I told him I could rake more than him."

"Can you?" Mags sounds like she really wants to know. "You're good, Darce. Your paycheck's almost twice the size of mine, and I'm no slacker."

Mags doesn't go around handing out compliments like Juicy Fruit; it means a lot. And it's the first time I've thought

about this thing without anger. "I dunno. He's stronger than
me. But I might be faster."

She lets loose a rare cackle, tossing her head back. "Ooh,
he must've hated you calling him out like that in front of his
buddies. Bet it got his panties all in a twist." She glances at
me. "Then this means that you guys definitely aren't—"

"No," I say flatly.

"Just checking." Then: "Good."

I'm nervous when we pull into Church Street. The
Levesques live in a nice white two-story house with a reno-
vated barn they use as a garage. I walk up to the door and
knock. After a minute, Kat opens it, her eyes half-lidded,
hair tangled around her shoulders. She wears a tank top with
no bra, her teeny-weeny boobs pitching pup tents against the
fabric.

"Hey," I say. "I called you."

"I know. Sorry." She squints at Mags's car, scratching her
hip through a pair of droopy boxers with the Playboy bunny
printed all over them.

"It's just my sister."

"Yeah. I can see that." She blows out a sigh, and stares
back.

"Are you and Kenyon okay?"

She hesitates. "He's sleeping."

"He's here? I thought he got arrested. Everybody's talking
about it."

She snorts and checks out her black toenail polish, disgusted with me or the world or all of the above. "They questioned him. It's not like they cuffed him or anything."

She's about to shut the door on me. I put my palm flat against it. "Well, I need to see him."

She opens her mouth, then glances back as a shadow steps from the stairs into the hallway.

"Kenyon?" I push past her into the house.

He's shirtless, wearing his baggy-ass skater jeans and nothing on his feet. Kenyon's blond—Kat's been dyeing her hair black or blue for years—with soft brown eyes and a sketchy attempt at a goatee. He stands with his hand on the newel post, maybe wondering if he can bolt upstairs before I catch him.

I'm not sure how to start, but pissed-off and yelling is out the second I get a good look at his face. The boy is *tired*. He's got shocked hollows under his eyes and his cheekbones are sharp, like he's lost weight. I have an edge to my voice all the same. "Why'd you tell the cops?"

"Look, I'm sorry, okay?"

"Why'd you give them my name, Kenyon?"

He goes off. "Because I didn't *do* anything to her, but they think I did and—I'm like Leatherface or something because they got my prints."

"Dude! Shut. Up." I've never seen Kat really mad before, and it's strange to actually see the whites of her eyes as she gets in her brother's face. "You're not supposed to talk about it." When he just stands there, looking beaten, she says, "You're such an idiot," and stalks off to the kitchen.

Kenyon and I look at each other. Mrs. Levesque's voice drifts down from upstairs. "Kenny? Who's here?"

He makes a frustrated sound in his throat and pushes through the door that opens into the garage. I don't know if he means for me to follow, but I do.

The light is on above the tool bench, and everything smells like sawdust and motor oil. This is where we do our drinking when Kat has people over. The Levesques run a furniture business, and Mrs. Levesque is all about yoga classes and spa weekends to center herself or whatever, so the twins basically have the run of the place most of the time. I lean against the chest freezer, watching him prowl. "They got your prints where?"

"Off the car. The stupid Fit. I had it." He sees my look. "I didn't take it. She gave it to me." I wait as he scrubs his hand across the top of his head, making his cowlick stand up in the back. "God, I've already explained this nine thousand times."

"Better make it nine thousand and one, bub."

He speaks slowly, like maybe I'm touched in the head. "She gave me the keys that night in the barrens. After Kat took you home."

"She gave you her car."

"Basically. She didn't give a shit. You oughta know. That

car was just her parents throwing more money at her to keep her out of the way. We were the last to leave that night. She said would I do her a favor and take the car."

"How was she gonna get home?"

"She said she had a ride coming. I don't know, I thought she wanted to freak out her mom by not bringing the car home that weekend or something. When I left, she was sitting by the fire alone. I slept it off at our camp on Alamoosook that night. Sent my dad a text, let him know where I was and everything. No big. I done it before. Next morning, Kat called me saying nobody can find Rhiannon, and had I seen her."

"So, what—you were too scared to tell anybody you had it?"

He gives me a naked look. "I'm not stupid, okay? The cops know me. They would've had my ass in lockup so fast, asking me where I put the body or whatever. They never would've believed I didn't steal that car. God, I was shitting bricks." Nervous energy sends him over to the heavy bag hanging in the corner, which he shoves and throws a left into, pulling his punch at the last second so it lands with a muffled *whump*.

I walk as far as the hood of Kat's pickup. "Come on, you could've told *somebody*. Kat would've tried to help you." He ignores that. "Where'd you hide it this whole time?"

"In the camp shed. Left it there all winter." He snorts. "Then back in June Dad started talking about opening up

GRIT

camp again for the summer. I freaked." He rubs his eye. He
and Kat are built the same, thin as whips with long-fingered
hands they can't seem to keep still. "I thought if I left it
somewhere they could find it easy, right? But nobody did, for
like, weeks. I couldn't take it anymore and called in a tip. I'd
wiped down the steering wheel and door handles and stuff,
but when they dusted for prints—*ding-ding-ding*—bells and
whistles." Another punch. "I'm the only person with a record
who ever touched that car, I guess."

Kenyon was busted for possession of a tiny bag of weed at
a school dance sophomore year. They let him off with community service and some drug counseling, I think. "They
gonna charge you with something?"

"Probably. But I told them I don't know where she is."

"Do they believe you?"

He tosses a dark look over his shoulder. "Do you?"

"Duh." And I do. Sounds like whoever picked her up that
night was the last one to see her alive. "I wanna know why
you threw me under the bus. I told the cops Kat and I were
out driving around that night." Kat backed me up, too. She
didn't want to get busted for trespassing any more than the
rest of us did.

He won't meet my gaze, and I think of all the times he
tickled my sides in the school hallway, or lugged me over
his shoulder through the parking lot while I shrieked and
laughed. "I gave them other people's names from the party,

too. Not just yours." He finally glances at me. "Sorry. Seriously. I had to give them something . . . you know, to get them off me."

My nails dig into my palms. He can't know why this matters to me so much. He can't know why Nell called Kat looking for me that night, hysterical, why I had to leave the party ASAP. He can't know what he's turned the cops onto, how this jar I've put over Nell could crack at the slightest pressure. But I know one thing. No matter what the cops did to me, I never would've thrown him under. Ever. All I say is, "Yeah."

We stand in silence for a long time, Kenyon pushing and punching the bag and watching it swing. When I've got my voice under control, I say, "Do you think Rhiannon's dead?"

"She must be."

It clicks, then. His sullenness, not asking any questions when Rhiannon told him to take her car. "You liked her, didn't you?" No answer. "Did she know?"

Kenyon puts his fist out very slowly and presses his knuckles against the leather, holding them there. "Wasn't gonna happen." His voice is quiet.

I say, "See you around," though I hope I don't, and leave. As I walk to Mags's car, the songs of crickets and the smells of a hot day cooling down to night strike me differently. In some way, everything's changed since I stepped into that house.

FOURTEEN

THE FAIRGROUNDS ARE deserted except for a line of cars belonging to the Princesses parked in a dirt lot behind the central pavilion where they hold the sheepherding trials every year. I hesitate for a second, watching Nell run to the gate, turn, and wave for me to come on.

Things just got real.

Mrs. Hartwell sent out an email telling everybody that the stage was good to go, so Sunday's rehearsal would be held here, where this whole crazy coronation is going to go down. My legs actually wobble as I follow Nell, crossing the track that runs around the huge sheltered stage, up the steps, into the thick of the other girls. The air smells like the ghosts of last year's onion rings and cow flops. I feel Nell's arm link through mine. She doesn't say a word, just squeezes and gives me a small smile that dents the dimple in her left cheek. For once, I'm not too stubborn to squeeze back.

Mrs. Hartwell wears electric blue and her cheeks are rosy. "A lot more impressive than the town hall, am I right?" Murmurs from us. Maybe everybody's as nervous as I am. Except Bella, of course; she's whispering with Alexis like Mrs. Hartwell doesn't rate the attention she'd give a mosquito.

Mrs. Hartwell points to a folding table set up on the ground below. "That's where the judges sit. Expect them to take lots of notes and talk among themselves as you go through your choreography—don't let it shake you! They're getting their first impressions down. During the interviews, they'll take turns asking each of you a handpicked question based on your bios, meant to learn a little more about you and your worldview."

That almost takes my knees out. I curse under my breath.

"Darcy? Is there a problem?"

I can't believe she heard that. I clear my throat, my voice drifting up into the rafters. "Uh . . . in front of everybody? I mean, they're going to ask us right in front of—?"

"Don't worry. We're going over all that today. You'll know what to do when the time comes." She smiles. "I won't leave you hanging. Now, Princesses, split into the same groups as last time, and I want to see two single-file lines waiting in the wings for my cue."

Once we figure out where the wings are, we're ready. Her cue turns out to be scratchy theme music blasting from two giant speakers. Each line hops out onto the stage like they've been poked with cattle prods.

For the most part, we all remember what we're supposed to do. Sounds silly, but it's hard work, thumping up and down those big risers, remembering when to pivot, all the while being loomed over by the huge grandstand across the track. I've seen the crowd at the coronation before. Most of Hancock County comes, and then some. Those bleachers will be packed.

We take a fifteen-minute break at the one-hour mark, and Mrs. Hartwell steps away to make a call. She brought juice and doughnut holes, which I scarf down, glad to have something to take my mind off how freaked out I am. I didn't sleep so great last night, either, my conversation with Kenyon running around in my head. Rhiannon. She really knew how to win people over. I think of all the time I wasted watching anime with her, trying to see what was so great about *Kiki's Delivery Service* or *Wolf Children*. I never figured out how she did that, got you to bend your rules for her and then feel good about doing it because it made her so bouncy-happy. Wonder who picked her up that night. Where they took her, how they hurt her. If we'll ever know.

"Now *that's* a healthy option," I hear Bella say quietly, but when I fix her with a death glare, she's facing away from me, checking out the food with Alexis. "Because they definitely hand out a crown for most cellulite."

Alexis giggles. "I know, right? Like I'm going to touch sugar."

"I've got a fitting for my dress today. Three weeks of cardio better have me down to size four or I swear to God I'll kill somebody."

"You went with the peach?"

"Obviously. It's my signature. People, like, expect it. Remember my Homecoming gown? Fitted bodice, lots of tulle?" Alexis *mm-hmm*s like it haunts her dreams. "This is way hotter. That was so, like, classic? This one's backless, slit up the side, spaghetti straps. Looks kind of amazing."

Alexis oohs, and then they both stare narrow-eyed at Nell as she pours herself a cup of juice and picks out a chocolate-glazed doughnut hole, not paying them any mind. "Then there are the people who wouldn't know style if it bit them in the ass."

Bella smiles, tilting her head. "You mean the people who will be wearing a piece from the Salvation Army's latest line to the coronation?"

They laugh. Nell looks up, aware of them for the first time, and I move in.

Bella's wearing a sundress, and I close my fist around the neckline, twisting it. She takes a stumbling step backward in her platform sandals. "What'd you say?" She puts her chin up, but her eyes give her away. She's scared of me. "Say it again."

"Don't touch me." Bella's gaze jumps around to the other girls who are watching.

"Now, that's not very nice." I'm so mad that I want to keep twisting, but considering where we are, I hold for a second more and let go, smoothing out the wrinkles before Mrs. Hartwell sees. I grab another doughnut hole and pop it into my mouth whole, then take Nell's arm and lead her away from them.

Nell shakes free before the steps. "Why did you do that?"

"Huh?" I'm surprised to see tears in her eyes. "Forget it. They're bitches. You should've heard—"

"It doesn't *matter*, Darcy. I don't want you doing stuff like that for me. I don't need you to."

Some part of me tightens like the last crank on a dial. My voice comes out low. "Bullshit you don't."

She looks at me, lips pressed together, like she's thinking a hundred things she can't say because I've made her swear on her life not to. She turns and runs up the steps, joining her group and shutting me out.

Great. Now she's mad. Only because she doesn't understand. She's got no idea how much little things like that matter. Letting people dump on your family, letting people dump on you. How can anybody take the high road with crap like that raining down?

Watching Bella walk her prissy self up the risers brings back everything Shea said about me the other night. How I could dress up as pretty as I wanted, but I'd still be trash. Maybe what I did to Bella proves him right.

Shea made it sound like he was coming to the coronation, like he'd be sitting right out there in the audience, watching me. I have a feeling he took the festival booklet home with him after Gaudreau's, too. Brought it home so he could keep twisting me in his hands.

Nell's still mad at me when we get home. She goes back to the trailer with Libby. I pour some iced tea and wander out onto the porch, where Mags sits on the floor, dealing solitaire onto the wicker table.

"How was Princess training?" She looks up. "Can you turn into a pumpkin at the stroke of midnight? 'Cause I'd like to see that."

"Jealous much?"

"Nope," she says simply, and it irks me because she means it. Mags has never been jealous of anything I have. Must be nice to be so steady and levelheaded that nobody can get a rise out of you, no matter how hard they try.

"Anyway," I say, "the coach turns into a pumpkin in 'Cinderella,' not her. That'd be dumb." Mags shrugs, and I blow out a long breath, propping my feet on the railing. I must look exactly like Mom.

Scraping sounds come from overhead, and I hear paint flakes sprinkling down onto the porch roof. "How's it going, Hunt?" I call.

The scraping stops. "Can't complain." Scrape, scrape. "Wouldn't do me any good if I did."

I nurse my tea, pulling on my lower lip, wishing something, anything, would happen to make me forget about being an awful person who wanted to beat up Bella Peront again because I could and it would be easy. Nobody's better at making me feel like this than Nell.

Maybe I've got a fairy godmother after all, because awhile later I hear a dual exhaust bellowing in the distance, getting closer all the time. Jesse's pickup blows past our house doing a good sixty miles per. He brakes hard down by the logging road and reverses onto the shoulder in front of our house.

There's somebody sitting in the passenger seat beside him, but I can't see who. Doesn't stop me from running up to the open window.

Jesse grins, leaning forward to see around Mason. It's like the weirdness after the quarry never happened. "Bored?"

"How'd you know?"

"Figured once you got out of Sunday school, you'd have some time on your hands." I laugh. "We're running over to Agway to pick up some stuff for my uncle. Wanna come?"

"Sure." I know I should tell Mom, but instead I step back so Mason can climb out and let me slide onto the bench seat. I look back at the house, see Mags watching, wave bye. Hunt's watching, too, turned partway around on his ladder as we drive off.

"Was that your dad?" Jesse says.

"No. My dad's dead."

"Oh. Sorry. I think I heard that somewhere."

This is one story I don't like to tell. I keep it short: "He worked on the crew that built the bridge. He fell."

"Jesus, that was him?"

"Yeah." I leave out that it was on account of a bet, that some of his buddies put him up to it, that his whole life turned out to be riding on fifty dollars and a round of beers at Ramona's.

It's hard to know how to act with Mason sitting silently to my right. Did Jesse tell him about us? I'm not sure what there is to tell. It feels like an awfully long time since he's kissed me.

Mason's hair is bleached almost white from the sun; he's so big that our thighs can't help but press together as Jesse tears up the asphalt between home and town. Mason's got his heavy forearm on the open window frame, where he drums his fingers, one, two, two, one.

Agway smells like cedar shavings and alfalfa. As Jesse holds the door for me, his hand finds its way to the small of my back, surprising me, so I don't keep my distance, either. Inside, Mason seems fascinated by the floor, and I wonder what he keeps in those pockets of his. Sounds like he's jin-gling change against keys. Guy's twitchy, something I've never noticed before, and when I catch a look he shoots Jesse over the top of my head, I can tell that he does know about Jesse and me. And seems to be warning him with his eyes.

Ignoring him, Jesse drops bags of mulch onto a flatbed cart. "I heard you're a Festival Princess. How come you didn't say anything?"

"Shea tell you about that?" I give a short laugh when he hesitates. "I bet he did. I bet he really talked me up." I swat at a peg full of trowels, making them clink together. "How can you guys stand hanging out with him?"

Another look goes between them, and Jesse shrugs. "He's all right. Sometimes."

"You just get used to him, huh?" I drop my gaze from his uncomfortable expression and look out the plate glass win-dow. "I hope I never get used to him."

Jesse cashes out, and then we drive around back to help load the big order of five-grain chicken scratch that his uncle called in. By the time we're done, I'm sweaty and feeling a lot better. Screw Shea and Bella. Nell will get over being mad at me by suppertime and everything will be fine.

We hop in and Jesse clears his throat, tossing his wal-let onto my lap as he pulls out into the street. Giving him a funny look, I open it, not seeing anything special until I part the billfold and laugh. "Aww." I pull out the little photo of me that Jesse clipped from a Festival booklet, flushing. "Think I look like a dork?"

He laughs. "No. You look beautiful." He flips my pony-tail. "You're gonna win. I know it."

I can't stop smiling. "Yeah, right. You see the other girls in the running? It's really Nell who—"

The *bloop-bloop* of a siren cuts me off. We all look in the rearview mirror to see a cop cruiser following us, lights flashing.

Jesse swears and pulls onto the shoulder, watching the cop park behind us and sit.

"You weren't even going ten over." Mason's deep voice startles me. It's like having the steering wheel jump into the conversation.

Jesse takes his wallet back and gets his license ready. We wait as the cop's footsteps crunch across the gravel, then look up to see a broad chest in a dark uniform shirt, a belt heavy with gear. Edgecombe leans down until he's eye to eye with Jesse. He's wearing aviator shades like a screw in a prison movie, and his salt-and-pepper crew cut glistens with sweat. I stare at him, but he ignores me, saying to Jesse, "Going a little fast today."

"Didn't know I was."

Edgecombe grinds his gum in his molars for a couple seconds. "License, registration, proof of insurance. Please."

It takes Jesse a minute to dig the slips out of the glove

box. By then, sitting in the cab with no fan or breeze coming through the windows has caught up with us. Sweat slides down my temples and my shirt sticks to me. Mason props his elbow on the window frame again and squeezes his forehead like he's got a headache.

Edgecombe goes back to the cruiser to run the VIN. We wait a long time. A horsefly gets into the cab, bouncing around, buzzing crazily against the windshield.

Edgecombe comes back and hands Jesse his ID and papers. "The speed limit on this road is forty-five. That's the law, not a suggestion." He steps back and hooks his thumbs into his belt. "Step out of the vehicle so we can have a chat."

Jesse's eyes widen. "Uh—"

"Darcy. Let's go." Edgecombe crooks his finger at me and puts his hands on his hips as a sedan passes us, throwing dust.

My pulse pounds at my throat as Jesse lets me out on his side; I can tell he doesn't like this, but there's not much he can do. I follow Edgecombe around the tailgate, squinting in the sunlight as I stand in front of him.

"These boys your friends?"

"Yeah."

He sucks air through his teeth, making a small *sssfft* sound. "Your friends let you ride around without a seat belt?"

I stand there, speechless. I was so busy talking when we left Agway that I didn't even think of it.

"It's state law that everyone wear a safety belt while riding in a motor vehicle. Did you know that?" I nod. "And you're under eighteen, which makes the operator of the vehicle responsible. Your friend is up for a fifty-dollar fine."

Did I say I was feeling better? I feel like roadkill on a stick.

We stand there in silence, our clothes rippling as another car passes. Edgecombe pulls his glasses off and hooks them over his chest pocket. His eyes are a deep shade of stump-water brown. "Darcy, I want you to think about something for me. Rhiannon Foss's parents, Charlie Ann and Jim, I'm sure you know their names. There's probably nothing they wouldn't give to see their daughter again. She's that precious to them. Most parents feel that way about their kids, wouldn't you say?" I nod again. "Imagine your mother in their position. How she'd feel if something happened to you." He waits, maybe for me to bawl and beg for mercy, I don't know. "You seem to keep putting yourself into danger-ous situations, and I'm curious why."

"I forgot about the belt, okay? I usually wear one."

"That's just one example. Not telling the truth. That can be dangerous. Especially when somebody's life is riding on it."

I clench my jaw, biting down until I think I can answer without screaming. "I don't. Know where. She is." I breathe in through my nose. "Have you been following me?" It's hard to believe somebody with the rank of corporal would be sitting at a speed trap. When he doesn't answer, I burst out,

"I'm telling you the truth, okay?"

He studies me. His mouth pulls into a grim smile. "But you're not exactly being honest with me, either. Are you?"

When he sees I'm not going to budge, he finally steps back and waves me to the pickup. Once I'm between the boys again, Edgecombe takes in the three of us for a long moment, then says to Jesse, "If I have to stop you again, I'll do more than ticket you. Understand?"

"Yessir." I'm glad Jesse doesn't try to be tough.

Edgecombe goes back to his cruiser, where I figure he must be making out the ticket, but then he starts the engine, pulls into the road, and drives away. I sag against the seat and say, "Sorry." Pathetic.

"No worries." Jesse's distracted. He's watching the cruiser disappear around the bend. "What'd he want?"

"He thinks I know where Rhiannon is."

"I heard they hauled Kenyon in."

"He borrowed her car and was too scared of the cops to bring it back, that's all." I stare out the window at the bright day, remembering Edgecombe's hound-dog eyes, tired and solemn, like he can see through me, like he knows me. Like he knows that, at the end of the day, I'll step up and do the right thing.

Don't know where he got a crazy idea like that.

FIFTEEN

MONDAY, I SET up by Shea without giving him a look. The rest of the day is a haze of berries, my rake flashing in the sun, the sound of my own hard breathing. Shea's always there, making it look easy, playing it up for the other guys. Laughing at me. Mason stays close, but more and more I get the feeling he's keeping an eye on me, making sure things don't go too far. I don't see Jesse except at lunchtime. He looks like he wants to talk, but we don't.

End of the day, I'm seventh on the board. Shea moves up to fifth. And Bankowski's still beating my butt in sixth.

"Go ahead. Drink." Mags watches me chug the Gatorade she bought me in three big gulps, then wipe the red mustache off with my hand. We sit in her car with the doors hanging open, our feet on the pavement of the Lehman's Formal Wear parking lot in the Bangor Central Plaza.

"Are you going to barf?" Nell leans between the seats. She's been a little stiff with me since Sunday, but this has her interested. "'Cause if you are, lean way out. I've barfed up Gatorade before, and it'll stain your shoes."

"I'm okay, guys. Seriously. Quit hovering."

Mags shakes her head. "You look like a boiled lobster."

"Awesome. Thanks."

"You do. You probably gave yourself heatstroke today." Mags grabs her wallet as we get out and walk to the shop. "Ready to give up this stupid race with Shea?" She says "no" at the same time I do. "'Course not. Wait till you're lying toes-up in the barrens instead. And you know what your tombstone will say? 'She never listened to her sister.'"

"No, it'll say, 'She never made it out of seventh place.' If I find that Bankowski, I'll break both his arms."

"He can probably rake with his feet," Nell says, surprised by our laughter as we step inside. "I'm only saying he's good, if he can keep ahead of you."

"Thanks, Nellie."

Mags floored it up to Bangor after work so we could go dress shopping at Lehman's before they close at six thirty. Nell's been set on coming here; Lehman's is *the* place to get prom dresses and tuxes, at least by Sasanoa standards. Nell has strict orders from Libby not to buy anything tonight. If she finds something she likes, she's supposed to ask them to put it aside so Libby can see it first and give the okay. Gag.

There's a row of headless mannequins in the window wearing formal getups, and classical music plays overhead. The lady working the counter does a double take at the sight of us; guess she doesn't get too many sunburned, calloused customers with wet hair from taking crazy-fast showers after a day of raking.

Nell's psyched, running from rack to rack, holding gowns up to herself in front of the mirrors as she chatters about some magazine article she read. "See, I have a cool, clear winter coloring, so I'm supposed to wear jewel tones—blue, red, purple. . . ." She points at me. "You're a warm spring, so you need pastels."

"Warm spring. Gotcha." I grip my purse tighter as I look at the price tags. Wish I could put my dress money right into my car fund instead. What's the point of spending two hundred dollars on a dress I'm going to wear only once?

Nell carries a mound of dresses into the changing room with her. I grab a couple from the sale rack without really looking at them. Mags parks herself in the mom chair outside, whistling a little.

I kick off my flip-flops and slip out of my shorts. "Hey, maybe I could wear your prom dress," I call to Mags. "You've still got it."

"Darce, I wear a sixteen. You'd swim in it."

I look at myself in the mirror, standing there in just my bra and underwear. Mags is right. I look worn out. I've always had something pinchable around my waist and hips, but now there's nothing to grab on to. It's all getting burned off in the barrens, battling with Shea. "You never did tell me what you and Will did after prom." I drag one of the dresses over my head.

"We went to a party at his friend's house."

"*And* . . . ?"

"*And* nothing. It was fun. Then he brought me home."

I open the door and narrow my eyes at her. "On prom night. You didn't get down on prom night?"

Mags laughs. "We didn't 'get down' ever."

I stare at her. The counter lady calls that they'll be closing in fifteen minutes. "You freakin' liar."

Mags shakes her head. "Truth."

I'm speechless as Nell bustles out in a dress that looks like a grape layer cake and flounces the ruffles in front of the three-way mirror, making a face at herself. "For a whole year. You never did it. Not once."

"Well, we messed around and stuff, but that's it."

"Why?"

Mags thinks for a second, scratching a mosquito bite on her elbow. "I dunno. Guess we weren't ready."

Nell lets out a cry that makes me think somebody must've

left a pin in her dress. "I love it!" Not the layer cake: whatever it is I'm wearing. Nell drags me over to the mirror, spinning me by the shoulders as I try to get a look at what she's so excited about. "How did you find the perfect one so fast? Mags, tell her how good it looks."

Mags give a thumbs-up.

I check out my reflection. The dress is knee-length, seafoam green, with spaghetti straps and an empire waist. Silver beadwork covers the bodice. The color's not bad with my hair, I guess, but my knees look like three miles of bad road from berry-bush scratches.

"You look like a mermaid." Nell pokes her head into my changing room and comes out carrying a matching wrap that must've been attached to the hanger. She drapes it around my shoulders. "You can borrow my shoes. You know, those strappy silver sandals? They'd go perfect."

I can't quite see whatever it is she's seeing, but I love the idea of not having to spend another second thinking about dresses. "Okay. What the hell. Thirty percent off, right?"

We go back out so Nell can keep looking. The associate working the bridal section is talking with the only other customer in the place, a petite brunette in her twenties. Her hair is long, grown almost down to her butt, and she talks with her hands, stroking the fabric of the lilac bridesmaid gown she's holding. "—think they'll love it. Sunday works for everybody, so we'll come up and do the fittings and everything then. . . . Oh, *shoes*, shoes, I meant to ask you about—"

I notice that Nell's standing very still. All the joy and energy have drained from her face. She watches the girl flutter her hands, resting on the satin of the dress and then lifting off again like butterflies. This bride's a stranger, but as I listen to her talk about her wedding plans, it hits home. Oh God. I know who this is without ever having met her, because of the look on Nell's face.

I press my hand against Nell's back, ushering her toward the counter so I can pay and get us the hell out of here.

"Nell? Don't you want to try on some more?" Mags stops her.

"They want to close," I say.

"But we might not get back up here again before the Festival."

Nell drags her gaze away from the bride and looks at us. "It's okay. It's not here."

"What isn't?" Mags says.

"The one. The dress I'm going to wear." Nell shakes her head. "I'll look somewhere else."

The lady at the counter boxes up my dress quickly, seeming glad to be rid of it and us. We almost make it—we're actually turning toward the exit—when the bride says, "Nell?"

My stomach is an elevator with a cut cable, dropping thirty stories. She's coming over and there's nothing I can do to stop it. Nell waits, and I can't read a thing in her face but sadness, like she's remembering something she once watched drift away from her, bobbing and listing until it finally disappeared under the surface.

The bride's smiling, getting these cute creases at the corners of her eyes. She's firm and tan, wearing a T-shirt from the Blue Hill Co-op and cargo shorts, so I guess she's kind of a crunchy granola type. "Do you remember me?" Hand to her heart. "Elise Grindle. Brad's fiancée? We met at school a couple times."

What's she think, Nell's some feeb who can't remember anything just because she takes special classes? But that's not what she meant, and I know it; it's my hate leaking out all over her, this nice girl who has no idea what she's putting us through right now. "How are you?" Nell says in a colorless voice.

"Great. Man, what a summer, huh?" Elise jerks her thumb over her shoulder. "I just picked out my bridesmaids' dresses. Took forever to decide." She laughs, then looks at us. "Are these your sisters?"

"Cousins." Mags shakes her hand. "Margaret. That's Darcy."

I don't want to touch Elise's hand, but I have to. It's soft and warm and it's all I can do to keep from wiping my palm off on my shorts.

"So you're going to be a senior this year, right?" Elise keeps smiling, trying to draw Nell out. "Nice. Brad really misses teaching at SAHS, you know. He's always saying that your class was the best he ever had."

"Oh, really?" Nell looks at a spot somewhere over her head.

"Are you here getting a dress for the pageant? Brad mentioned you were nominated as a Princess. Good for you."

Something the size of a fist lodges in my throat. He mentioned. Just casually mentioned across the breakfast table: *Oh, honey, remember Nell Michaud? Isn't this nice, says here she's a Bay Festival Princess this year. That'll really boost her self-confidence. She always struggled.* I step back, crushing my dress box under my arm. "We have to go."

If Mom was here, she'd cuff me in the back of the head, but Elise rolls with my rudeness pretty well, stepping back and smiling again. "Oh, okay. Nice to see you again, Nell. I'll tell Brad you said hi."

Even though she didn't. None of us did. But Elise soon-to-be Ellis is too caught up in her dream wedding to see two inches in front of her own nose, and I hate her for being happy and blind. And the worst thing, what I can't get over as she walks back to the bridal section with her long, wavy brown hair hanging down her back, is how much she reminds me of Nell.

We all get into Mags's car, and she takes the interstate ramp, I-95 South. I feel shaky and sick, like we've survived a disaster, a hurricane tearing through. Nell sits, looking down at her hands, not talking. Finally, Mags says quietly, "What just happened in there?" She waits. We all sit and wait, listening to the sound of the wheels beneath us, and we don't talk.

SIXTEEN

MAGS WATCHES ME at breakfast. I say, "What?" hoping if I sound pissy enough, she'll stop. She wants answers. I'm not giving any.

I wonder if all the lying I've done for Nell has changed my looks somehow, made me older, harder. I definitely don't feel the same as I did sophomore year, before everything happened. I remember hearing a song once that said something like, *I wish I didn't know now what I didn't know then.* Wish to God it worked that way, for Nell and me both.

"Is Nell okay?" Mags stares me down.

Mom's upstairs getting ready for work, and I want to kill this before she comes down. "Yeah. Of course."

"Are you sure? Seems like something's off."

"She's fine. When is she ever not fine?" Because I make sure of it. Mags thinks she takes care of everything, but really, it's me. See how good a job I'm doing?

I got a look under Nell's surface last night, and what I saw made me heartsick. I really thought she'd get over it. I figured she just needed some time, a new school year, to take her mind off everything. I should've known Nell would be different. She feels things too hard.

The day is whisper-still and dripping with humidity. Thunderstorm weather. We need a big one to roll in and break it wide open. Since I can't put my anger away—Elise tore the lid off yesterday—I use it as fuel to rake against Shea. He doesn't have as many followers today, probably because some of them decided it's no contest.

"Are you even on the board anymore?" Shea calls over at one point while we're both topping off boxes and stacking new ones.

"Guess you don't know how to read."

"It's tough when the writing's waaay down at the bottom."

"Fun-ny. I haven't had so many laughs since the Fourth."

The other guys in earshot go "Ohhh." That one hit home, but I won't check to see how he took it, won't waste the seconds. "You loved it," he calls back.

"Oh, yeah. All three inches of it."

The guys bust up laughing, can't believe I said it. I grab my rake and walk back down the row. Not my fault if he doesn't know better than to mess with me today. I hear him slam a box down, then another, hard enough to crack the plastic.

Thunder rumbles around four thirty. Storms love the Penobscot, come booming across the river with enough power to rattle our windows. We're packing up our gear when the first crooked finger of lightning touches down over the water. Duke and Mr. Wardwell get the last load secured to the truck while Mrs. Wardwell crabs at them to hurry as she folds her chair and magazines.

Nell reaches us, the wind whipping her hair free of her handkerchief. Thunder booms overhead, followed by a flash up on the hill that makes everybody flinch.

"Holy crap." Two drops of rain spatter the lenses of Mags's glasses. "That hit close."

We're leaving the field when we hear shouting. A couple people run down the hill toward us, yelling and gesturing back at the cabins. Flames lick over the rise.

Mr. Wardwell curses. He and Duke get into his pickup and tear up the road. There's confusion, shouting, people following them to help—but a lot of people not moving, too, milling and muttering or hanging around their cars to see what everybody else is going to do. Somebody whistles, and I see Jesse dropping his tailgate for us, waving us in. Mason's standing in the bed, and he gives Mags a hand up.

The cabins sit in a clearing at the peak of the hill where the barrens border on the neighboring property; you can see them when you drive down Back Ridge Road, five little buildings with rusty tin roofs and matchstick porches. Jesse pulls into the driveway and we pile out.

Smoke and flames boil out of the roof of the second cabin from the road. Some migrants throw water from gallon pails, and Mr. Wardwell hauls ass around the first cabin with a garden hose unwinding behind him. Mrs. Wardwell drove up in the flatbed, and I see her grab a crying little girl and swing her up into the truck like she weighs as much as a sack of flour.

Everyone starts dousing the flames, using anything that will hold water. Somebody hands me a plastic bowl, and Jesse gets an old caulk bucket. I run to the hand pump everybody's drawing from, and then back to the cabin, passing Mags and Nell as they run for refills.

The water I throw disappears into the smoke; I can't even tell if it hit the roof, if I'm making any difference at all, and I can't stop coughing. Mr. Wardwell's soaking down the walls and porch with the hose, his face ruddy, white hair kicking up in front with sweat. "They on their way?" he yells at Duke, but Duke's still on the phone with 911.

The grass catches a little, and some migrants stomp it out, only to have another piece of burning insulation drift down and light up a few feet away. Migrants run out of the cabins on either side with their arms full of stuff: backpacks and bedrolls and plastic bags of food and dishes. One guy carries a Jack Russell terrier, squirming and barking like she's ready to take on the fire herself.

I don't know how long we throw water before I notice that I'm wiping rain from my eyes. It's finally coming down. The cabin's still burning, but soon it's more smoke than flame, and the other cabins are drenched, so they won't catch. We keep the water coming anyway until the fire trucks show up.

As we all stand back so they can turn the hose on it, Mags, Nell, and I lean on each other, exhausted. Nell rests her head on my shoulder while I put my arm around Mags, catching my breath and checking out the migrants' turf.

It's not much more than a scrubby patch up here, really, with two Porta-Johns by the tree line and a little fire pit in a ring of stones. The cabins have been tagged all over by Sasanoa wannabe gangstas. The Wardwells have covered it with big patches of gray paint, but I can still read the word *spic*, and more f-bombs than I care to count.

Little kids have started appearing on the porches of the cabins at the far end. I can't believe how many families are crammed into these five little houses. There's a skinny, freckled, hard-faced lady standing with a man and a little boy, watching what's left of the cabin roof collapse. Whatever they had inside, something tells me they couldn't afford to lose it.

★ ★ ★

"We got to talk," Jesse says.

I don't want to hear this. I want to hear *you were awesome up there, Darcy,* or *you look hot with your hair wet* or anything other than the breakup words. Mags and Nell are waiting for me in the car, the engine running, the wipers going. I sit with one leg out of the pickup, one hand gripping the door.

He says it fast, like somebody on the verge of wussing out, and he doesn't look away from the dash. Mason's waiting in the rain for me to let him slide into the seat, and I tell myself that Jesse wouldn't do this to me in front of one of his buddies. He wouldn't be that cruel.

When he finally looks back at me, his expression doesn't give much away. "Drive-in tonight? It's supposed to clear up."

I sag like a popped balloon. The drive-in isn't a breakup place. You can't make a quick escape after ripping somebody's heart out at the drive-in. I scribble my number down on a take-out napkin and let in Mason, who makes a point of not looking at me at all.

"You should see how crappy those cabins are." I towel off my hair as Mom, Libby, and the girls set the table for supper.

"I've seen them," Mom says. We were late getting home; as soon as we came through the door, Libby went off on Nell about not calling before Mags could shout over her about the fire. Now Libby's tight-lipped, banging dishes down.

"They don't even have power or running water or anything." I hang the towel over the back of my chair. "And there's, like, fifteen people to a cabin, at least."

"Not that many," Mags says.

"Close enough."

Mom shrugs, refusing to get bent out of shape like I want her to. "I'm sure they're glad to have roofs over their heads. Better than sleeping in tents or their cars. Growing up, I remember a potato farmer up the road had a bunch of junked buses for the migrants to stay in during harvest time."

The screen door opens and Hunt leans in, soaked to the bone from rushing around collecting his tools. He lifts a hand to Mom. "Taking off." He starts to duck out again.

"No, stay," I say. "We're having fried chicken."

"Can't. Thanks."

"At least take some with you." Mom goes to the cupboard and pulls out Tupperware. "We got enough pasta salad to feed an army."

Hunt steps in and waits by the counter, his gaze resting mildly on Libby for a second before checking out the kitchen, the chipped cupboards and the shuddery old Frigidaire covered in alphabet magnets and clippings from the plays Nell's been in over the years. The photo of sophomore year's one-act play *The Tempest* has yellowed and curled at the corners. You can see Nell in the far corner, playing the part of Ceres, a spirit with one line. "Hunt, you ever seen those migrant cabins?" I say. "I mean, up close?"

"Private property up there, isn't it?"

"Yeah, but there was a fire today, and we went up to help. It *sucks*. People got their kids stacked in there like cordwood."

"Darcy exaggerates." Mags looks at him over the top of her glasses. "A lot."

Nell shakes her head. "I dunno, I wouldn't want to use those outhouses. I wouldn't want to pee over that hole in the middle of the night with daddy longlegs and—"

"Nell," Libby says sharply, as if saying "pee" is right up there with cussing out somebody's mother. "You don't need to worry about those people. You need to worry about yourself. You can't even see your way to putting my laptop away after you use it or taking care of your dirty dishes on the coffee table. I shouldn't have to be picking up after you all the time."

"Sorry," Nell mumbles, turning a napkin over in her hands.

"And don't talk down into your chest. Throw your shoulders back and look people in the eye." If I had a nickel for every time Libby's said that, I could finally pay to have her trailer moved to Outer Mongolia. She clears her throat and starts loading her plate. "Well, maybe this fire will finally end it. Maybe Bob and Evelyn will have the sense to tear those cabins down and stop courting trouble." Plop goes a dollop of butter. "Tell those people to keep right on driving next harvest."

Hunt says, "Those people need the work."

Stillness settles over us like a sheet shaken out over a mattress. I watch Libby stop, holding her knife, and turn his way. "So do the people of this town. People who live here year-round and pay their taxes."

"You see about as many year-round residents turning out for berry raking as you do ditch digging. It's hard work, and most people don't want to do it. The Wardwells hire migrants because they need the hands. Can't fault them for that any more than you can fault somebody for traveling to where the work is. Especially when they got kids to feed."

For Hunt, that was a speech and a half. I try to keep the smile off my face as I watch Libby set her knife down carefully, color rising into her cheeks. "If you think bringing in ex-cons and illegals to work side by side with our children is understandable, you got a problem. And that little Foss girl's blood is on your hands, and the Wardwells', and anybody else's who thinks the same way."

Mom says, "*Lib,*" but Hunt doesn't hesitate.

"I've known the Wardwells half my life. They're decent folks. They probably believe what I do, that almost all of us sprung from people who come over on a boat or a plane or maybe had to sneak across a border or two. Turning away somebody who wants to work just because their home's on wheels or they ain't the right color is wrong, and if you don't think so, I'd say you're the one with a problem." He takes the stack of covered dishes from Mom, who looks like you could knock her over with a stiff breeze. "Smells good, Sarah. Thank you." He nods our way as he leaves. "Have a nice evening."

It's the quietest meal we've eaten together in a long, long time.

The phone rings while I'm doing the washing up, and even though I run, Libby gets to it first. After a second, she holds the extension out to me like it's got eight crawly legs and antennae.

Instead of hello, Jesse says, "You guys got a landline?"

I wonder when the last time was that he had to deal with a girl's family when he called to ask her out. "Mom won't pay for us to have phones. Nell's the only one who's got one."

"Oh. Well, rain's stopped. You up for the show?"

He'll pick me up in an hour. I've got butterflies; this isn't just a hookup. I could tell by the sound of his voice. What-ever it is he wants to tell me, it sounds like it's eating at him.

Upstairs, I look through my clothes; nothing seems right. I notice some T-shirts I never wear anymore, a pair of track pants that never fit me right. I bring them downstairs with an extra fleece blanket, passing Libby and Mom at the table with their coffee.

Mags and Nell are sprawled on the porch floor playing

Hearts. I poke Mags's butt cheek with my toe. "Maybe tomorrow we could bring some things in for the people who lost stuff in the fire. Like donations."

Nell lights up like I knew she would. "Yeah! Like clothes and food." She takes off for the trailer, and Mags goes to her room to dig around.

We end up with two bags of pretty good stuff. Libby watches me like she's got a nasty taste in her mouth, and finally, she can't hold it in anymore. "Well, aren't you Mother Teresa. Your mom can barely afford to keep you in clothes as it is, and here you are, giving them away."

"I buy my own clothes."

That stops her barely long enough to take breath. "Doesn't stack up next to rent, bills, and groceries, does it? You got no idea how much it costs to run a household. This family is the one who needs donations, for God's sake." She ticks away with her nail at a crack in her mug. "Don't see *us* holding our hands out."

Mom sets her mug down hard. "I've got some stuff to add to your bag, girls."

She comes down from the attic with her face set. She's carrying Dad's big winter coat, his steel-toed boots, and his wool camp blanket with *Prentiss* stitched into one hem. Mags and I look at each other, wide-eyed.

Libby stands up. "You can't give those away! What're you thinking?"

"Well, which is it, Lib? Either I can't keep them because it's been years and I got to move on, or I can't give them away because they belonged to Tommy. Make up your mind." Mom drops the stuff into a trash bag, tying it with sharp movements. "God knows you two never liked each other, anyway." She looks Libby in the eye. "But he was never too scared to make a commitment to me, or to his girls. Even you can't argue that."

We stare. Libby's cheeks drain pale, and she pushes her chair back and leaves the house quietly, not even slamming the door behind her. I don't understand what just happened, other than that Mom schooled Libby somehow. Being a know-it-all is what gets Libby through the day, and now she's had her mouth shut for her twice in one night. We girls slip out in different directions and leave Mom in the kitchen with her smoke and memories.

When Jesse pulls into the driveway at dusk, I step out the door to meet him. Nell's voice startles me from the swing. "You going now?"

She's sitting with her legs tucked to the side, playing Matchmaker, a game she made up when we were kids. She lays all the face cards on the table, then pairs up the king of spades with the queen of clubs and so on, until everybody's a couple. Then the jack of diamonds comes along to steal the queen away, that kind of thing. Her version of solitaire, I guess. I haven't seen her play it in a long time, but I recognize the lay of the cards.

"It's *Peyton Place* this week." She's got the joker in her hand, slipping him between each king and queen like she can't decide who to split up next. I can't see her very well, really, until she turns her head, catching the glow from the kitchen window. Her face is full of loss. "Tell me about it tomorrow?"

"Sure." Jesse flashes his brights, but I hesitate on the steps. "Don't stay out here by yourself too long."

She doesn't answer. As I cross the yard, I look back at the light in Mags's bedroom window. I wish sisters really had a psychic link, so she'd know to come downstairs right now and be with Nell. She needs someone, but tonight, it can't be me.

In Jesse's truck, he leans over and kisses me deep, catching me off guard. As we pull out, I check Nell in the side-view mirror, but I can't tell her from the porch shadows anymore.

Libby's always saying how bad I am. God knows she's not the only one. But when I see our good girl sitting out there in the dark, mourning some sick excuse for love, playing make-believe because she isn't allowed the real thing, I think maybe I've got the better deal. I've got more freedom than Nell will ever know.

S E V E N T E E N

SOMETHING'S DEFINITELY UP with Jesse. We were late to the movie, so we parked in the way back, and he's been nice and everything, but underneath it all, he's tense. I catch him checking out the other cars like he's looking for somebody.

"Want popcorn? I'm buying." It's the only thing I can think to say to break the silence.

"I got it." He stuffs a twenty in my hand before I can argue, then goes back to scoping out the tailgates in front of us.

I slam the door behind me. On the way, I stop to use the gross bathrooms around back of the snack shack and projector. I pause under the fly-specked bulb outside, look-ing for Kat's pickup. It's in its usual spot. Wonder if Kenyon's over there, holding on to whatever secrets he didn't want to share with me the other night. What would Rhiannon say if she knew he was still carrying a torch for her? I can hear that dry laugh of hers now, see her flick her greenish-hazel eyes up, like he's just too, too pathetic, the way she did whenever we'd gossip about people. But I guess she thought she could trust him.

When I come out of the bathroom, Kat's standing at the edge of the light. She wavers a little, like she might step back out of sight, then says, "What up, chiquita?"

"Not much."

She's wearing black shortalls with a skull-and-crossbones patch safety-pinned to the bib, a cami so thin it sags to show her breastbone. She sticks her hands in her pockets. "Here with the girls?"

"Not tonight." I know better than to say who I came with.

Kat rakes her fingers through her hair sideways, mak-ing it rest funny. "Sorry about the other night. I was pretty freaked."

"He's your brother. I get it."

She cuts her eyes at me, checking to see if I really do. She's probably smoked half a bowl since sundown, but I guess she finds whatever it is she's looking for, because relief flickers over her face. Then she slides back into her stoner thing like a favorite pair of sneakers: "Stop by the truck, if you want. Bet you could get Braden Mosier to drink Jaeger out of your belly button."

"Come on. Gimme a challenge." We smile a little. So maybe we'll never be besties. What we've got is still worth having. I could let her go, but I'm not quite ready. "Hey . . . who do you think Rhiannon was waiting for that night?"

Kat shrugs. "Somebody she knew pretty well, I'm guessing. Rhiannon was smart. She wouldn't meet-in-person with some creeper. Not saying she didn't do a lot of random stuff that night, but . . ." Her gaze lingers on me.

I remember Kat's expression that night when her phone hummed and she read the caller ID, holding it out to me. *For you. I think.* My stomach rolled. *Michaud.* I'd saved Kat's number in Nell's phone for emergencies only, life-or-death.

Darcy? Her keening voice, tear-choked and faraway. *Please, please come get me.* A gasp. *I wanna go home.* Then she started sobbing, hard.

Took forever, but I found out where she was—outside that convenience store Chase's on Irish Lane in Hampden, a half-hour drive away—but I couldn't get her to say how she got there, if she was hurt, nothing. I said, *Call home, I don't have a ride.*

She cried. *I can't. I can't tell. Mom can't find out. Please, Darcy.* Ice went through me. *You wait,* I said. *I'll get there.*

Kat was too drunk to drive me. She laughed and sprawled

over in the scrub grass when I asked to borrow her truck. Lots of people did the same—*Ha-ha, Darcy can't drive, no way, she'll put it in the ditch*—and I was breathless and scared and about ready to call home when—

Rhiannon stepped up to me, for the first time in nearly a year. I'd almost forgotten how her face looked straight-on: heart-shaped, high cheekbones, her mouth fuller since she'd started outlining it with lip pencil. She held out her car keys in the firelight. When I didn't move, stunned, wondering if maybe somebody'd roofied me, if this whole thing was a bad trip, she said, *Just take them.*

In spite of every mean, nasty thing I'd ever wished on her, how I hated her in the way you can only hate your best friend, I took them. Not thanking her, just running to the Fit. Because Nell needed me.

"Why'd she do it? Why'd she give me the keys?" I'm asking myself as much as Kat, a shaky edge to my voice.

Kat lets her gaze slide over the peeling siding, where people have been scribbling for-a-good-time-call graffiti since the 1970s. Half the girls on that wall are probably grandmothers now. I'm on there, fourth down from the left, written in blue ballpoint beside something filthy about a girl name Jennie. "I dunno. Maybe she heard karma's a bitch."

So maybe she knows. Maybe Rhiannon told her what really went down between us sophomore year; she's the only one who could've. I take a few steps away, feeling stripped in front of Kat. I don't know which feels worse, the lies or the truth. "Stay out of jail, lady."

She watches me go, hugging one thin arm. "No promises."

I buy more food at the snack counter than I really want and get back into the cab with Jesse, turning it all over in my mind. On-screen, all the people in this wicked uptight town called Peyton Place are having a picnic with three-legged races and pie-eating contests and stuff. I hold out a package of Twizzlers to Jesse. When he doesn't take any, I bite into one, letting his gaze burn on me until I can't stand it anymore.

When he kisses me tonight, it's like he can't get enough, or like he thinks he won't get another chance. He presses me back against the door, and we slide down together; the popcorn spills into the darkness under the seat. His hands move up under my shirt, over my stomach and bra and around to the clasp, which I know he won't be able to open because no guy ever can, so I help him.

I lie there for a couple seconds with my eyes closed before I realize that he's pulled away. When I look, he's facing the wheel again, shoving his hair back with one hand. I prop myself up on my elbow. "What now?"

"I shouldn't—" He breaks off, shakes his head. "Not supposed to be doing this."

"Why?"

He gives me a look, kind of unbelieving, then shakes his

head again. "Tonight wasn't gonna be like this. I told myself we were really gonna talk and . . ." He swears, looking out the window. "Then I did it again."

"Did *what*? What's the problem?"

"What do you think, Darcy?" When I throw my hands up, he says, "I feel like a piece of shit, hooking up with you. But you're so—" He breaks off again. "Nobody knows about us. Well—Mason. But I didn't tell anybody else what we been doing."

I make a little sound in my throat. A piece of shit. That's how I make him feel.

Jesse's eyes are dark in the half-light. "I never cheated with anybody before. I mean, I'm no saint or anything, not saying that, but I don't screw around. I always said I never would."

I swallow down an acid taste, getting it now, why he's been running so hot and cold. "You have a girlfriend."

"Huh? No. I'm talking about you and Shea." All I can do is blink. "Come on. He told everybody about the Fourth, how you guys finally did it up at the quarry. Surprised he didn't put up billboards, telling everybody what a stud he is."

This isn't exactly news, but I still flush all over, not sure if I'm ashamed or just furious. I try to keep my voice level. "What's that mean?"

"He's wanted you forever. He always says—well, he talks about what he'd like to do to you, with you, whatever. Says you like him, too, that you flirt and come on to him all the time."

"I do *not*." I spit it out, thinking of the Fourth, what I can remember of it: drinking way too much, until I was fighting to keep my head up, and then Shea beside me, smiling with those good white teeth and tawny eyes, being all nice, for some reason. I knew what he was about—how he and some other boys threw rotten crabapples at Rhiannon and me in seventh grade and ruined Rhiannon's new white hoodie, how he'll say or do any mean thing to get a laugh—but that seemed pretty fuzzy right then. I can't say if I flirted back, but if I did, I was mostly joking, even when he started kissing my neck. The first time he asked me to go for a walk with him, I said no; the fourth time, I caved, grateful when he put his arm around me to keep me steady. I didn't plan to have sex. That's not why I went out there. "I never led him on, that's crap." I'm choking on my words. "I bet Mr. Big-Badass-Stud didn't tell you that I never even called him after, that I don't want anything to *do* with him." Jesse's quiet. "Yeah. Didn't think so."

"What about in the barrens? You guys are always going back and forth, giving each other hell."

"So?"

"So I figured that meant you were still hanging out."

"You mean hooking up." I stuff myself back into my bra. "No. We fight all the time because he's an ass. I told him

I'd out-rake him, and his ego can't handle it."

"You can't win."

"God, Jesse. Thanks for having my back."

"No, you don't get it. You can't beat him." When I look at him, his head's down, his fists resting on his thighs. "Duke . . . helps him out every harvest. He messes with Shea's numbers, gives him credit for more boxes than he actually raked. How do you think Shea affords the payments on that crotch rocket of his?"

I just stare. Shea's Ninja, black-and-poison-green, waxed to a shine. I look down at my clenched fists. "How long have you known?" My voice is soft.

"Since the first week of raking this harvest. He told me and Mason, made us promise to keep our mouths shut."

I nod slowly, working my fists, letting my nails bite into my palms. "No wonder all the guys have been laughing at me."

"Nobody knows but us, Darcy. Even that was a mistake, I think. He got so caught up in bragging about all the money he's making that he let it slip." A weak laugh, like maybe I might join in, like we might still be in this together.

"The Wardwells got no idea?"

"Bob trusts Duke. End of harvest, things don't quite match up, they blame it on miscounting, scales being off, whatever. All part of the business. Duke never takes enough off the top to get anybody worried. I guess he thinks he's helping out his nephew."

I breathe out through my nose. "And you're okay with this?" My voice is almost a whisper.

Jesse shrugs. "No. But what am I gonna do, tell on them? Duke's got kids and bills and everything, and he's on layoff most of the winter. He needs what he makes harvesting. Mason and me aren't gonna be the reason he gets fired. And Shea"—he looks over, but I won't meet his eyes—"we been friends since we were twelve. I know he can be a douche. But with you and me . . . I mean, I already thought you were cute and all, and when it seemed like you liked me . . ." He gives up on catching my gaze and looks out at the night, his voice flat. "But Shea, he's in love with you."

I laugh harshly, startling him. "Oh, yeah. He loves me." Me, kissing Shea in the dark, running my nails over his back, laughing a little and not taking it seriously. "That's gotta be it." Things moving faster, too fast, us on the ground and him reaching under my skirt and tugging down my underwear, pushing my legs up before I can stop him. "That's how come he calls me a slut, and trash. That's how come he treats me so good." I can feel Jesse's surprise and I can't stand it, won't wait for him to ask questions. I won't answer his damned questions. "Take me home."

He begins to say something, then swallows his words and starts the engine. I face the window rigidly the whole way, watching woods and lit houses stream by without really seeing them. Shea, loving me. Jesse, not loving me at all.

When we reach my house, he leans over, saying, "Don't go yet," like it's still not too late, like we can save this.

I shrug him off. "No. I thought you were . . ." *Somebody different.* I shove the door open. "I'm done."

I cross the yard, breaking into a run, getting one clear image of Nell's cards scattered all over the table by the wind before I'm through the door, with the sound of his engine roaring away in my ears.

Upstairs, I fall asleep in my clothes, my mind raging, headphones on, and the stuffed dog I'm too old for squished under one arm. Nobody comes to check on me, and I'm glad.

Around one a.m., I thrash awake, sure that the car is out there again, positive that if I'd opened my eyes a second sooner, I would've seen the headlights track across my wall. I go to the window, but when I part the curtains, there's nothing out there but the night.

EIGHTEEN

RHIANNON'S WAITING FOR me at the kitchen table the next morning. I sink into a chair, puffy-eyed from a bad night of sleep, and see her splashed all over the front page of the *American* again.

A Year Without Rhiannon. That's the headline, with a smaller one underneath: *Twelve Months After Her Daughter's Disappearance, Sasanoa Mother Seeks Answers.* There's a big photo of Rhiannon's mom staring off down Route 15 with the barrens behind her, the snow fence unraveling to the left. Charlie Ann looks older, and I think she might be getting her hair dyed at Great Lengths now, because it's a brassier shade of auburn than I remember. So it's almost the anniversary.

Crazy to think that this time last year, I was picking up the phone and hearing Charlie Ann's voice. *Did Rhiannon stay over? Was there a party?*

The next photo is of Rhiannon, a candid of her lying on her stomach across her bed with her fuzzy slippers on, her gaze tilted up, chin propped on her hands. The last photo is of the Fit being towed out of the woods.

"You should read it," Mags says, sitting next to me with a bowl of cereal. "It's a pretty good article." She doesn't say anything about seeing a car parked on our road again last night, so either she slept through it or I dreamed that flash of headlights across my wall. I shrug, don't say anything.

Mom finishes wiping down the counter and sits by me. "You got in early last night."

I look up. She almost never says anything about when I come and go, as long as I don't show up wasted. While I watch, something unspoken passes between her and Mags. For the first time ever, I get the feeling they've been talking about me.

Mom coughs and crinkles the cellophane on a fresh pack of Kools, keeping her eyes on what she's doing. "Everything good?"

I bite my lip for a second. "Yup. It's all good."

When I woke up this morning, I thought hard about not going to work. The harvest is almost over. The barrens should be cleared by Saturday at the latest, and Bob will probably send most of us home before then because he won't need as many hands. I'd lose only a couple days' pay. It might be worth it to dodge Jesse, Shea, the whole stupid mess.

But that'd be chickenshit, and I know it. Shea's cheating all of us, every single person who busts their back in the heat while he does the same work for extra pay. If Jesse's too gutless to do something, then I guess it's on me. So, I put on my cutoffs, tank top, and cowgirl hat, lay the SPF 50 on thick, and get ready to survive this day.

Nell comes knocking, and on our way out the door, we grab our bags of donations for the migrants who lost their stuff in the fire. I'm surprised to step into the first hint of fall crispness in the air. It'll be seventy-five by noon, but right now, I've got goose bumps on my legs.

I brought the front page of the *American* with me. Wait till Libby shows up and sees that somebody messed with her morning ritual of coffee, toast, and paper. I read the Rhiannon article on the ride in, Nell reading over my shoulder. The reporter gives the facts of Rhiannon's disappearance, then talks about Charlie Ann's "quiet resolve and determination": "Somebody out there knows the truth. It's been a year. Maybe this story will help them find the courage to come forward and bring Rhiannon home."

It mentions Rhiannon's dad only once, which isn't surprising, since Jim and Charlie Ann divorced when Rhiannon was nine and have that awkward on again, off again thing going on. Once he even moved back in with them for a whole year, until the day Rhiannon came home from school to find him gone and her mom mopping the kitchen floor with a vengeance, saying that he wouldn't be coming back and to stop asking about it. I remember Rhiannon called me, crying so hard she could barely talk.

"Wow. Look," Nell says, and I glance up to see a big new poster stapled to the telephone pole in front of Gaudreau's. It's printed on white poster board with Rhiannon's sophomore-year photo, a full-color five-by-seven, dead center. *Missing—$5,000 Reward for Information.*

It's a parade of Rhiannons all the way down Main Street, her face smiling out of every business, bulletin board, and telephone pole. We even pass the people hanging them up, some guy stapling a poster in front of the post office while a woman waits in the car. I think I catch a glimpse of auburn hair, but I'm not sure.

We're called up to headquarters before work begins for the day, sitting in clusters on the grass, knowing something big is brewing. This time, Mrs. Wardwell stays in her chair, watching her husband with a tired but not-too-mean *I give up* kind of look. Bob stands with his fists on his hips, working his mouth around his dentures like the words he's mulling over have a bad taste.

"I got something to say, and then I ain't gonna bring it up

again. But I never thought I'd see you people—some of you I known for years—walk away from folks needing help. That's not what small-town livin's supposed to be about."

I notice Jesse looking at me. He sits beside Mason with his forearms resting on his bent knees, looking up at me slantwise from under his hair, which has gotten shaggy this summer, and shot through with reddish sun streaks. He doesn't look like himself without a grin. I can see how badly he wants to say something to me. It hurts to see him hurt, no matter how mad I am at him. I turn away. I didn't make him lie, didn't make him set me up as a fool, or be so totally blind to what's really between me and Shea.

"Now, you know who you are, so I ain't gonna go namin' names, but the ones I seen drivin' off down the road while we were putting that fire out . . ." Bob jerks his chin. "Well, there ain't gonna be work here for you next year. If the woods had caught, or one of them little kids had been inside—" He steps back, shaking his head. "Just don't be coming around looking for work." He claps his hands together once. "Get to it."

You can feel the shock, people looking at each other, whispering, maybe the migrants most shocked of all. The faces of the locals who left yesterday are like hard masks as we get up and spread out across the rows. A couple of them leave, just plain leave, without a word to the Wardwells or anybody else. I watch Shea brush off his jeans, giving him time to feel me looking and meet my eyes. He grins. This time, though, he must sense that something's changed, because he doesn't give me any crap as I follow Mags and Nell into the barrens.

But he follows me. And sets up two rows over.

I rake hard because I want money. I rake hard because that's how I like to work. I'm not killing myself anymore to try to beat Shea in a rigged game.

His presence beside me is like heat, like weight, something I've carried around on my back too long. Can't believe how he's steered my time and energy toward him this August, feeding his lame love/hate thing, while all I could think about was proving how tough I was. I fill a box and close the top, letting my gaze meet his, staying cool as I can, not giving him a reaction.

He pushes his hat back and wipes his brow. "Looking rode hard and put away wet, Princess. Rough night?"

"You'd love to know."

"Nah. I'm not into sloppy seconds."

"From what I hear, you'll take whatever you can get." I drop an empty box on top of my stack with a bang. "And I hear you take handouts pretty regular."

"What, you mean like the handout you gave me at the quarry? I do okay. You worried about me?"

"No. But you should be."

I let him think on that one. When I glance at him next, his cockiness has faded into watchfulness. He gets back to work, but he's moving slower, sizing me up.

At lunch break, I wait until Mrs. Wardwell makes her usual mosey over to the Porta-Johns before grabbing the bags of donations from Mags's car. I carry them up to the camper and set them inside the open doorway—the Wardwells will figure out who they're for—mostly because I don't want us to look like kiss-asses in front of the locals who were basically told not to show their faces here next harvest.

I go back down the steps. Everybody's eating lunch in the grass below. I see Nell's blue bandanna, the sun shining gold off Mags's hair. Then somebody grabs my arm hard enough to make me gasp, pulling me into the shadows behind the camper.

Shea presses me back against the cool metal, leaning down to get in my face. "Who've you been talking to?"

I push on his arms. "Let go, idiot."

"Not till you tell me what the hell you were hinting at back there."

"What do you think?" Our noses are almost touching. "I know you're cheating. We're all busting our asses while you pull in double—" I jerk against him, then go flat against the camper, breathing hard. "Tell Duke to stop, and I won't say anything to anybody."

"You think we're dealing? You want to, like, shake on it or something?"

"Fine. Then I'll tell everybody. Hope you like washing

186

dishes at the Harbor View diner next summer—"

This time he slams me back so hard that the aluminum ripples. I curse, lunging at him until he grabs my wrists and pins them. I'm strong, too, and I don't make it easy for him. "You're not telling anybody." He's breathing hard on me. "You just love screwing me over, don't you? You been after me all summer, giving me shit."

"You got that backward."

"Bouchard told you, right? He's the one." I fix my gaze on sunlight caught in a spiderweb. He swears. "Knew it. He can't keep his mouth shut. Just like he can't keep it in his pants when some little hoochie like you shakes her ass at him. I don't even blame the guy." He turns my chin back. "That's the plan? You're gonna spread for all my friends before you work your way back to me?"

"I'm never gonna touch you again. And just so you know, I liked Jesse way before I ever hooked up with you. But I *never* liked you." Using all my strength, I twist my wrists free and push past him. "Stay away from me."

A few seconds later, he says, "Hey, Darcy," and when I glance back, he catches my upper arm and pulls. I stumble. He sweeps my left foot out from under me. I go down.

I don't remember seeing the trailer hitch, but I guess I must've, because I almost get my hands up before I hit it. My forehead and nose slam metal. My teeth clamp down on my tongue.

I see fireworks, smell blood, taste blood, and gag as I roll onto my side.

Cradling my face, I ride the wave of pain until it drops me, and I can breathe again. Sitting up, I wipe away tears—I'm not *crying*, it just hurts—and see a watery image of Shea walking away across the field. He didn't even stick around to see how messed up I am; going by the warm wetness on my face and the way my head is throbbing, I'm guessing very.

I'm too dazed to do much more than put one foot in front of the other, touching my fingertips to my nose, wondering if it's broken, how you can tell. All I can think about is getting to Mags's car so I can lie down in the backseat where nobody can see me, but I've got to cross the field to get to the road. A big hazy shape closes in to my right; must be Mrs. Wardwell coming back. She drops whatever she's holding and says, "Holy crap."

I try to hide my face, skirting the boulders, going faster and faster until I run smack into Mason. It's like he's been waiting for me. I try to go around him. I've got blood trickling down the back of my throat now, making me cough. He leans down, says, "God," under his breath, holding my shoulder as he checks me out.

Then Mason, all six-four, two hundred and thirty pounds of him, goes after Shea. Shea's standing around with some guys, shooting bull like any other day, when the heel of Mason's palm hits him square in the chest, knocking him back. "What the hell is wrong with you?" Mason's voice booms across the barrens.

Most everybody scatters, only a couple heroes stepping between Mason and Shea, trying to keep them apart.

I haven't moved, watching this whole thing like it's happening on TV. Then Jesse runs up. The moment he sees my face is awful, almost worse than hitting the trailer hitch in the first place. His expression goes slack, like somebody in shock. I can see him putting two and two together. Everything that makes him Jesse—my Jesse—falls away, and he loses it.

He's on Shea, grabbing for his throat, smashing his fist into Shea's face twice before the other guys can tackle him to the ground. He rolls free and throws his head into Shea's stomach, bringing him down, where they roll, punching each other's ribs, really ripping each other apart, not like some fight in the school hallway that's mostly for show.

Mags has me, then, and Nell presses in on my left. I let Mags hold my head to her chest, worrying my hair with her fingertips, her heart pounding beneath my ear. She yells something at Shea, but I can't understand it.

For a few minutes, not even Bob and Duke can pull the boys apart, and it looks like we're going to have to let them fight it out. Finally, Duke gets his arm around Shea's neck in a sleeper hold, and it's either Shea lets Duke drag him back or passes out. Jesse gets slowly to his feet, wiping his face with his forearm, one eye already swelling shut.

There's nothing but the sounds of breathing, bugs humming in the bushes, and Nell's tear-choked voice as she says to me, "Oh no, oh, your poor face," and dabs at my lips and shirtfront with her unrolled bandanna.

Bob's deeply flushed, his eyes snapping. He stoops and grabs Shea's ball cap, throwing it at his chest. "You do this to her?"

Shea's dusty, bleeding at the mouth, and the collar of his T-shirt is ripped. He looks at me with this remote expression, like he doesn't even know me. Underneath that, though, there's a hard smugness that blows my mind, a real satisfaction. All I can do is stare back as he says, "She wasn't supposed to land that hard."

Jesse makes a choked sound and takes a run at him, almost getting ahold of him before the guys pull him back. Bob walks up to Shea. "Get your ass off my property."

Shea pulls out of Duke's hold, spits blood into the dirt, and walks away without looking back. Duke squints after him, rubbing the back of his neck.

Bob turns to me. "You want me to call the law, dear?"

"No," I say quickly. With my luck, they'd send Edgecombe, and I can't deal with him right now.

Mags draws back. "Darcy. You have to press charges."

"No." She opens her mouth again and I say, "Drop it," in a tone that actually seems to get through to her.

Bob wants me to go to the hospital, but when I say no, he settles for Mrs. Wardwell calling Mom at work. The conversation's pretty short. "She'll meet you at the house," Mrs. Wardwell says, then watches us go. I think of Jesse, but I don't look at him.

We pass Shea on 15. He's taken his shirt off and tucked it into the waistband of his jeans, like he wants to feel the sun on his back.

NINETEEN

THE GIRLS HELP me wash up. Warm pink water trickles into the sink. Terry cloth slides over my face. The soft white smell of Ivory takes me back to baths with Mags when we were little, Mom sitting on the edge of the tub, trying to dig the potatoes out of our ears.

When I'm clean, I see that my nose is swollen clear up to a lopsided egg on my forehead that's already turning purple, and my eyes have an owlish look that probably means they'll be black in the morning. Sexy as hell. Nell takes a breath, looking at me, her face pale and stricken in the mirror.

The door opens and we hear Mom set her purse on the counter, the *chink* of her keys dropping into the little Pyrex bowl with a pattern of red hens on it. She comes to the doorway and looks at me, then at my tank top, lying on the floor with a rusty stripe of dried blood down the front. Mags picks it up and shuts it away in the washing machine, like she can block the memory.

Mom breathes out slowly, then steps back. "Better get some ice on your face, bring down the swelling." Her calmness helps me feel more normal, too. I follow her out to the kitchen table, where she hands me a bag of frozen peas and puts the kettle on.

Mags comes in, gripping the back of a chair. "She might have a concussion."

"Come on, I'm fine."

"You are *not fine.* She's not fine, and we should be on the phone to the cops right now, getting Shea Gaines's ass hauled in." She stares at Mom's back. "Aren't you even going to ask what happened?"

"When your sister's had a second to catch her breath, yeah. And I'll be asking her, not you, so back off." Mom drops the whistling kettle onto a cold burner and reaches for two mugs. "One busybody in this family is enough, thank you very much." Mags bangs the legs of the chair down and heads for the porch. "Margaret, don't you slam that door."

The door slams. Nell watches me from the hallway, wavering, like she's afraid of what will happen next if she takes her eyes off me. "Go on home, Nellie," Mom says, pouring hot water over bags of Red Rose.

After a second, Nell goes, shutting the door carefully. Mom adds sugar and brings us both aspirin. She pops hers. "Headache?" I say.

She nods. "You, too, I'm guessing."

I snort, which hurts. The cold of the peas and the steam from my mug coat my face in clammy dew. I sip tea, waiting.

"How'd you get hurt?"

"I told a guy off. He didn't like it."

"Derek Gaines's kid?"

"Maybe. I dunno his dad's name." I think she's going to call Shea's dad, maybe right after we're done here.

"Is it over?" The way she asks it surprises me. It's woman-to-woman, not mother-to-kid. "I need to know if you're gonna be safe now."

I sit there in the kitchen where I've eaten meals, done homework, scrubbed countertops, and learned to bake, hoping I've got the guts to cross this next bridge. Finally, I shake my head. I just don't know.

"You feel dizzy or sick to your stomach since it happened?" I say no. "Want to go to the doctor?" No chance. She sits back in her chair, clearing her throat. Her gaze flits to the pack of smokes to her right, then away, like she's putting off having one. "Next week, you're gonna be a senior. When you turn eighteen, there won't be much I can do about your choices. Libby thinks something needs to be done about you.

Your sister told me she's worried, too." I look up sharply. "Don't get mad at her. You're lucky to have Mags. She was born a mama bear and she's always gonna be there for you, whether you want her or not. I guess what I want to know is what you think we should do about you."

I know it's a big deal, her talking to me like this, like a grown-up. It scares me, too, though, being handed the wheel when I'm not sure if I'm ready to take it. I owe her more than a shrug, but as usual, when I really need words, they won't come.

Mom waits, then presses her fingertip against a few crumbs, brushing them into a paper napkin. "You're like me when I was your age, you know that. Sometimes I can't believe how much."

"Really?"

"Oh, yeah. You and me would've been tight. Ramming the roads Friday nights, seeing how many shots we could take before somebody stopped us. Your grandparents and Libby liked to blame all that on your dad, but it was me. Grampie and Gramma tried to make me act right. They pushed, so I pushed back harder. Guess I always figured it'd be the same with you, so I didn't push at all."

"Probably smart."

She half smiles. "But it seems like the way we're going now isn't working, either." She looks at my bruised face. "I barely survived being young. When I think of some of the

195

stuff I did, stuff I tried . . . it's scary to think of you in my place. And sometimes it's hard to know when things stop being fun and turn into a habit." She hesitates. "You come talk to me about it, if you ever need to."

I don't tell her not to worry, or that I'll change, here and now. Neither of us would believe it. As she stands and dashes the last of her tea into the sink, I say, "Was Libby as sweet and innocent growing up as she says?"

"Not really."

"Huh. Figures, the way she keeps Nell on a leash." I shrug. "Maybe if Nell's dad had stayed, Libby would've had a husband to nag, so Nell could take a whiz without asking per—"

"Nell's her whole life." Mom's look is sharp, and I drop my smirk. "And nothing would've been better if her dad had stuck around. He let Libby chase after him for a commitment for almost two years, and then dropped her as soon as something better came along." Mom stops, her shoulders bunched. I don't say, *But I thought they were engaged,* because I'm pretty sure she just let a family secret slip. "Don't you ever throw any of that in her face."

"Okay." I take a breath and set my peas on the table, feeling my nose. It's numb.

A sneaker scrapes outside and I turn to see Nell step up to the screen door.

"Sorry," she says to us. Mom waves a hand. "It's just that . . . we got rehearsal." She looks at me. "What're you gonna do?"

★ ★ ★

A blue velour curtain hangs on the stage, and some volunteers staple bunting to the facade and grandstand as Nell and I walk up the steps. I was too sore to put on makeup before we left, so I wore my pink Red Sox cap, pulling it low. The stares are almost enough to turn me around; Bella grabs Alexis and they smother shocked giggles. Nell's grip on my arm is the only thing that keeps me from going after them like I was smashing pumpkins on Halloween. Still holding tight, Nell walks me up to Mrs. Hartwell and says, "My cousin got hurt at work today, but she still wants to rehearse. Is that okay?"

Mrs. Hartwell blinks quickly. "Well—of course. Goodness, you poor thing. What in the world kind of work were you doing?"

"Blueberry raking," I say, and leave it at that.

Mrs. Hartwell puts us through our paces, having a great time stepping and clapping along and getting her whole body into it. The Festival's coming together around us, and it makes me feel like I've swallowed a handful of tadpoles. Three days until the coronation. Three *days*. I'm going to have to get up here in front of everyone, and pretend I belong, all the while looking like I used my face to stop a Mack truck. The aspirin's faded and my head throbs dully with every step I take, every thump of the sound system.

Once we're all seated on the risers with our legs crossed, Mrs. Hartwell says, "At this point, you'll be called by name to the microphone center stage, where you'll be introduced to the audience by the emcee. The judges will ask you the question they've prepared for you. Now, there's no reason to agonize over the interview. You're all experts on yourselves, right? If you receive high marks for your answer, you'll move on to the final round, where you'll be interviewed again. The judges will confer, and then announce Miss Congeniality, second runner-up, and the Queen." A guy drives a tractor around the stage, raking the dirt track smooth for Saturday. In the distance, a white tent rises like a huge mushroom cap.

One girl raises her hand. "How many of us will make it to the final round?"

"Anywhere from three to seven. But there was one time that ten girls qualified, and we were all here until the wee hours." Mrs. Hartwell's gaze lingers on each of our faces like we're something special. "I won't be seeing you all again before Saturday, but you have my number and email, and I want you to contact me about anything at all. Even if you just need somebody to talk you off a ledge." She laughs, even though that doesn't sound too far-fetched to me. "Now, I'm going to start calling your names one by one, and we'll practice interview entrances and exits."

When it's time to go, I wait for Nell as her riser empties out, hugging myself, wishing I'd brought a sweatshirt now that it's getting cooler at night.

Mrs. Hartwell's voice makes me look over. "It's really not

so bad." She gathers her purse, bottled water, and clipboard, then touches her cheek. "Your face. The bruises won't be gone by Saturday, but good makeup can take care of that. Green cover-up. Apply it with a sponge under liquid foundation. Works wonders for reducing discoloration."

I put my hands in my pockets, then think of Mason, and pull them out. "I was thinking . . . maybe I should skip." She stops what she's doing. "I mean, I'll look like a prize jackass with my face like this."

She stands, big purse under her arm. Her powder-blue shadow makes her eyes intense. "Do you want me to talk you out of it, or talk you into it?" I hesitate. "I get the feeling you've needed a lot of talking-into since this process started." She nods at Nell coming down the steps. "Like maybe you're here for somebody else?" She's got me; I don't try to cover. "Well, I'll tell you what I know. You're no quitter. If you were, you never would've come here tonight, looking like you do. I know how tongues wag. That took guts." She smiles, tugging her cardigan together. "Think you can finish what you started?"

It's a thought, looking at this like a challenge, not a chore. Almost like making it onto the board in the barrens. After a second, I nod. "Okay. I won't bail." I take a few steps back, then say, "What was it like, when you won?"

It takes her a second to get my meaning. Then she laughs. "Oh, hon, I was never Festival Queen. I was never even a

Princess." You could knock me over with a tiara. "I wasn't . . . well, let's just say I wasn't the type of girl who gets chosen for things like this. I was quite a bit heavier in high school, and so shy." She laughs again. "Scared of my own shadow. I couldn't have gotten up in front of all those people, even if I'd had the chance."

"Then why do you do this?" I can think of about a hundred things I'd rather do with my August than spend it herding a bunch of teenage girls around.

"Because I enjoy it. My sister Gwen was Queen back in 1989. She passed away about fifteen years ago. I guess I like to stay involved because it reminds me of her, and how we were that summer." She gives a soft laugh. "Young."

"I'm sorry."

She can tell I mean it, that I get how it feels when you talk about somebody you loved who died. "Thank you. But it's nice to say her name out loud once in a while. Way too much time goes by without me saying it, I think." She touches my shoulder. "Go on home and get some beauty sleep."

TWENTY

WE'RE ON THE roof, the three of us, wearing jeans for the first time in months and sharing the last Coke from the fridge. The phone rings downstairs. None of us move.

Mags pokes me with her toe. "You know it's for you."

I grunt. After bringing Nell and me home, Libby handed me my phone messages, her face stony as Mount Katahdin. Jesse called three times while I was gone. And there was one hang-up, too, which must be my fault, apparently.

"Why don't you want to talk to him?" Nell sits up on her elbow, her hair sliding over her shoulder.

"I just don't."

"But he defended your honor." Mags and I snort. "Well,

he did." Nell sits forward, hugging her knees, wearing that look she gets whenever she drifts into one of her big-screen fantasies. "He came to your rescue, like a knight or Gregory Peck or somebody."

I gulp the rest of the Coke without thinking. Mags sets the can on the windowsill, annoyed. "He got into it with Shea because it's been a long time coming, that's what I think." It sure as hell wasn't because he loves me; he made that pretty clear. I picture Jesse playing with his phone, waiting for me to call; why, I don't know. I wonder what his bedroom looks like at his uncle's place. I'm guessing medium-messy, a couple centerfolds on the wall. And books. I get the feeling he reads.

Mags takes her glasses off and rubs her face. "Darcy doesn't need a knight, but if she did, I think she could do better than Jesse Bouchard."

That reminds me of what she told me in the dressing room of Lehman's. I turn to her. "He must've at least asked you, right?"

Mags stares at me. "Who?"

"*Will.* He asked you to have sex and you said no, right?"

She bursts into exasperated laughter. "What's your issue? We talked about it sometimes. It just never happened. Not every guy pushes, you know. You do know that, right?"

"Duh," I say, flustered, not knowing it at all. Except for Jesse. And when he didn't push, I got mad at him. "So you've really never done it?"

"Well, considering the last boyfriend I had before Will was in sixth grade, no, I've never done it." She looks at me blandly. "How many times have you?"

They're both watching me, but I feel Nell's gaze the strongest. I know she's going to hold up whatever I say as some kind of lens to see herself through. I can't lie. Not to her, not about this. "Four. I mean, with four guys, not four times." There's a silence. "It's not that bad."

"Did anybody say it was?"

I shrug. The bridge lights flash over the treetops. Scarlet, then blackness. If I'm ever going to tell them this, now's the time. "You know who my first was?"

Mags looks surprised when I say Adam Morrow. "I didn't even know you knew him."

"I didn't." All I knew was he was beautiful. Beautiful on the soccer field, the red and white of his uniform bringing out the color in his cheeks on those fall afternoons when Rhiannon and I would sit on a blanket on the sidelines and scream for him. Beautiful at school, passing by the water fountain I'd stake out between periods every morning, just to catch a glimpse. It was one of those hopeless crushes that twist your insides because you love him so much, and you know it'll never, ever happen. He's perfect, and you're nobody. "Rhiannon liked one of his friends. Having crushes on them was what we *did*. I mean, we talked about it all the time, what we'd do if they liked us back, how it'd be the best thing ever and totally change our lives."

Mags watches my face, the wind stirring strands of her hair. I don't look at Nell, because I can imagine her expression exactly: lips slightly parted, hanging on words that I should've told her a long time ago, before it was too late. "I never would've talked to him in a million years. Seriously, who does that, ask out their mega-crush like it's nothing?"

"Rhiannon." Mags's voice is flat.

"Yeah. If she wanted something, she went for it. She didn't even tell me first. She asked a friend of a friend to tell the guys that some sophomore girls liked them, and when they said they'd be down for hanging out with us on Halloween . . . she set it up."

"Were you scared?" Nell sounds soft.

"I got really mad at her, at first. But I let her talk me into it, fill me up with how hot I must be, a senior wanting a hookup when he barely knew my name. We got Rhiannon's mom to drop us off at the school gym for the dance. Soon as she drove off, we walked up to the soccer fields and met the boys." Rhiannon and I almost ran up the hill, giggling crazily with nerves, our breath steaming in the cold air. Trojans in our pockets because we weren't stupid, you know, we read *Cosmo*. "We made a pact. Said this was gonna be the night. We were gonna give it away, 'cause there couldn't be anybody better to give it to, ever."

The boys, parked at opposite ends of the lot, car engines

running. Rhiannon smiling at me, looking way more fearless than I felt, saying, *Have fun.* Disappearing into the Mustang.

Then I was inside the Explorer, with the smell of his cologne and the heater and a pine air freshener just out of the package. Being this close to him lit a fire in me, smoking and crackling away. I must be beautiful. I must be something. He'd showed up. "I was scared, but he didn't make me do it or anything. I mean, it was my choice." Pulling his weight down on me, dragging his lip between my teeth, letting my body take over to block out the confused, crazy messages my brain was sending. "I'm saying it wasn't horrible or anything. But when it was over, he was like, 'This was your first time?' and he sounded, like, shocked. Because you've gotta figure any girl who goes after a guy the way I did must have some mileage on her, right? Even if she's only fifteen."

There's the softest sound of Mags drawing breath through her teeth. I can't stand her feeling sorry for me. That's not why I'm telling them this. "He tried to make it nice. He'd laid out blankets in the back, and I could smell that he'd washed them. It wasn't like this awful thing."

"You keep saying that."

"Because I know how you are. You'll waste all this time hating him and there's no point. I mean, he doesn't even matter, really. It was totally awkward after and neither of us could think of anything to say. Finally I said see ya and got out."

Into the freezing dark, walking faster and faster, ditching the girl who'd gotten into the backseat of that Explorer twenty minutes ago because I didn't want to know her anymore. "The other car was gone, and Rhiannon was standing under the streetlight, shivering like she'd been out there for a while. All she wanted to do was go back to the dance, so we went." In the girls' room, watching her run hot water over her hands, trying to get the feeling back, her face pinched and frowning in the mirror, me asking, *Are you okay?*

"Was she okay?" Nell's voice is hushed.

I bite my lip, literally counting to ten before I speak. My words still come out tightly. "She didn't do it. She changed her mind."

"What?" Mags.

"She got into the car and changed her mind. The guy must've been pissed, because he kicked her out and left." I can still feel how the whole room seemed to fall away, leaving us together in a pocket of sickening silence, even with the bass pounding on the other side of the wall and girls coming and going. Rhiannon's quick, sharp little movements, like she was disgusted with me.

"I was like, 'You were the one who set the whole thing up,' and she was like, 'I didn't make you do anything.' That was when I walked away. She was right. She didn't make me. But she still let me put myself out there alone after we'd agreed to do it together and everything. I mean, not that I *wanted* her to sleep with somebody, I just . . . hated feeling tricked. So I borrowed somebody's phone and called Mom, said I was sick and wanted to come home."

Mags watches my face. "You never told anybody what happened?"

"What could I say?" I brush at some dirt on my pants. "I thought Rhiannon would call and say she was sorry, but she didn't. We didn't talk at school on Monday, either. Or the rest of the week. By then everybody was whispering about what happened on Halloween, except nobody was talking about Rhiannon being part of it. So I figured she was the one who ran her mouth, and made herself look good."

"That bitch." Mags sits very straight and stiff. Rhiannon's lucky she's missing, because my sister's mad enough to come down on her like a 185-pound landslide right now. "She's embarrassed about punking out, so she trashes you."

"And I heard her talking about me one time. Saying how easy I was." I shrug. "So now you guys know."

"I always wondered why you stopped being friends." Nell jumps when Mags brings her heel down against the shingles. *"Shhh!"*

"Damn it, I *never* liked her." Mags simmers for a few seconds, then says in a rough voice, "Sorry, Darce. Really. That sucks."

"It's done." I tuck my chin into the collar of my fleece. My words speed up, because I want to get this out while I've still got Nell's ear. "The point is, your dream guy is just a guy, and he can stomp all over your heart. But then you got to move on, because he's sure not wasting any time worrying about you. You got to protect yourself, or somebody worse will come along and smell blood in the water and they'll come at you, too, and it won't ever end." As I say it, it hits me, what Shea really did, on the Fourth and today. I reach for the bruises, stop, and force my hand back down. "You got to be smart. You know? Smart."

Even in the dark, I know Nell's eyes are wet, and she's checking out her shoes. When it's time to go inside, she climbs off the roof without saying good night, and I see her wipe her face with the back of her hand. Guess I hurt her. Good.

Maybe she learned something.

TWENTY ONE

WE'RE DOWN TO the last hundred rows of the west field, but there's plenty of work for everyone because lots of people ditched today. That happens at the end of harvest, but this time, it's got less to do with running out of berries and more to do with Mr. Wardwell telling the locals where to stick it. Good thing he's not running for dogcatcher.

Now that Shea's off the board, Bankowski's made it to first place. Nell sings "My Darling Clementine" while she rakes, and it's nice, kind of, because it helps keep my mind off Shea. I'd like to think that he'd never show his face here after what he pulled, but yesterday he didn't seem to care if he got caught, or what anybody thought of him. I remember

Mom's question: *Is it over?*

I practically jump out of my sneakers when Jesse comes up beside me at lunch. I swallow a dry lump of sandwich, my heart thumping. Mags and Nell get really interested in what they're eating.

He hunkers beside me. He smells good, like sweat and outdoors. "You get my messages?"

I slap a horsefly.

"So, are you okay or what?"

"I'm good." My voice is low as I pick at my sandwich. "You?"

His left eye is purple, burst vessels speckling the white, and there's a scrape down his cheek that looks pretty nasty. "Been worse."

I watched him for a few seconds earlier: he's moving slowly today, biting his cheek as he rakes, like something hurts inside. Bruised ribs, maybe. He and Mason rake close together. Mason must've been in the middle this whole time, listening to Jesse and Shea both talk about me when the other one wasn't around. He must've known something bad was going to go down sooner or later. I glance at the road again.

"You heard from him?" Jesse knows who I'm worrying about. "If he's bothering you, tell me."

"Come on. You went after Shea yesterday for you, not me." Nell flinches at my tone, pulling her knees in, making herself small. "Shea busted my face. You liked my face better the way it was, so you hit him." I breathe out slowly, letting the shocked silence settle over us. "I'm sorry you got hurt. But it wasn't for me."

He watches me for a long moment. "I was stupid about Shea. I'm sorry, okay. I didn't see how things really were with you guys. But if you're still mad about the raking thing . . . I mean, Shea's done. Bob's never gonna let him back into the barrens."

"Yeah. But he never got nailed for it, either." I squeeze my sandwich into a tinfoil ball and chuck it down. "He got away with it, 'cause nobody did anything."

Jesse stays where he is, white-lipped and quiet. His hand grips his knee, and I can see the ground-in dirt around his thumbnail, the kind you need pumice soap to get out. "So that's it, huh?"

I squint off. "Guess so."

He stands. Then I feel his hand rest on the top of my head for just a second. His fingers slide away. "Take care of yourself, Darcy."

"I will," I say faintly, but he's already gone.

It's blue twilight when Libby and Nell get home from Bangor. I look out the living room window and watch Nell run across the grass, hugging a long garment bag to herself. Her face is lit up, hair bouncing around her shoulders as she hops over the first step and disappears into the trailer.

I guess Nell found it. The dress she's going to wear.

"Show us." Later, Mags flops onto her bed, giving Nell a look. "Come on, you're really not going to show us?"

"No. It'll ruin the specialness." Nell works a sponge around in a little palette of green concealer.

"At least tell us what color it is."

"It's the one. That's all you need to know." Nell touches my shoulders and lifts my chin with her hand, our reflections moving together in Mags's vanity mirror as she lightly dabs my forehead and nose, then uses a little brush to spread the concealer around my eyes, practicing to see if she can fix my face for the big night. I look like I did a face-plant in a bowl of pistachio pudding.

"You know about this stuff, right?" I watch Nell in the mirror as she starts smoothing her fingers over my skin. "'Cause, no offense, but this looks . . . kinda . . ."

"Green covers redness and blotchiness really well. Mrs. Hartwell told you it would work, didn't she?" She's so gentle that her fingertips feel like wings brushing over my face. "The heat from my skin helps blend it. Your fingers really are your best tools for applying almost any makeup."

"Look out, Pauline's School of Beauty," Mags murmurs, smiling as she flips through one of her yearbooks.

"Next, we build with foundation." Nell lays it on heavier

than I ever do, but you really can't see the green through it. I sit up a little more, watching.

Mags turns pages, then snorts. "I'm sorry, but what a moron."

She's stopped on a page of candid photos. Her thumb rests on a shot of Kenyon. He's half-turned at a table in some classroom, wearing a ski cap and hoodie, eyes heavy-lidded, looking even more like Kat than usual. "He's not a moron," I say. "He's just . . ." I don't even know if we're still friends, and here I am, sticking up for him. "He got scared and screwed up."

"Holding on to that car for a year? That's more than a screwup. How could he seriously not know that was the worst thing he could've done? He'll be lucky if he doesn't end up doing jail time."

Nell steps back. "Done."

I'm almost back to normal. If you really stare, you can see something isn't quite right with my face, but I'll be far enough away from the crowd on Saturday that nobody will be able to tell. "Wow. Thanks a lot, Nellie. That looks much better."

She smiles and shrugs like it doesn't count, gathering her tools. "I'm smart with makeup."

"You're smart with lots of things. Don't run yourself down," Mags says, setting the yearbook on the pile of novels on her nightstand.

I'm still thinking about Kenyon, picturing his fist slowly meeting the heavy bag, the tightness of his jaw, the focus of his gaze when I asked if Rhiannon knew he was crushing on her. *Wasn't gonna happen,* he'd said, not like somebody feeling sorry for himself, but like he knew for sure, like it was a fact. "You think he was lying to me the other night?"

Nell glances at me, then down at her packet of brushes. "He lied to everybody for a year."

"All he had to do was tell his parents," Mags says. "You know they would've smoothed everything out for him, like they did when he got caught with weed at school. Everybody knows they've got more money than God."

"Gimme the laptop," I say. Mags raises her eyebrows at me and doesn't move. "*Please.* Please gimme the laptop, Your Highness."

I private message Kenyon, and keep it simple: *Y r u lying?*

The next morning, I oversleep and wake up to Mags's big foot kicking my door. No time to see if Kenyon's messaged me back. But at least I poked him. He knows I suspect something.

The last day of the harvest is probably the most beautiful day of the whole summer. Hot but dry, the blue sky full of those big, rolling clouds that really do make animal shapes. We'll be outta here by noon and everybody knows it, so the attitude's pretty relaxed, people calling back and forth between rows, laughing. We girls work close by, not talking much, just feeling the sun and making our last few hours count.

Mr. Wardwell blasts his truck horn three times when the field is cleared, and everybody walks up to headquarters and stands around in a loose knot. Mrs. Wardwell gets to her feet. "You all know we give something away at the end of harvest to whoever raked the most. This year's a first. We never had a lady up here before. Therese Bankowski, come up and get your check."

I watch a hard-faced, freckled woman break away from the group. It's the woman from the fire, the one whose family lost their stuff. She's rangy and strong, shaking hands with Mrs. Wardwell—the tendons stand out in her forearms like baling wire—and taking the check for seven hundred dollars with no more change in her expression than if she was being handed a grocery store receipt. My gaze meets Jesse's through the crowd. It's a long look, neither of us wanting to be the first to break it.

"Awright, people. We brought in some good berries this year." Mrs. Wardwell drops back into her chair, massaging one foot through her moccasin. "Last checks are in the mail."

"And don't let the door hit ya ass," Mags whispers. I smile on reflex, watching Jesse step back, move away with Mason. Mason, I'll see at school on Monday. Jesse, I don't know when I'll see again.

Locals move toward the line of parked cars, heading home to houses and trailers. Migrants move toward the cabins; starting tomorrow, they'll be heading north to potato country, or the next under-the-table construction or food service job. Wonder if they'll come this way again next blueberry season. If I were them, I wouldn't.

As we walk downhill toward Mags's car, I hear a whoop. Bankowski's spinning her little boy around by his hands as he giggles crazily at the sky.

The barrens really deserve their name without us rakers. Nothing left out there but the flatbed loaded with the last day's haul, some pickups, and the toilets to prove we were here at all. I stop, squinting against the sunlight as I watch Jesse's pickup pull onto 15 with the rest of the locals streaming back toward town.

Mags stops with her hand on her door. "Forget something?"

I take off my hat, toss it into the car, and climb in after it. "Not a thing."

TWENTY TWO

IT TAKES ME a second to recognize the gold SUV when it pulls into our driveway later that afternoon. We're on the porch playing I Doubt It, and I stand, leaning against a column as Kenyon gets out of his mom's car. Didn't take long to flush him out of the weeds.

He looks up at our house for a second. He's never been here before, and the place does look kind of sketchy right now, scraped bare except for fresh butter-yellow paint up to the top of the first-floor windows. He stops at the steps. "Hey." He sees my bruises but doesn't ask; knowing the Sasanoa grapevine, he's already heard the whole story.

I nod. Nell's curled up like a cat on the swing, studying

him openly while working her fingers through an old afghan Libby knitted that we keep thrown over the backrest. Mags sits on the floor, watching him over her cards with absolutely no expression, her foolproof trick to make somebody feel unwanted. Kenyon checks out our setup—table with cards, change, and a bag of cheese puffs—then says to me, "Can I talk to you?"

Mom's at work, but we go up to my room for privacy anyway. It isn't too messy except for a pair of dirty underwear that I kick under the bed. He goes over to the window and looks out at the road. "I got your message." He reaches up and flicks the bunch of dried buttercups distractedly, making them sway. "So I'm a liar, huh?"

"I think you're bullshitting, yeah."

When he turns around, he has a hunted look. "Don't go around saying that."

"Why not?" I keep my face hard. "You threw me under. Why shouldn't I do it to you? Why shouldn't I go right to the cops?" Bluffing, but he might not know that.

"Darcy, seriously. Just leave it alone."

"What's the deal, Kenyon? The truth. You owe me."

He curses softly. He looks skinnier than usual, his Bob Marley T-shirt and skater jeans hanging off him. His jawline's so sharp it almost looks delicate, the sun turning the fine blond stubble transparent. "I told you. She asked me to take her car."

"You said you borrowed it."

His voice is so quiet that I strain to catch his words. "She had to get away."

I sink slowly onto my bed, hands curled in my lap. My room seems very still now in the afternoon quiet, almost like one of those shadow boxes we made in elementary school: tiny bed, tiny bureau, miniature people. Whatever I'm feeling, you can't call it relief, exactly, but it's heavy, stealing my strength and voice for a long time. When I finally speak again, it's in a whisper. "From what?"

"I don't know. I don't know what. She couldn't tell me. Not wouldn't, but like, *couldn't*, you know. Like it hurt too much." He shrugs and sniffs. "She was messed up bad that last year. We kind of talked around it a bunch of times, but the night of the party, she started crying. Saying she couldn't stay here anymore."

I try to fit the memory of the bubbly, smart-ass fifteen-year-old I knew into this frame. Doesn't go, and I shake my head. "Because of her parents or something?"

"Kind of. She said they wouldn't miss her 'cause they were too wrapped up in their own drama. That's the reason she raked blueberries last year, so she could make some money of her own to bring with her. She didn't want the car, didn't want the cops putting out an APB and catching her. I told her I'd hide it at our camp until she got away."

"She burned her bag on purpose."

"She wanted to make it look like maybe she was dead. That way people would keep searching for her right here. Plus, I think she just didn't want any of that stuff. Anything that made her who she was. Not her ID, nothing." He looks down. "I didn't really think about what would happen if I got caught with the car until I sobered up."

I fold my arms. "She bother telling you where she was going? How she was getting there?"

He shakes his head slowly. "She promised to text me after, but she never did." He meets my eyes. I see a guy who has had his heart carved out. "I don't even know if she's okay."

I try to hold back, I really do. I don't even breathe for what feels like a full minute. "Well, that's awesome. She didn't tell you anything so you couldn't blow her big stupid plan, and now you're on the hook for it, and you don't even hate her. Christ, Kenyon, does she have to come back here and literally kick you in the balls to make you realize that she never cared about you? She never liked you, she *used* you, and now you're gonna go to jail because of her."

He doesn't move, just keeps on watching me, his eyes steady, his mouth in that slanted line. "You can't tell anybody."

"Why not? She treated me like dog crap. I'm supposed to keep secrets for her?"

"She *was* right. You hold a grudge forever." I stare. "She

told me what you did with that guy in the parking lot. How you let him pop your cherry." His mouth twitches. "Then you blamed her for it."

"Because it was her *fault*. It was her *idea*. Then she went around telling everybody what a slut I was. She tell you that part?"

"Yeah." It takes me a second to process what he said. "She wasn't into it that night like she thought. So she got out of there. What'd you want her to do, jump him anyway?"

"*No.*" I hunch, going through all the dark, ugly baggage again, pulling stuff out and holding it up and remembering how bad it all makes me look. "If she hadn't run her mouth." My voice is thick. "She didn't have to do that. We could've stayed friends."

"She talked shit about you before you could do it to her. Typical sophomore. She thought it was her fault that you gave away something special. Like maybe if she'd never set it up that night, later you never would've"—I watch him mull over his words—"been with so many guys."

I've got two words for both him and Rhiannon, and they ain't Merry Christmas. "So she tried to fix it by making fun of me?"

"She never said it was smart."

I put my head in my hands, working my fingers into my hair, my nails over my scalp, until it hurts. "You know where she is, don't you? She told you."

He shakes his head. "All she told me was she had a friend picking her up. Late, after everybody left the party. I don't know who." He lets out a breath. "She talked about killing herself that summer."

That takes the wind out of me. We're quiet. None of this makes sense. Sly-smiling sophomore-year Rhiannon, the version who knew how to dress all fringe with her messenger bag and Chuck Taylors, who hung out in the smoking woods with the stoners and under the bleachers, offing herself. I can't picture it. But then, I didn't really know that girl. "You gotta tell the cops." He doesn't move, doesn't answer. "Don't be stupid, Kenyon. The cops think you did something to her."

He walks to the door and stares into the hallway, watching dust motes drift in sunlight. "We should let her go, Darce."

The stairs creak as he goes down.

When I open my eyes the next morning, sunlight lies in four windowpanes across my bed. I listen to the sounds of Mom and Libby moving around downstairs, the toilet flushing.

The Bay Festival starts at ten thirty a.m., one hour from now. Over at the fairgrounds, they'll be gassing up grills, hanging 4-H banners in the livestock stalls, counting out cash drawers. Only nine hours until Nell and I need to be at the pavilion for tonight's coronation.

I take a deep breath, pull the sheet up over my head, and

sink like I'm in quarry water.

Downstairs in the kitchen, Nell starts to sing.

"I can't believe she's going like that."

Hours later, Libby's voice carries upstairs to my open door. I roll nude pantyhose, slip my toes in.

"Not that I'm surprised you're gonna let her. If she wanted to leave this house stark naked, you'd say okay." Her voice drops to a hiss: "For God's sake, she looks like she got beat up by a pimp." Mom snorts and mutters something. "You think that's funny?"

"I think you're being ridiculous."

"Wait and see if everybody isn't saying the same thing tonight. She's gonna be up onstage in front of the whole *town*, Sarah. This ain't the kind of thing people forget. This story's gonna follow her. You want that?"

I fasten my strapless bra. Nell did my makeup an hour ago before she went to get ready. My only slightly mangled face stares back at me in the mirror. I hear the thud of Hunt's ladder against the side of the house as he shifts, spreading his brush across the clapboards.

"And let me tell you something else." This I have to strain to hear: "I saw a boy come out of the house yesterday while you were working."

I feel Mom's hesitation. "Jesse Bouchard?"

"I don't know. He wasn't one of Nell's friends." Another

way of saying he's trash.

I slide the mermaid dress, all sea foam and silver, over my head. I can almost see Mom situating herself around this news, filing it away for later. "They're allowed to have friends over. No rules against boys."

"Maybe there should be."

I spray my hair, wrap a strand around my curling iron, rolling it so close to my scalp it burns. Libby makes a disgusted noise. "I'm gonna go check on Nellie." Our back door will be lucky to stay on its hinges after what Libby's put it through this summer.

I stump downstairs in Nell's silver kitten-heeled sandals. Mags leans in the kitchen doorway, eating an apple and acting like she wasn't waiting for me. She checks me out head to toe. "Nice."

I shrug, looking at myself, then back at her. My heartbeat's like some crazy kid banging cymbals. "Curls too much?"

"Nah. Wait." She comes over and smooths one ringlet back, which I figured she'd do. "There. You're good, butthead."

"Hold up." Mom comes out of the kitchen with a small white box. My heart ratchets up that much more, because this is as close to misty as Mom ever gets, that quiet smile that crinkles the corners of her eyes.

It's a corsage from Weaver's, a white rose and baby's breath.

I can't think what to say as Mom slides the elastic over my wrist. "We got you both white because Nell wouldn't tell us what color her dress is." She steps back and sighs, looking me over. "Well. You know we'll be out there tonight." She gives my chin a quick snip between thumb and forefinger like she used to when I was kid, then pecks my forehead. "Love ya." I close my eyes a second, and then she moves away, going to get the camera while Mags holds the back door open for me so we can meet Nell.

We wait in the yard, me fidgeting with my wrap, twisting from side to side, my heels digging divots in the grass. Finally, Libby comes out of the trailer. She's crying a little.

Nell steps out from behind her, and none of us can speak. Turns out the corsage will go perfectly, because her dress is pure white organza with one ruffled strap, the bodice fitted to the waist. The skirt is layer after layer of ruffles, belling out and nearly hiding her open-toed heels. I've never seen her wear her hair like that, side-swept and pinned in place with a rhinestone comb that matches her earrings. Her makeup is intense, smoky eyes and deep red lipstick with a high gloss. She looks like she stepped right out of old Hollywood. I've never met this woman. She sure isn't my cousin Nell.

"Well," I hear someone say behind me, and I turn to see Hunt standing beside Mom. He looks at Nell, tries to find something more to say, then takes off his old ball cap instead.

That opens the floodgates, and we're all telling her how

beautiful she is, how she doesn't even look like herself, and Libby keeps on crying as she smiles. Nell says to me, "Told you it was the one," smoothing her hand over her dress.

"You were right," is all I can say back.

They take a million pictures of us together, standing side by side, the mermaid and the starlet.

TWENTY THREE

THE FAIRGROUNDS FLASH neon. The Ferris wheel's studded with a thousand bulbs. The Thunderbolt cranks techno as the cars slam forward and back. Shrieking and laughter are everywhere. The air's thick with the smells of hot grease, fried dough, cotton candy, and manure.

I wish this was any other summer. I'd be waiting in line at the Zipper, eating a corn dog and checking out the guys from Bucksport and Ellsworth while Mags tells me to put my eyes back in my head. Any other year, my biggest worry would be where the party's at tonight and how much beer they'll have.

This year, I'm standing backstage at the pavilion with fourteen other girls in gowns and heels, everybody whispering and giggling half-hysterically and checking their makeup in compact mirrors. I'm holding Nell's forearm with both hands, too freaked to even talk about how freaked I am.

She smiles. It's weird to see flashes of our Nell through that sophisticated stranger's face. "Don't look so worried," she whispers. "We'll be okay. We've been practicing our butts off, right?"

Everybody stared at her when we got here, and the stares had nothing in common with how they'd looked at me in my ball cap and raccoon eyes on Wednesday. Maybe Nell Michaud the special ed kid isn't so funny anymore. Maybe she stands a chance in this. Her style is totally different from everyone else's; most girls wear pastels and the shellacked updos they specialize in at Great Lengths. It was pretty sweet to see Bella, all decked out in a glittery peach dress slit halfway up her butt crack, gape for a good ten seconds before she remembered to pick her jaw up off the floor.

Mrs. Hartwell comes in and holds up her hands for quiet. "Showtime, girls. Best of luck to you all. Remember, the judges are watching for smiles and energy, so let's keep it up, up, up. Head over to your wings. I'll be rooting for you." She gives us a big thumbs-up and takes her place at the edge of the curtain.

Nell has to pry her arm out of my grip, giving a little wave as she leaves me for stage left.

You can hear them out there, a crowd of a couple hundred

people all shifting and talking and eating fair food at once, sounding like one giant monster with its tentacles coiled through the grandstand, waiting for its annual Bay Festival sacrifice of girl meat. I try to remember that Mom and Mags are out there, and lots of people from school, too, like Kat. And maybe Jesse. Maybe Shea.

Mrs. Hartwell hauls on the pulley, and the curtain opens with a clatter. My eyes fill with spotlight. My breath is gone, my brain wiped of anything but light.

Dance music blasts from the sound system. The first girl in our line walks out onto the stage, smiling and doing exactly what we rehearsed. The crowd cheers. One by one, the girls climb the risers to hit their mark. I'm next, but I can't move. The girl behind me shoves my shoulder. Please God, get me to the fifth riser.

I don't know what pulls me up there, but then next thing I know, I'm in my place. I didn't freeze, I didn't fall. My first real thought is Nell, but she's exactly where she should be, smiling straight into those lights, all charcoal hair and white organza and red, red lips. I straighten my back, angling myself out like I'm supposed to, and force my head up. It's dusk now, and the bulbs studding the grandstand turn everything into glare and shadow. You can't see any faces in the crowd.

"Welcome to the forty-third annual Bay Festival Queen Coronation," says the emcee into his mic. Applause. "Our judges this evening are Alden Mercer of Mercer's Appliance and Repair, Cathy Browning of Riverview Realty . . ."

We sit with our legs crossed as the intros finish and the Q-and-A segment begins. The judges work from the bottom riser on the opposite side to the top riser on ours, so I get to sit and watch most of the other girls go first. The cold sweats have dried, but now my stomach is nauseous and tight. Nobody's ever gotten a crown after barfing on their shoes in front of most of Hancock County, I don't think.

The questions are kind of dumb—"What makes you blush?"; "What do you think is the most interesting facet of your personality?"—but Bella gets nailed with, "What advice would you give the next generation of girls on navigating high school?" She hesitates for a second, then delivers this incredible load of crap about high school being a "stepping-stone to the rest of your life" and how important it is to balance academics with extracurriculars. This from the captain of the basketball team who bullies most freshmen into quitting within the first two weeks.

When it's Nell's turn, I squeeze the edge of the riser until I realize that Libby's probably doing the exact same thing in the stands right now, and force myself to sit back and take a breath. Nell's standing at center stage now. The judge asks, "If you could change one of your physical characteristics, which would it be?"

She takes maybe two seconds before answering. "I

wouldn't change anything. I think what some people call flaws are what make us special, and beautiful. The trick is to learn how to bring those features out, not try to cover them up."

The applause is big. Really big. The judges thank her and off she goes.

The girls standing between me and my moment in the spotlight are disappearing fast, and none of them get applause like Nell did. I watch them dwindle down to three, then one, then none.

By the time I'm crossing the stage, filling my lungs is like blowing into a couple sandwich bags with holes poked through them. I stop where I'm supposed to, keeping my gaze on the mic as I stand there, pinned by hundreds of eyes.

"Darcy Prentiss, age seventeen, from Sasanoa," the emcee says. People clap just like they have for everybody else.

In the silence that follows, I wait for Shea to yell something nasty from wherever he is. Nobody speaks. There's a rustling of papers as the judges, who sit at a long table hung with bunting, shuffle their sheets of questions.

A paunchy old guy dressed in a light-colored suit and a loud tie clears his throat and says into his mic, "Miss Prentiss, in your opinion, what are the benefits of growing up in a small community?"

My silence is total. I may as well have never spoken before in my life, and never will. Time grinds down like a bare knee

GILLIAN FRENCH

over gravel, and every twitch and tic of the judges' faces are magnified times ten as I try to produce a single half-bright thought.

"I don't really like living in a small town." Somebody's finally talking. I guess it's me. "Maybe when I'm old I'll look back and think it was great, but right now, I guess I'd like to know what it's like to go to school with different kinds of kids. People who do and say and wear different things. And I'd like to know what it's like not to have everybody know everybody else's business all the time." I'm rolling now; there's no stopping this, for better or worse. "We're lucky not to have to worry about being shot in the street and stuff like that, though. And it's nice to be able to walk from school to the Quick Stop for lunch."

I run out of positives and stand there, sweat popping out all over me, my legs trembling down into my sandals. For the first time, you can hear the fair sounds again, screams from the rides and crazy music.

One of the judges stops gaping long enough to thank me, and I go back to my riser.

The rest of the girls and I who didn't make it to the next round are flagged down and ushered out the stage door during a ten-minute intermission by Mrs. Hartwell, who's still smiling and telling every disappointed, crying girl what a good job she did, how nicely she held herself out there. "Darcy," she says. She takes in my big relieved grin and laughs, shaking her head. "You were truthful. I'll give you that."

I feel awesome, all light and bouncy. I could eat about fifty corn dogs, wash them down with two gallons of Moxie, and ride the Zipper until they shut off the midway lights. I'm off that godforsaken stage, and Nell was chosen for the next round.

Bella and Alexis made it, too, and along with a couple other girls, but I'm not worried. Nobody can beat Nell tonight. There's something special about her in that lily-white dress, something glam and so-not-Sasanoa. She's taking that crown home and we're going to nail it to the roof to show who's got class.

Some of the girls leave right away, which, judging by Mrs. Hartwell's expression, is a sore-loser thing to do, but the rest of us go stand by the fence along the grandstand to watch. I can't see Mom or Mags, but they're probably up toward the top of the bleachers so Libby can take pictures.

When the lights come back up, Nell and the four other girls who are left sit in a row on the bottom riser closest to the judges. Somebody's brought out a fancy throne with red velvet cushions, which is where is the Queen sits for photo ops.

The judges start calling them up for questions one by one like before, but these questions are hard: How does social media affect young women's body images? How can schools encourage girls to foster a lifelong interest in science and math?

When Nell's standing back in the spotlight, they ask her, "Who is your role model, and why?"

She wasn't ready for it. Neither was I. I have no idea what she's going to say. After what feels like a long, long time: "Rita Hayworth." She pauses, leans down to the mic. "She's an actress. From the forties."

One of the judges leans forward. "And why?"

Nell thinks. "Because she always knew what to do with her hair." She shows us exactly what she means, doing the head toss we saw Rita Hayworth do in *Gilda* at the drive-in this June. The crowd erupts, hooting and whistling so loud that the judges have to wait a couple minutes so their "thank you" can be heard. I laugh my butt off. So maybe she didn't sound brainy like Alexis or Bella. She still brought the house down.

When the Q and A is finally done, the emcee tells us that the judges will now confer, and starts thanking all the sponsors. I shift from foot to foot and finally kick my sandals off, squeezing my hands together as I wait.

It takes nearly twenty minutes, but eventually the results are taken over to the emcee. "Without further ado, the title of Miss Congeniality goes to"—big pause—"Eleanor Michaud!"

I scream. Nell screams. The dance music cranks up, and

she runs out to the meet one of the judges, the old guy in the suit, who gives her a bouquet of white, pink, and yellow roses. He slides a satin sash trimmed with glitter over her head that says *Miss Congeniality* on it, and awkwardly sets a little tiara on her head, so as not to mess up her hair. So she didn't win Queen—it's a bummer, but she's still shining up there.

Cameras are flashing everywhere. Nell's crying. Behind my hands, two tears roll down my cheeks before I can wipe them away.

When the applause dies down, Nell's sent to stand beside the throne while second runner-up is announced. Alexis. I'll give her credit for looking honestly shocked as she rushes out to get her sash and tiara.

Drumroll time. If it's Bella, I'll eat my pantyhose.

"And this year's Bay Festival Queen *is* . . . Rachel Pelletier!"

It's the tall, gorgeous blonde who answered the science and math question; I think maybe she goes to Bucksport. Everybody's on their feet as Mrs. Hartwell comes out with the rest of the judges, bringing the crown and a huge bouquet of roses and a little velvet cape they drape over Rachel's shoulders as she takes her seat on the throne.

I work my way back over to the stage, waiting for Nell to come out as people leave the pavilion for the next event on the festival schedule, probably the country music band lined up for nine o'clock. Bella comes out first, looking like she swallowed a quart of vinegar. Her buttoned-down mom's waiting for her, and Bella blows right by her, the two of them sniping at each other all the way—"I *told* you not to wear that dress, it was totally inappropriate for a pageant like this,"; "God, Mother, enough!" Fun times in the Peront house tonight. Then again, it's probably never real fun.

As I wait, I keep an eye out for Shea, but I don't see him. He probably never even set foot in the pavilion tonight. He didn't have to. He knew I'd do the work for him, worrying that he might show, wondering what he might do. I guess nobody can psych you out better than yourself. "Darce!" I look up to see Mags raise a hand in the crowd. Feels like I haven't seen her in about a year.

They're still taking pictures onstage. Nell's crying as she smiles, hugging her roses. I really don't think she could've been happier if she'd taken Queen.

My gaze moves across the dirt track, back over the crowd, maybe hoping for Jesse, I don't know. Instead, she snags my attention, over by the grandstand post.

I watch her standing there, wearing a moss-green North Face T-shirt, cargo shorts, and Birkenstocks. Elise Grindle.

She's smiling and talking to the guy she's with, the guy who no doubt fed her some line about turning out to support Nell tonight. How Nell was always one of the special ones. I almost don't recognize him in his street clothes: a sport shirt, jeans, boat shoes. He holds the leash of a yellow Lab that's sitting with her tongue hanging out, food watching.

They step away from the grandstand, Elise slipping her hand into his back pocket. I stare at his back as they join the leaving crowd, moving so easily. They have a *dog*. Might as well be a kid. Another building block of a phony life.

I step out into the midway, barefoot, arms hanging at my sides, making people stream around me. He sat right there with his eyes all over Nell tonight, cool as could be. Now he's going back with Elise to their apartment on Irish Lane, where he'll keep playing house with her, and it makes me feel so damned ugly I could cry. Because it's not over. It never was. And some part of me always knew it.

TWENTY FOUR

NIGHT.

I open my eyes, and know that the car is out there. No headlights on the wall this time. I don't need them.

I don't think that I ever really slept. Last night was one long after-party: riding home with everybody crammed into Mom's Subaru, all of them talking at once, the smell of roses and hair spray, Nell spent and glowing, Libby an absolute mess, like she never dared to believe her baby would place. Mom let us drink some cheap champagne, and Mags clapped me on the back, said I'm the best loser she's ever seen, and that she practically blew an artery laughing when they asked me about small-town living. It was a good night. Should've been the best. But I watched it all from some high, cold place where the air was thin and all I could do was count the minutes until right now, 2:03 a.m., when I have to decide what to do.

I get out of bed and put my jeans on underneath my sleep shirt. My mermaid dress lies in a pool on the floor, silver sandals beside it, my corsage wilting on the vanity. I pull on my hoodie and go downstairs, walking along the edges, Nancy Drew–style.

Outside, it's misting. The grass is dewy under my flip-flops, and I slip and catch myself as I follow the roadside ditch into the woods beside our house.

It's darker than I expected. No moon tonight. I pull my hood up and hunker down between some trees, waiting for whatever's going to happen.

The car's idling. Still no headlights, but as my eyes adjust, I can see it there, maybe fifteen feet away, by the faintest dashboard glow.

I wait long enough for my legs to get stiff and my nose to start running before I see the tiny light drifting along like Tinker Bell in the blackness. It's on the opposite shoulder, coming our way. A penlight.

The light drifts across the road. When it's almost to the car, he switches on the headlights. She's painted in halogen, my Nell, wearing her navy-blue raincoat with the pattern of little white whales on it, her face a dark hollow inside the hood. She's reaching for the passenger door. In a second, she'll be inside, pushing her hood back, turning to smile at him as he takes her away, away from us.

I throw myself forward, not knowing where I'm putting my feet until I'm on pavement. I say her name, just say it, but in that night silence, it might as well have been a scream.

Nell spins around, wincing in the light. We stay that way, pinned.

Then, very slowly, the car glides backward. From the corner of my eye, I watch him pull a gradual U-turn and accelerate away, leaving her. Leaving us facing each other in the blue glow of her penlight beam.

She runs, but I'm faster. I get a fistful of her raincoat and we go down together on the wet grass of our front yard.

"You *promised*." I slap her hood back. She gives a high, thin scream. "You said you'd never see him again and you did!"

Nell shields her face. "I'm sorry, I'm sorry," she sobs.

"Don't tell me you're sorry! You lied! You lied! You know how hard I tried to keep you safe? You know how many times I had to lie so nobody would find out? Then you sneak around behind my back and do it anyway! Goddamn you!" This roar comes out of me, and I bring my fists down on the ground beside her head, making her scream and roll to the side.

She manages to get up on one foot, her jacket hanging on by one arm. Lights come on in the house and trailer. I shove her back down, and she cries out miserably, her shoulder grinding into the mud under me. "I love him."

"*No, you don't!* You don't even know what you're *talking* about! He's a goddamn pervert, you don't love him!"

I shake her until somebody catches me under the arms and pulls me back. "Stop! What the hell are you doing?"

I kick and swing as Nell staggers away, hugging herself, watching me with huge, stunned eyes. When she sees that Mom's really got me, she bends double and shouts back, "You don't know, Darcy! You don't love anybody, so how can you know?"

Libby runs across the yard, jerking her old terry-cloth robe around her. "Nellie? Baby, what—?"

Libby reaches for her, but Nell pulls away and Libby nearly falls, gasping as her baby turns and runs from us, across the yard and down Old County Road into darkness.

Late morning. I'm at the kitchen table, but nobody's getting me cups of tea and aspirin today. I sit alone, head in my hand, picking at the place mat.

Nell's gone. Mom and Libby got into the car and went after her last night, leaving me with Mags, whose middle-of-the-night fuzziness wasn't helped by the champagne she'd slugged down before bed. "What *is* it?" she kept saying, holding the door frame like it was keeping her up, as I huddled on the couch, not answering. "Why can't you tell me what it is?"

Mom came back alone. They couldn't find Nell. Libby was still out looking. I expected a million questions, but all Mom said to me was, "Go to bed." In those three words, I knew I'd undone everything we'd built at the kitchen table the other day, the way she treated me like a grown-up, an equal. I went, and lay there with my eyes open until dawn. I'm so scared I feel numb. I know Nell couldn't have gone to *him*, not with Elise around, so she could be anywhere. Hurt. Alone.

Now a cop car pulls into our driveway, and the porch floorboards creak as Libby, Mom, and Mags all go down to meet him. It's Edgecombe, of course. Dispatch must tap him for any call from 36 Old County Road, or else he's got a nose for trouble like a bluetick hound.

He unfolds his big self from the driver's seat and stands looking up at our house for a second, reminding me of the way Kenyon stood there the other day. What are they seeing in our half-dressed place that makes them think twice about coming in? Hunt isn't painting today; Mom must've called him this morning, because he came at first light, then drove off again, searching. Now he's out in the driveway, leaning against his pickup and doing what he does: keeping quiet.

I lay my head on the table and wait for the sound of the

screen door opening, the scrape of the chair pulling out next to me. Edgecombe doesn't speak. I lift my gaze and see him watching me, lips pressed in a line, fingers twined together on the table. A drop falls from the faucet like a shot.

Libby comes through the screen door, marching straight at me. Her face is dead white, her hair flying loose from the sloppy braid she slept in last night. "You *talk* to him. You hear me? You tell him where she is!" Edgecombe stands and takes her shoulders, moving her back. "She was hurting my baby last night," she yells, straining against him until Mom comes in and holds her. Libby sobs. "Oh, Jesus, what if she got in a car with somebody—what if somebody picked her up—"

Mom looks at me for the first time all morning. I shrink away from the flint in her eyes. "Start talking."

"I don't know where she is." God, déjà vu, but a different girl, a different day.

"Cut the crap!"

"It's true!" I could do it, light Nell up right here in front of everybody. Tell them about Irish Lane in Hampden, where I drove that night last August to pick Nell up after she poured her heart out to him. Tell them to go ask *him* what happened, ask *him* how come I had good reason to hit and cuss her out last night, just let the whole messy thing spill everywhere.

Edgecombe's gruff. "You all need to calm down so we can sort this out. Libby, I'm going to tell you the same thing I told you over the phone. Nell's eighteen. House rules aside, she can come and go as she pleases. We can't get involved in that." He lowers himself back into the chair, watching her gasp and wipe her nose on her hand. "She hasn't been gone long enough for me to make out a missing person's report. But"—he puts up a hand before anybody can jump on him— "I'll do what I can to help you find her." His gaze settles on me. "Darcy, you two were outside fighting around two thirty this morning. What was it about? And don't say nothing. That isn't going to fly this time."

I sit, gripping the edge of the table, looking back at them. The screen door opens, and Mags comes in. "I heard some of it." She stands, arms folded. "Darcy was calling Nell a liar. I could hear it all the way up in my room. By the time I got out on the porch, Darcy had Nell down on the ground, telling her she didn't love somebody, some 'he,' that she didn't know what she was talking about."

"Oh God." Libby starts shaking her head like a horse with the wind in its ears. "I knew it. I *knew* it and I let it go and now look." She points at me. "You little whore. How could you? You took my baby and dragged her into something dirty and—and cheap with you, and now look, *look*—"

This time when she goes for me, it takes both Edgecombe and Mom to haul her back and out the door onto the porch, where she stays, crying into her hands. I hunch in my chair, breathing low, staring at the tabletop.

When Edgecombe comes back, I say, "Check the quarry.

Drive-in. Twice Is Nice. She likes the library, but it's closed today." And I'll swallow my tongue before I say more. Libby made up my mind. Nobody's going to do Nell the way she just did me.

Edgecombe gets Hunt to go to the drive-in while he checks the other places in town. I go upstairs to my room, ready to wait it out until Nell comes home. She'll be back any minute. She has to be.

I'm doing a shoddy job of making my bed when I sense somebody behind me, and turn to find Mags standing in the doorway. She isn't wearing any expression, just looks tired and burnt out like the rest of us. I sit, figuring we'll talk now. She'll say how crazy Libby is, and I'll say, *God, I know,* but what she says instead is, "What is wrong with you?"

I'm too surprised to answer. She doesn't wait for me to anyway.

"I've been beating my head against this all morning. Trying to figure out what would make you hurt Nell. I got nothing. You'd cut off your own arm first. You guys have always been like that." She makes a sound in her throat. "When we were little, I used to get jealous sometimes. I thought you two made better sisters than you and me. Like maybe Nell and I were switched at birth or something." Normally I'd make a joke here, but I can't, not to this cold-faced Mags I hardly recognize. "You've been weird all summer. Pulling more dumb-ass stunts than usual, acting like you want to see how far you can push everybody. All I can think is you want somebody to stop you, to put the brakes on, because you can't do it yourself."

I don't know what to say. Outside, the Subaru's engine coughs to life. Mom, going out looking again.

"You're like him, you know." Mags shakes her head. "Dad. You worry everybody to death, then show up laughing with five or six beers in you and big stories about where you've been. He wore everybody out, too. Then he went and got himself killed and left us with nothing but a pair of old boots and some drinking stories."

"Don't say that. He was a good guy."

"But he didn't take care of the people who loved him. You don't remember what it was like, or maybe you don't want to." Her voice is hoarse, talking over me before I can argue. "He was reckless with his own life, get it? He pissed it away up there on that girder for fifty bucks, didn't think twice about his wife or two little girls waiting at home. Mom's still so crazy over him that she'll never see it that way, but you need to open your eyes. I'm sick of this."

It could almost be me saying how I feel about Nell. But I'm not like her—I don't need anybody babysitting me, hovering over me—and helpless anger binds my tongue.

Mags breathes out, fixing her gaze on me. "Are you ready to tell me what's going on with you and Nell?"

I hold my breath so long that tiny starbursts appear around

her, my big sister, standing there so self-righteous she ought to be wearing a halo like a church-window saint. "I *can't*," I say, trying to force in every bit of feeling I have so she finally gets it.

She stands still for a long second before turning back to the hall. "Then I'm ashamed to know you."

She couldn't have taken my breath away faster if she'd sucker punched me. I listen to her go downstairs. Then I whirl and rip the quilt off my bed, heaving it against the wall, clearing the junk off my vanity top in one swipe, kicking the stool over.

When there's nothing left to trash, I storm into Mags's room, grab the laptop, and message Kat. *Come get me?* She's always on her phone. In less than thirty seconds she sends back a thumbs-up. On my way out, I knock over Mags's can of pens and pencils, scattering them across the floor.

Fifteen minutes later, nearly noon, I see Kat's pickup pull into our driveway. I run downstairs and out the door. Libby's sitting on the porch, and she's on her feet in a second. "Where do you think you're going? Hey! I'm talking to you!" She shouts after me from the railing, "Don't you dare—Darcy Celeste, *freeze!*"

Words I haven't heard since I was about nine, and I give them the respect they deserve, climbing into the cab and slamming the door. "Go, go, go." Kat gives it gas and swings the pickup in a circle, taking us to town.

TWENTY FIVE

FILLING MY BELLY with vodka and beer. Hope nobody wants these pretzels, because I'm eating them all. No wonder Kat weighs ninety-seven pounds: she called three ice pops and a handful of green olives supper. That was hours ago, at her place, before she sent texts and got everybody out here, quarry-side.

Hard edge to the night, and it's not just me. Everybody's drinking more, laughing louder, forcing it. End of summer, almost back to school and senior year and the big unknown after graduation. I'm not the only one who feels like their world is ending.

"Remember Mr. Eldon-Tower?" Kat's loud and doesn't

know it. "God, he was *suuuch* a freak. Remember?" She duckwalks around the bonfire while all us girls shriek laughter, then drops back onto the granite slab, her sweet, earthy, weed scent settling over me. "He wrote my name on the board once for, like, nothing. I literally did nothing and got in trouble." She grabs more beer and gives me one, because she knows I'm hurting without having to ask what it's about, which makes me love her. Mags is stupid to always be dumping on Kat. Oh well. She hates me now, too, so there you go. I gotta stop eating these pretzels. They're soaking up my buzz.

Shea's here. One minute I'm singing with Kat and Emma and Maddie, feeling really floaty and good, and then he's standing over there, back from the firelight, beer in his hand, with that sophomore—I guess she's a junior now— who pulls her thong up so high you can see it over the top of her jeans. He's watching me, a hint of a smile playing at the corners of his mouth. *Smiling.* Sonofabitch shouldn't be here. Nobody invited his ass. I'm not scared, but I guess my heart is, because it starts sprinting without me.

Kat feels me stiffen, sees Shea, blinks like she can't focus too good. "Screw 'im. I'll take care of ya." Slings her arm around my neck and pulls me back down into the singing.

A couple girls get into a shouting match and one of them shoves the other, sending her down so close to the pit that we see sparks. Makes me think of Nell last night, her shoulder grinding into the mud under me. Not that she's been off my mind for a second all day. I try not to picture her lying white and stiff with unblinking eyes in a ditch somewhere, but I can't help it.

Jesse shows up with Mason and a couple other guys, wearing his plain white T-shirt and worn-out jeans, that sexy-as-hell Springsteen uniform that still melts me. He and Shea see each other. Major unspoken friction. As I watch, Jesse presses his lips together and keeps moving through the crowd to the other side of the clearing. Guess he decided Shea isn't worth it. It doesn't bug me that Jesse's here. I mean, live and let die or whatever.

Not sloppy drunk yet, because I can tell where Braden Mosier's lips begin and mine end. When you're sloppy, your faces feel like one big warm glob, which can be nice until later when you wonder who saw you sloppy-globbing and how many people they've told. I close my eyes and think about Jesse in the field, sweet hay under us, my fingers in his black hair.

Braden's chewing my earlobe like Double Bubble and whispering, "You're so hot." I go into a giggle fit because, come on, seriously. "What?" he says. I think he's mad. "What?" And I'm just so done.

★ ★ ★

Moon is out. People toss things into the quarry: empties, rocks, a flaming log. "God," Maddie says, standing at the edge looking down, "that's like . . . really, really far."

I've been clique-hopping, pretending not to be freaking out since Kat forgot about taking care of me and went into the woods to smoke even though she *knows* I'm too drunk to have good radar. So I keep moving, keep acting like I'm having the best time. That way Shea can't come up from behind. I chug more beer, washing down the acid in the back of my throat, and say to Maddie, "Don't you ever swim here?" I'm loud and laughing.

"You *jump*?"

Burp. Tastes awful, coppery. "It's not that high."

"Are you serious? It's like forty feet."

"Show us, Darce." I hear him but don't turn. I catch enough of him from the corner of my eye: Shea, sitting on the ground, forearms on his knees, that sophomore curled up beside him. He talks in that way he has, like we're buddies, like we're both in on the joke. "You done it before, show us."

Other people start in: "Yeah, show us, Darcy." "If you ain't scared, do it."

"Okay." I turn my back on Shea, holding up my hands, stumbling a little. "Okay, goddamn it, I'll do it." I toss my beer. "Us girls come here all the time." Us girls. Nell, in her little-kid underwear, tightrope-walking the cliff's edge. Mags, swimming out to the deepest point and yelling that the water's fine. All of a sudden I don't care what happens. All gone to shit anyway. "Didn't you hear about the guy who found his ring here? People been doing this forever." Something is not quite right about that, but all I really remember is Jesse smiling and telling me stories.

Shea's voice rises over the crowd. "Wait a second. Don't you usually do this with your titties hanging out?"

Big laughs. I turn slowly to look at him, seeing it in his face, that it was him who spied on us that day. His sophomore wears this sour look, like she's actually jealous of me. I could tell her all about him. How easily she can end up on the ground under him tonight, how fast it can all happen and how afterward she'll walk around in a bad-dream haze, trying to remember if she ever said no or just thought it, counting the days until she gets her period and crying when she finally wakes up to find blood on her underwear. I'm too fuzzy to think of a comeback, grateful when Kat calls out, "Pig," from the smoky darkness. He raises his beer to her.

I go over and grab Kat's hand. "Come with me."

She snorts, shaking me off. "No freakin' way."

"You'll break your damn neck." It's Jesse. I glance around, but I can't find his face in the crowd. "It's too high and you can't see where you're going."

Everybody boos and catcalls. I wave him off. He didn't get around to talking to me all night, so he can keep his opinions to himself.

I run forward, reaching the edge, seeing that yawning

darkness ahead of me, and slam on the brakes, hard.

"Awww, come on! Chickenshit!" They're all yelling, making fun of me, and I look back at the orange faces in the firelight. These people aren't my friends, not like Nell, not like Mags. Now I'm so mad that I don't say a word. I back way up and plow, throwing my arms out to the side, taking off.

For a second, I fly.

Falling. Falling. Hurtling black. A flash of moonlight off the water. A thought—*made it, I'm clear*—before I split the surface and my left arm explodes in pain so stunning that I sink into white shock.

I drift through whiteness. Slowly it darkens to gray, then black. My feet float above my head. My hands drift out.

My eyes jam open. *Can't breathe.*

I kick but there's no up, no down. I'm swimming through space. I thrash and grab. Nothing. I'm drowning. This is what it feels like to sink with your lungs screaming for air.

I swivel and scissor my legs. Could be heading straight to the bottom. It isn't until I feel air buoy me, pulling me up the last couple feet, that I know I chose the right direction.

I break the surface with a gasp that echoes across the quarry. Can't get enough air. I drag it in, coughing and shaking my head, trying to clear my ears.

"I see her!" somebody yells from above. "There she is!" A cheer goes up.

My left arm throbs. I can't use it. I do a lopsided dog paddle to reach the silhouette of one of the dinosaur-back rocks, scraping my knees as I crawl up onto it. I lie on my side, shaking all over, my left arm tucked like a broken wing.

Time passes. I hear my own breathing, sometimes a laugh or a screech from the party, and then sneakers scraping over rocks. "Darcy?"

Jesse. I sit up, even though I'm pretty sure he can't see me. "Be right there."

"You okay? Jesus, when I didn't see you, I thought . . ." He stops like he's listening to my harsh breathing.

"I'm fine. See ya."

"You don't sound fine." For some reason, this breaks me. My throat closes and there's no stopping the tears. I duck my head and sob down into my chest.

"Hold on. I'm coming out there."

"Don't."

Liquid sounds as he lowers himself into the water. "Keep talking. Right or left?"

Finally: "Right. On the last big rock." I clear my throat. "I'll come to you."

As our eyes adjust, we meet each other. His arm goes around my waist. He keeps me above water on the way back in.

We go up the path, dripping and silent, avoiding the party

and going straight to the road where everybody's parked. I can't stop crying. I don't know where these tears are coming from, but there's no holding back, no getting a grip. He opens the door of his pickup for me and I get in, hiding my face in the hand I can use, ashamed to know myself, ashamed to be me.

We drive through town. No hotdogging this time, no more can-you-top-this. We're both soaked. It's late. I take deep breaths and blink a lot, trying every trick I know to suck it up and stop crying. Nothing works.

Jesse pulls into the Irving station's all-night pumps and parks, putting his hand on my shoulder. I shrug it off, not because of him but because I don't deserve a second of this poor-me bull. I choke out, "Mags is gonna kill me," before a fresh wave of sobs hits. I cry ugly, crumpled face, open mouth, the whole bit.

He lets me go for a while, then says, "What hurts?"

I motion to my arm. He turns on the dome light and touches me gingerly, elbow to wrist, testing the joints a little, watching me wince. "You hit rocks, huh?" Shallow scrapes ooze blood. "You're lucky you aren't dead."

That gets me going again, and it's a long time before I can speak. "Mags is right. I'm like him." Jesse waits. "Our dad. He always pulled numb-nuts stunts until he died, and it was his own fault."

"I thought he died building the bridge."

"He fell 'cause he was screwing around." I knuckle my eyes, picturing that December day I'm glad I was too little to remember except from Mom's stories, when the Penobscot Narrows Bridge crew was up there freezing their sacks off in thirty-mile-an-hour winds and snow. "Somebody tied a Christmas tree to the rebar. Even had lights. The star blew off the top, and Dad's buddy bet fifty bucks that nobody was willing to climb back up and set it straight before the storm really hit. Foreman had gone home. Dad didn't fasten his harness right. He fell." I close my eyes, nauseous, thinking of my own fall, how Dad had dropped at least a hundred feet farther than that through gray freezing sky, with all that time to think about what was happening to him. I hope his neck broke when he hit. Kinder death than drowning in the dark salt river.

Jesse's quiet a long time. "So you think it's like a curse? You have to be your dad?"

"I dunno. Mom says I'm like she was, in trouble all the time."

"So you got all the bad stuff, and Mags got all the good." I nod. "Come on. You got a brain. You don't have to play some role just because your family says so. You can do better than getting wasted every weekend."

"I didn't see you turning down any beers tonight."

"Didn't say *I* was smart. All I got is good taste in women." He surprises a laugh out of me and shrugs. "I came because I was hoping you might show. Then when I saw you, figured you'd just ream my ass again, so I stayed away."

Good figuring. I fish a paper napkin out from between the seats and blow my nose.

"Mostly I wanted to tell you that I thought about it, and you were wrong." Jesse's mouth is set. "About it being some guy-ego thing that made me go after Shea. He hurt you, and yeah, I lost it. Same as I would've if you were my best friend or my sister. Didn't have anything to do with sex. You don't let somebody you care about get beat on. Ever. Bet you feel the same way."

I nod, thinking painfully of Nell, and look down at my sneakers.

"Let me take you to the ER for that arm." He waves me off before I get three words out. "Costs too much. I know."

He takes me home, driving slow. I lean against the door, watching dark woods go by.

We get there and he idles, looking at me. "Kamikaze Darcy. Wait and see if they aren't all calling you that in homeroom on Tuesday."

I sit there with my matted hair and wet clothes, and somehow, I feel almost shy. "Well . . . thanks." I reach for the door handle, then glance back. "Almost said see you at school."

He looks down, half smiling. "See you around."

There's nobody in the kitchen. At the sound of the door, Libby comes out of the living room, but her expression falls flat at the sight of me, and she leaves again, not asking where I've been or why I'm all wet.

I go upstairs and take a long, hot shower with my left arm raised, because even the spray hurts. While I'm drying my hair, I hear voices below, and put on Mom's bathrobe to step out into the hallway.

It's Nell. She's back. The tension that's been driving me for the past twenty-hours or so dissolves so quickly that I almost fall down in a heap. I stand there, straining my ears.

". . . nobody was home, so I figured you were over here." Nell's voice is quiet, dull. "I just wanted to tell you that I'm back."

"Where have you *been*?" Libby. "I was ready to lose my *mind*. You got any idea what you put me through?"

"I needed to go somewhere to think. That's all. It's nothing bad, Mom. I just had to go think."

"*Don't give me that.* You tell me what's going on! What's Darcy gotten you into?"

"Nothing. You always think everything's her fault. I'm the one who ran off. Now I'm back. And I want to go to bed." Nell pauses, using the firmest tone of voice I've ever heard from her. "Good night, Mom."

"Nellie Rose, get back here." I can almost see Libby standing in the hallway, shoulders rigid as Nell's footsteps head toward the back door. "Nell." Sounding weaker. "Baby. What is it? You can tell me." Her voice breaks as the door closes.

I step back and see Mags standing in her bedroom doorway at the end of the hall, wearing plaid pajama pants and a T-shirt, obviously listening in on the conversation, too. I want to go to her, but before I can move, she turns and walks back into her bedroom.

Another door closes.

TWENTY SIX

I WAIT UNTIL the house is asleep, then creep downstairs and out the back door.

Nell's window is dark. I tap on the screen—shave-and-a-haircut. A minute later, she slides it open for me.

It's been a long time since I did this, and it isn't as easy to climb through her window as I remember, especially with my bad arm. I try to boost myself up and pain shoots up my forearm into my elbow. I catch my foot and almost crash into her nightstand, which would be a disaster, since Libby's probably snoring away on the couch with her Louisville Slugger under her arm.

Nell lies on her back in bed, staring up at the old glow-in-the-dark constellation stickers on her ceiling. I slide under the sheet beside her, resting my arm across her stomach. It feels like months have passed since yesterday. The James Dean collage looks down at us. She has a still from *East of Eden* up there, Cal and Abra's kiss at the top of the Ferris wheel.

"I'm sorry I hurt you," I whisper.

Her profile is lit by moonlight, and I can follow the trail of freckles across her nose. Fairy kisses, Libby used to call them; Nell loved that. "It's okay. I lied to you." She doesn't apologize this time, just lies there with her hands folded over her chest, looking at the stars. I close my eyes.

"So where were you?"

She shrugs one shoulder. "In the woods."

"The whole time?"

"I went to that field where the lupines grow, even though the lupines are all dead now. It's quiet there. Then I found seven dollars in my coat, so I walked to Smiley's and bought some snacks." She pauses. "I didn't go see him, if that's what you mean. He wouldn't like that."

I remember the car driving smoothly away, leaving her in the dark and the rain. "You know that's wrong, don't you?" After a beat, she nods a little. "You guys been messaging each other all this past year?"

"Only since June. I blocked him last August when you told me to. He made another profile. He missed me."

I breathe in, trying to stay in control, not letting my anger get bigger than me. He's like some poison she drank that's eating through everything until it reaches her heart. Or maybe it started there. "Nellie, he's going to marry her."

"I know."

"I didn't do right by you. Last August, after I picked you up that night, when I told you I didn't want to hear about it—him—again, I left you hanging with nobody to talk to. I wasn't being a friend to you. I'm sorry."

She turns to me, surprised. "Darcy, you're always my friend."

My eyes start to sting. Thought I'd cried out every drop in my body. "I'm not done. You shouldn't have listened to me. I think maybe it was too big a secret for us. Maybe somebody else would've known what to do better than I did." She faces back to the ceiling, lying still. "I'm not saying I'm gonna tell. But I've screwed things up pretty bad, huh? You and me . . . we're in the same spot we were in that night. Nothing's gotten any better." She doesn't speak. I have to force the next words through my lips: "You can't keep sneaking around in backseats with him. That's me. That's not you. You should be the one planning some fancy wedding, and it should be with some guy who doesn't expect you to share him with anybody, or keep his secrets." She's quiet. I shake her gently. "You know?"

A little nod. Her breath catches, and I realize she's crying, and has been for a while. I touch my head to hers, and we lie there with moonlight across her sheet in patchwork squares. "We got to do something," I say. I'm talking to myself, though, because now Nell's asleep.

After a while, I dream that I'm at Elise Grindle's wedding, and for some reason there's water pouring down the middle of the guest tables, swirling through place cards and favors, sweeping flowers and floating candles down the white cloth into my lap.

I make it back into my own bed before morning, and wake up with a crusher of a hangover and a forearm I carry around like it's equal parts ground glass and rusty nails. I accidentally touch it off the bathroom door before I'm fully awake and yelp. So much for feeling better in the morning.

I wash up and put makeup on my bruises, which have started to fade and turn yellow around the edges, then dress carefully in nicer clothes than usual, jeans and a three-quarter-sleeve shirt that hides most of the scrapes on my arm. It's a gray, wet day, but the rain's holding off for now, and I hear Hunt's ladder *ka-thump* against the clapboards now and then as he paints.

The house is quiet, mellowing after the past couple days of drama. I eat breakfast alone, wishing somebody would come talk to me but not holding my breath; Mags's car is gone and Mom's out in the garden, giving me the cold shoulder. Nell will probably be on house arrest until she's thirty, unless Libby can get her into a good convent first. Me, I know what I have to do, even if it turns my guts to water. I just need to find a way to get myself out there.

Hunt comes inside around noon, washing his hands and filling his mug with what's left in the coffeepot. I quit channel surfing and straddle a kitchen chair, watching him move around, knowing his way around the kitchen almost as well as I do now. "Can I ask you something?"

He glances back at me. "Shoot."

"Did you really buy this place so you could live here with your wife?"

Mom would skin me if she could hear this, but Hunt doesn't get all huffy. He takes a swallow from his mug and pulls his bag lunch out of the fridge. "I did."

"How come it didn't work out?"

He's got ham and Swiss, looks like; he eats it right from the wax paper. "Well"—he chews—"sometimes, after you been together awhile, you don't fit the way you did when you started. Life gets in between. If you let it." Another bite. "We let it."

"I heard you started building her a barn so she could have horses." Sounds like a spoiled-brat thing to want, if you ask me. He nods. "How come you planted all those lupines on the foundation?"

He doesn't answer right away. "Lupines were my mother's favorite flower." The way he says it, I know his mom must be dead. I guess he's pretty old to still have a mom kicking around, anyway. He's got some grays and all.

I watch him eat, then scrub my face and hunch over the table. "Everybody's mad at me. Mom and Mags aren't even talking to me."

His gaze is sharp, but not judgey; quiet or not, I don't think Hunt misses a trick. "They got good reason?"

"No. I mean, yeah, there's stuff I can't tell them right now. Not because I don't want to, because I can't. And they all hate me for it."

"Nobody hates you around here."

"Libby does." That trips him up. "She thinks I'm turning Nell into some kind of tramp. Stupid." I start to lean my elbows on the table, then pull back, not wanting him to see me wince. "I'm not what she tells everybody I am."

"No, you're not." He brought a chocolate snack cake with him, and he takes the plastic off, offers me half, then takes a bite when I shake my head. "I was hoping maybe you'd win Queen. Show 'em a thing or two."

I laugh. "Were you there?"

"I caught some of it."

"Then you know how bad I tanked it. Whatever. I don't care. I'm not really Queen material anyway."

"I thought you deserved your shot." The way he says it makes me sit back. He starts balling up his trash.

"Was it you?" I watch him push back from the table. "Hunt, did you put my name in for Princess?"

His embarrassment shows only in the set of his shoulders,

and how he keeps himself busy rinsing his mug, swiping crumbs off the place mat into his hand. "I was in the town office getting the sticker for my truck, figured what the hell. You're as good as any of those girls on the ballot. And you're funny and you got some grit, which ought to count for more than it does."

I sit there, blinking, not sure what to do until it comes to me to say, "Thank you," for something I didn't even know I was thankful for until I found out it all happened because he thinks I'm worth something.

I tap my fingers on the table, almost letting him escape back to painting before I catch him at the door with, "Are you sorry it didn't work out with your wife?"

He shakes his head. "That was some other guy. Some kid. Couldn't speak to it either way."

"Then you should go out with my mom. Don't wait around anymore, or she'll think you don't like her enough." He stands there with his fingers on the door handle. "Trust me, girls hate that. Guys are always saying we're impossible to figure out or whatever, but it's pretty simple. Let her know how much you like her."

He has to clear his throat twice before saying, "I'll keep it in mind."

"Good." I hesitate, then decide to go for it. "Listen. I guess you probably don't have any reason to go into Hampden today. But if you're going, I could use a ride. I'll give you gas money."

He turns, considering me, resting his shoulder against the door.

"Don't worry, I'm not scoring weed or anything. It's just something I have to do." I look up at him. "But if you're not going, it's okay." Part of me really hopes he'll say no.

"I need some things from True Value. Could swing by the one on Main Road North." He opens the door. "Run and tell your mom."

Mom glances up when I stop beside her. When she sees it's me, she goes back to yanking weeds, her brows drawn.

"I'm going into Hampden with Hunt." Nothing. "We'll be back soon." Nothing. "Okay?"

She talks to the dirt. "You checking in with me now, Darcy?"

"Do you want me to?" She rakes her gloved fingers through the soil, digging at a root. I'm ready to stand over her all day until she answers me, but Hunt starts the engine, and I know if I waste another second, I'll never do this. "Whatever. Bye."

As we leave, I watch her sit back on her heels, her hands on her thighs, but she never lifts her gaze from the ground.

We have to cross the bridge to get to Hampden. *Thump*, the pickup tires cross the meshed steel teeth binding Route 1 to the bridge, the vibration sending a sick ache through my arm. Gray girders fly by, railing streams past. I stare down into the Penobscot, daring it. *Come and get me.* The water's the color of rusty iron today, churning and boiling and paying no mind to Tommy Prentiss's youngest girl.

Hunt doesn't talk. He's probably the only person on the planet who wouldn't push for answers on this little joyride. I sit close to the door, blood roaring through my veins, knee jumping. At first, I think I'm psyching myself up. Maybe I'm glad this is finally happening. I'm gonna face it and end it, slay the dragon, like in that Saint George picture book Nell used to check out of the library when we were kids, running her fingertips over the drawings of the beautiful knight lying bleeding in his armor.

We drive through Frankfort and Winterport, and cross the Hampden town line. My nerves are on fire. Hunt slows to twenty-five. "Where do you need to go?"

"Irish Lane, up here on the left."

"Which house?"

"Just drop me at the store." He pulls into Chase's lot, and I can almost see Nell, half-hidden around the side of the building like she was that night, curled into herself like she'd been punched in the stomach. She'd lifted her hand to block the headlight glare, not recognizing the silver Fit until I honked. She got in slowly, like everything hurt, her shoulders shuddering and twitching. I'd never seen her cry like that. "I'll meet you back here."

"I'll wait."

I'm so cranked up that I have to clench my teeth to keep from snapping at him. "I'll be fine."

"I'll wait."

I know stubborn when I see it, so I turn and walk stiffly away down the sidewalk, sucking air in short bursts. Why can't your body remember how to breathe when you're scared?

I walk only a couple minutes before I recognize the place. Nell told me all about it sophomore year, back when the world revolved around Mr. Ellis, the drama coach and ed tech who helped Mrs. Hanscom out in the resource room. She grubbed every detail of his life, keeping them like a magpie hoarding shiny, precious things. Mr. Ellis lives in an apartment house in Hampden. Mr. Ellis is gonna get married, and it's gonna be beautiful. Mr. Ellis says I diagram sentences faster than anybody in class. Talk, talk, talk, till we all rolled our eyes and teased her about it. We should've known something was wrong when she went silent. *I* should've known.

His car's parked in the side lot. I picture him driving the half hour to our road once a week or so, sitting there in the dark, waiting for that fairy light to drift out to him. I stand on the sidewalk, hugging my good arm across my middle, looking up at all the windows. If Elise is home, I'm outta here. But there aren't any cars near his, and they'd probably park together. Most people do. I step over the curb onto the lawn.

The metal mailboxes fixed to the siding by each entrance

have numbers and names spelled out in reflective stickers. *#2 Ellis/Grindle.* There's green carpeting that looks like Easter basket grass covering the steps. My air slows to a trickle. I ring the bell.

Chimes play inside. I want the place to be empty, but somebody's coming.

Brad Ellis opens the door and we look at each other. He wears this half smile, looking tolerant, like he expects me to tell him I'm selling Christmas cards for the senior class fund. He must know who I am. Even if he didn't get a good look at me in the rain the other night, I used to wait for Nell at the resource room door before lunch all the time. Then it hits me. I'm standing on a teacher's doorstep, about to nail him to the wall. Christ on a crutch.

"I'm . . . Darcy." Mouth's too dry. "I go to Sasanoa?" Stupid. He knows that. "Nell's cousin." He keeps right on looking. "I need to talk to you."

He smiles, giving a puzzled tilt of his head, and steps back. "Sure. Come on in."

I figured I'd say it right here on the steps, tell him how it was gonna be, and then go. But he's waiting.

I slide past him into an entryway, passing a spindly little stand with a basket of potpourri on it under a sign reading *Home Is Where the ♥ Is.* I smell a pumpkin spice candle burning somewhere. I don't want to go any deeper and I stop, turning to him as he brushes by me into the next room.

Living room and kitchen, separated by an island. Nice leather furniture in the living room, more folksy decorations. "Take a seat," he says over his shoulder, walking around the island into the kitchen and pulling back a chair for me at the table.

I sink stiffly into it, knees angled out, fists in my lap. Should've stayed standing. The candle burns on the countertop, the jar smudged with soot. By the stove, some wrought-iron hangers dangle just-for-looks oven mitts. I don't get the point of that.

"Can I get you something to drink?" He moves the same as he did in school, quick and loose, kind of absentminded or something, like a poet or an artist. Maybe that's why he directs the plays. His hair's all over the place, brown and wavy and long enough to push back behind his ears, and he isn't dressed much differently than at school, either: light-blue oxford shirt untucked over khakis. But he's in his stocking feet. Gray argyles.

"No." What am I gonna do, sit at his table drinking iced tea? He must know why I'm here. I straighten my spine, but my voice doesn't sound right. "I'm gonna say this and then I'll go."

He looks back at me, kind of puzzled, kind of amused. "Okay." His brows are thick, his gray eyes intense, trying to give me the feeling that he's listening very closely to my every word.

"I know what you been doing with Nell." He doesn't blink. "You can't see her anymore. Or message her, or anything. I won't tell if you promise to leave her alone."

He gives his head a small shake. Still the smile. "What?"

"Stay away from her."

"Stay . . . ? What do you mean?"

Heat jets up into my face. I stare at him, out of words. When I swallow, it makes a click.

He sits back slowly, his hands loose on the table. He's not a big guy. Much shorter than Shea. He's maybe got an inch or two on Jesse, but slender, fine-boned. Probably ran cross-country or something when he was my age. "Nell was my student," he says slowly, like he wants to understand. "We haven't seen each other since I took the job at Hampden High. Am I missing something here?"

I work my lips over my teeth. My voice is hoarse. "You've been messing with her."

He blinks twice, quickly. He pushes back from the table, looking down at his stocking feet on the linoleum for a second. "Uh—wow. Darcy." He goes to the fridge and pulls out a carton of soy milk, leaving the door open as he reaches into the cupboard for a glass. "I think you're confused about some things."

I watch him pour a glass of milk and set it in front of me. "I think . . . Nell may have misconstrued what I said to her before I left SAHS. She was always one of the best kids we worked with in resource. Really special. And I told her so. I said we'd always be friends." Staring fixedly, he sits, putting his fingers to his temple and rubbing lightly. "Maybe I shouldn't have."

Disbelief crackles through me. I sit forward. "I *saw* you."

He presses his lips together, nodding. "Mm-hmm. What's happening here is coincidences and appearances adding up to look like something more. I . . . must've fed a need in Nell that I didn't realize was there. A crush." He looks at me with clear, startled eyes. "It's my fault. She sent me a friend request last year. I accepted it. I wasn't her teacher anymore. There was no ethical reason not to. I just . . . didn't know."

I've never seen lying like this. He's almost got me believing, questioning everything Nell told me as she cried, how she'd fibbed to Mags that night about wanting to go to the summer theater production of *Anne of Green Gables* happening at Hampden High School, how she'd said she was meeting a couple girls from drama class so Mags would drop her off there before going over to Will's house. How she'd walked to Irish Lane, up these steps, and rang the bell, because she'd decided she had to tell Brad that he couldn't get married because she loved him and he loved her, bursting with her pure and wonderful decision.

She'd told me how she'd fibbed to Libby so she'd pick her up late from play practice sophomore year because Brad had begged her for alone time. How he'd kissed her that first afternoon, and it led to fooling around in the prop closet, backstage, in his car, and twice in this apartment, in his bed, before Elise asked to move in and he'd told Nell that she had to step back and get some perspective. He'd made a commitment to Elise. That was a serious thing.

"It's really too bad." He shoves his hair back and it wings out over his left ear, the waves separating, making him look young. "I'm not so much worried about myself. The administration knows me. It shouldn't be difficult to explain the situation. But if people believe this story . . . well, you know how bad it will be for her. What people will say. It's not fair and it isn't right, but it's always, always harder on the girl. Nell doesn't need that kind of stigma hanging over her."

I can't decide if he's way smarter than me, a really good actor, or both. My mouth's open as I watch him slide sideways in his chair, hooking his arm over the back, frowning. "I'd hate to see it. There was this girl in the high school I went to. She made some . . . questionable decisions with a teacher, and . . ." A soft, bitter laugh. "Let's just say there were far-reaching consequences." He flicks his hand as if pushing the memory away, then says distractedly, "She ended up transferring. Drink your milk, Darcy."

In another room, a clock chimes. The kitchen's still, and we're even more still in it. My nose and throat are choked with cinnamon-spice. I look down at the milk I didn't want, off-white, in a dimpled glass.

I throw the glass. It slams against the cupboard doors under the sink, shattering, and milk sprays everywhere: cupboards, linoleum, a splash across the oven door. I look at it, breathing hard, then look at Brad, who's staring at the spot where the glass had been a second ago.

I get to my feet. Milk's still dripping. "If you mess with her again, I'll tell everybody." My voice is uneven, but it sounds like my own. "I swear I will."

He lifts his gaze to me, eyes half-lidded, his expression perfectly flat. Footsteps thump, and the front door opens with a scrabble of claws on hardwood. I turn to see Elise come in with the yellow Lab on a leash, both breathless. She sees me and smiles, her hair pulled back in a high ponytail, wearing shorts and running shoes. "Oh! Hi. I didn't know anybody was here." She glances at Brad, but he has a new face on now, one she's used to seeing. Her gaze goes straight to the puddle of milk and the broken glass on the floor.

I leave. Go past her, feeling the dog grab a quick sniff at my jeans, out the door into the shock of fresh air, surprised to see it's still daylight, it feels like I've been in there so long. I take the steps two at a time even though it sends sick jolts through my arm, and hit the sidewalk running. I'm Nell a year ago, running from him, from the words *I care about you, but* and *I can't hurt Elise this way, you have to understand* and finally *at least let me drive you, don't just leave, Nell, how are you going to get home—*

Hunt's truck is parked at the curb. He followed me—if I'd looked back even once, I would've seen him. Weak with relief, I climb in, shut the door, hit the lock, and let my head fall back against the seat. Hunt's asking me something over and over, but all I can do is breathe and wait for the darkness to stop spinning behind my eyelids.

TWENTY SEVEN

I START SCHOOL on Tuesday with a cast on my arm. The ER doctor said I'd fractured my radius. From Irish Lane, Hunt took me straight up to Eastern Maine Medical Center and stayed with me through it all; he did real good, too, considering he doesn't have any kids of his own. The nurse let me pick what color plaster I wanted. I went with hot pink.

So I'm back at SAHS, in the stink of dust and old books and horny kids and hot lunch. This place never changes. The freshmen still show up wearing stiff new jeans and hoodies and melt in the sweltering classrooms by ten a.m. The locker rooms are full of smoke, ditched butts unraveling in the toilet bowls. The hollow bounce of basketballs echoes down the hallway from the gym. And the flyers for the fall one-act play tryouts are everywhere I look. School sucks.

I've got study hall second period. I ask for a library pass so I won't have to sit around playing what-I-did-on-my-summer-vacay. I pass some kids in the hallway. "Cliff divah!" one of them calls, fist-bumping me. "Badass mofu."

I kind of smile, not remembering him being at the quarry, but whatever. Maddie's wasting time at the water fountain, and she gapes at my cast as I go by. "You broke your *arm*?" Sounding thrilled.

I get more stares and a devil-horns sign in the library before I drag out a chair at one of the long tables and drop into it. I'm not stupid. For every person who fist-bumps me, there's another two talking about what an ass I made of myself, how I had my tongue down Braden Mosier's throat. I got this whole place figured out, and it's a friggin' bore. Never thought I'd say this, but I'd rather be raking berries.

There's a stack of one-act play flyers on the table. They're doing *The Crucible* this year, directed by Mr. Brassbridge, the freshman English teacher. Nell will try out, get a part with a couple lines. Our family will go to opening night, and I'll sit there, trying not to picture Brad Ellis pressing Nell up against the backstage wall sophomore year, the two of them touching each other in the dark behind the scenery after everyone else had gone home. Wonder what he said to Elise about my visit. The milk on the floor would be easy enough, but the way I ran out—that would take some work. Not that I don't think he's up to it. Brad Ellis snows better than a January nor'easter. Scary-good.

"Darce. Heard about the quarry." Jake Curtis, my chemistry lab partner from last year, claps my back. "Nice."

I nod. The librarian's got her eye on me; she's pretty strict about your actually doing something like homework or reading while you're down here. I get up and wander over to the shelves under the windows, tugging out a couple yearbooks like Mags and I do when we're bored. I sit, leafing through last year's. Dedicated to Rhiannon, of course. Her picture looks back at me. Strange to think of her the way Kenyon knew her. Depressed. Messed up. Talking suicide if she couldn't get out of Sasanoa.

I open our sophomore yearbook, which was where I was headed all along. Brad Ellis, Ed Tech, looking perfectly nice in his photo, right next to Mrs. Hanscom, Special Education.

He pops up in some candids, too, kids hugging him, giving him bunny ears, having a tinfoil swordfight with a senior during a rehearsal. Forgot how popular he was. I close my eyes and see his mouth moving, telling me about this girl he knew, and far-reaching consequences. His slim forearms against the table. His hair looking soft and a little out-of-control, making him seem younger than he is, young enough so girls can fall in love with him.

I reach drama and pictures of *The Tempest*. Nell onstage

in a gauzy veil and leotard, her hair pinned up. The spring musical's next. They did *Tommy* that year. Nell doesn't do the musicals, even though she loves to sing; Libby keeps her to one play a year so she doesn't get behind in her schoolwork. There's a curtain-call shot, and when I see her, I have to lean so close that my nose touches the page, and even then, I'm still not sure who I'm looking at.

A girl who looks like Rhiannon peers out from between two seniors, half-bleached in light. Easy to miss with all the leads hogging the applause up front. Her hair's pulled back and it looks like she's all dressed in black, which is what stage crew wears. I never knew she did drama. She never did when we were friends.

There's no cast and crew list or anything, but there's a candid from the cast party of Mr. Ellis getting a bouquet of roses from everybody. He's smiling.

I sit back slowly, my mouth gone dry. Out in the hallway, some girl shrieks like she's being tickled. A mumbly teacher voice hushes her.

I could find out if Rhiannon worked on the crew of *Tommy* pretty easily. I could ask around. I don't really hang out with anybody who does drama except Nell, but she might know. Maybe she's known all along.

But she can't know all of it. Even with how she feels about Brad, I can't see her keeping quiet about this. I mean, if one plus one really equals two here.

Jesus. Even I can do that kind of math.

* * *

I go to lunch in a haze, passing the line for soggy pizza and tater tots.

Shea's sitting at the first table to the left, legs stretched out to take up a bunch of seats. Don't see his junior around. He sees me. His gaze goes to my cast, then travels up to my face, and he smirks as the guys around him bullshit and arm-wrestle and pay us no mind. A whole school year with him. Awesome.

"There she is." Kat climbs off a stool at a crowded table, touching my cast. "Holy shizz, I heard you busted some-thing. Everybody thought you were *dead*, man. Like straight to the bottom." She pulls me over to the table, pushing me down onto a stool. "You guys blind? Move over. Chick's hurt." She squeezes her bony butt in next to me and pushes a bag of chips my way. "Tell these losers you really did it. You jumped the quarry."

Everybody's asking me questions at once. A two-pack of cupcakes lands in my lap. I open the plastic with my teeth, letting them swap half-truths and whole lies, just eating my cupcakes and letting the whole story get bigger than life without even having to say a word. When I finally glance over at Shea, he's turned back to his buddies.

I'm the only senior riding the bus home. Humiliating. Nell never got on, so I guess Libby must've picked her up to make sure she came straight home.

The house is quiet as I dump my backpack on the floor and the mail on the table. No big fat bill from the hospital yet, but it's coming. Mom's still at work and Mags is out picking up applications for waitressing jobs. If she was speaking to me, I would've asked her to grab some for me, too.

I go upstairs to Mags's room and sit on her bed, resting the laptop on my knees. I stare at the screen. It's been so long since I actually wanted to get in touch with Rhiannon. I've deleted and unfriended her from every account I have.

Except my sent folder. I never clean that out. I scroll through practically every email I've ever sent. About two years back, early October, I hit a big chunk of replies to Rhiannon Foss. I open one and hit reply without looking at the message. I know what we were talking about. Those beautiful senior boys we thought we were in love with.

I sit staring at the blank email. *Are you alive? Are you ever going to read this?* It feels fake to begin with, "How are you?" For the longest time, I didn't care. Who knows if she even uses that account anymore; the email will probably bounce right back. Even if she gets it, there's a good chance she won't answer me anyway. Guess I've got nothing to lose.

I try to put myself in Rhiannon's shoes for once. Where would she go if she was hurt and messed up and needed to get away? I'd say Camp Mekwi, but a place like that wouldn't hide some runaway. Maybe her camp friends would, though. If she kept in touch with them. Maybe if one of them is older, has their own place, they might let her crash with them, and keep it a secret. Maybe that was who picked Rhiannon up from the barrens that night, and took her away from Sasanoa.

I type, *Did you leave because of him?*

The cursor blinks. I hit send.

Supper is painful. Nobody's talking, and Libby and Nell don't even come. I get the message, loud and clear. Nell can't be my friend anymore.

I stab at my food. The faucet drips. Another job for Hunt, but Libby isn't around to complain. He's almost done painting the house, only a small section near the roof left bare. I'll miss having him around. I want to ask Mags which restaurants are hiring, which places seem like you'd get the best tips, but I don't bother, not with her face looking like it belongs on Mount Rushmore.

Mom's got another headache. Her color's bad. She's eaten maybe three bites of food with her aspirin, coffee, and nicotine. When I get up and start filling the sink to wash dishes as best I can, she says, "Darcy—"

I jerk around. She looks at me for a second, her eyes flicking to my cast, then away. She taps ash into the tray. "Leave it."

I stand there, then slam the faucet closed and go upstairs, ignoring Dad in his frame, holding that little blond girl I hardly remember being.

They stay downstairs, clearing the table and pretending

I've fallen off the edge of the earth. I take the laptop out of Mags's room and bring it into mine, mostly to piss her off. If she wants it, she can come get it.

She doesn't. Two nights later, it's still there. I'm curled up in bed at seven thirty, dozing because I've got nothing better to do.

I wake up to the sound that the laptop makes when a new email pops up.

Holy crap.

The email stands out in bold. Sender Rhiannon Foss, no subject. It hits me hard: tight chest, eyes open so wide that they burn as I stare and stare. I'm scared of what she might say after all this time, after everything that's happened. I'm scared to feel what's coming next.

I double-click. There's no message. Only a link.

It brings me to a page on a poetry site. The poem's called "The Uses of Sorrow" by a lady named Mary Oliver:

> *(In my sleep I dreamed this poem)*
> *Someone I loved once gave me*
> *a box full of darkness.*
> *It took me years to understand*
> *that this, too, was a gift.*

I press my hand to my mouth. The words won't let me go. I see myself in them. I see the night of the boys waiting in their cars for us. I see Nell, and Mags, and the summer behind us. And beneath all that, like some underground stream, runs Brad Ellis.

I see Rhiannon standing in the cold that night after I got out of the Explorer, hands jammed in her pockets, her expression closed off to me. *I changed my mind.* Or maybe her feelings for somebody else had. Even before that, I hear her say, *Isn't she in special ed?* and then making sure we started hanging out at her house, far away from Nell.

That was freshman year. That far back? Had he been working on her longer than Nell, adding them both to his chain? Rhiannon wasn't in drama freshman year, but that didn't matter, not for him; he could've talked to her in the halls, planted the seeds, charmed her into turning out for stage crew the next year. Later, selling the whole *I don't want to hurt Elise, but I can't seem to get you out of my mind* thing? Had both she and Nell been trying to tell me in their silences, in their looks? Rhiannon, holding her car keys out to me, eyes deep wells in the firelight. Understanding everything. *Just take them.* And later, after I dropped Nell off at our house and took the Fit back to the barrens, I just left the keys in the car and went to find Kat, who was finally sober enough to drive me home. I never even told Rhiannon thanks. I never saw her again.

I make a soft sound, jerking away from the computer, leaving the bed. I'm in the hallway before I know it. My feet take me to the place I always go when I'm hurting.

Mags reads in bed, her glasses on the nightstand. I stand there in the doorway until she notices me, raises an eyebrow, and looks back at her book.

I bite my lip. "Mags." My voice wavers, and I take a couple steps in. She doesn't look up. "It's about Nell."

My face is in the lamplight now, and she finally gives me her full attention. Some of the hardness fades from her eyes. She lays her book down. "So talk."

It's bad. My words weave a long snarled string, tangling Mags into the mess Nell and I have spent a year making.

Her eyes go wide, her mouth goes grim. She shakes her head like she's got too many words to let out. At one point, she slams her fist against the wall, sending a hollow vibration through the upstairs. I wait, shoulders hunched, to see if she's going to pound me, take the hurt and anger out on me like I almost hope she will because we've beat each other up before, we know how to deal with that. Instead she stares dully at her hands. If she could make it better with her fists, she would. Out of all of us, it never should've been Nell.

"How could you not tell me this?" she finally whispers.

"Because you would've made us do something."

"Goddamn right."

"Like tell the school or the cops. Then everybody would've ripped Nell apart. You *know* they would've. She was seventeen when they did it, not some little kid. Everybody would say, there's the girl who slept with the teacher and got him fired. There goes that slut."

"So you were gonna just keep on swallowing it. Taking it on you. Letting us all think—" She cuts off. Then Mags's arm goes around me and holds on tight, so tight my shoulder pops. It feels good.

Finally, she says, "Come on," nudging me out of bed, leading me to the hallway.

Mom's watching her little bedroom TV in the dark, a pillow hugged under her arm, another behind her head. She sits up, her face watchful as we come in. Mags guides me, her hands on my shoulders.

The blue glow flickers and flashes across Mom as she takes us in. Then she reaches over and turns on the light.

TWENTY EIGHT

AROUND ONE O'CLOCK on Saturday, Edgecombe pulls up to our house, but he doesn't come in. He walks through the side yard to the trailer, a big guy with big strides and his hand hitched in his equipment belt. Mags and I are on the porch playing Whist. We like Hearts best, but like I said, you can't play with two people.

I go over to the railing, watching him walk up the trailer steps and knock. After a second, the door opens partway, and he goes in. I guess they've been waiting on him.

"We playing or what?" Mags doesn't take her eyes off her hand, holding our can of Moxie out for me to sip.

He's in there a long time. We play two more hands of

Whist and a full game of Spit, pretending to care about winning quarters and dimes.

They could've come to the station with us on Friday afternoon. Mom says it would've been better that way, if we'd all gone. But you can't make Libby do anything she doesn't want to do. And right now, she doesn't want anything to do with us.

Eventually, we hear the screech of the trailer door again. Mags goes with me to the railing. We're hoping to see Nell.

Edgecombe steps out into the daylight. I catch a whiff of Libby's hazelnut coffee on the air, picture her asking, *Cream or sugar?* and pushing a plate of of Nilla Wafers on him while Nell sits there, ripped wide open with all her most private parts on display. It was hard enough for me to talk about, and it really wasn't my story to tell.

Just walking across the station house to Edgecombe's desk felt like a journey. He sat over some paperwork and a steaming Colby College mug he must've brought from home. He didn't look smug, like I'd expected, or like he was going to give me some big lecture. There was heavy stuff going on behind his eyes. Almost like I'd proven something to him. I dunno, maybe that's stupid. He took us into a private room with folding chairs waiting for Mom, Mags, and me. When we were situated, he leaned forward, clasped his big hands, and said to me, "When you're ready."

Now he turns and says something quietly to Libby, who

comes out onto the step. She looks sick, washed-out and rumpled, like she slept in her clothes last night. Maybe I was wrong about the coffee and Nilla Wafers. Edgecombe puts a hand out and she gives it one stiff shake. He looks around her to speak to Nell. Keeping a grip on her shoulder, Libby lets Nell step out into the sunlight.

My heart gives this big leap at the sight of her, then shrinks back just as quick. You can see it in her face, a tightness that wasn't there before. She's grief-stricken, eyes swollen, standing with her hands behind her back, a little girl being good for Mom, but it's too late for that and there's no going back.

Edgecombe starts toward his cruiser. He sees me sitting on the railing, and, his eyes as grave as ever, gives me a nod. For Rhiannon, I guess. For telling him about the email and camp friends and giving him a place to start. We've put that to bed. For better or worse.

When I turn back, Nell's looking at me. Her light's been snuffed out as cleanly as a cup over a candle flame. I open my mouth to say something, but she's going now, pulled inside by Libby, who acts like she can't even see us. Maybe if I'd waved, Nell would've waved back. It's too hard to speak right now.

I end up on the swing, dragging one foot slowly over the rug. Mags plunks back on the floor and crackles the cards, using her mad shuffling skills to flash the matches by me, king-queen-jack, jack-queen-king. "Don't let them make you feel bad."

I pick at the fringe of my cutoffs. "Nell hates me."

"She does not. She's just all turned around." She frowns, chopping stacks together. "It was never your secret to keep."

The September day I meet Jesse at the quarry is clear and cool. I wear jeans and my fleece jacket, the left sleeve snug over my cast. I can hear the sound of Mags's engine fading away down the road behind me as I come out into the clearing and see him standing by some of the granite slabs, a backpack sitting at his feet. Behind him, the swamp maples are turning red; that's the first sign of the leaves changing every fall. Pretty soon this whole place will be fringed with orange and gold.

He turns when he hears my sneakers crunching over rock. He's wearing a gray hoodie, the usual beat-up jeans. "Hey," he says. "Thanks for coming."

"Sure." I don't have any brainstorms after that, so I scuff my foot back and forth. I don't feel as awkward as I thought I would, though, considering the last time I saw him, I bawled like a baby. Guess I know now that Jesse wouldn't laugh at me about something like that.

"How's the arm?"

"Itchy."

"I should've taken you to the ER that night."

"I wouldn't let you."

"Still." He looks at me for a second, then clears his throat, putting his hands in his pockets. "So what you been doing?"

"School. Work. Mags and I are waiting tables at the Harbor View." A nod. I don't tell him that I've been putting a little money away for after graduation, letting myself think about traveling, for real. Not sure where I want to go or how I'll get there. Guess I'll figure that out when the time comes. "So . . . are we out here because you heard?"

"I heard something. Figured it was bullshit." He sees it in my face and curses softly. "Sorry." A pause. "She's gonna have a rough time of it."

"She already is." I don't tell him about the ladies watching Mom and me and whispering at Hannaford. Or the kids yelling stuff at Nell from across the school parking lot, then taking off, tires squealing.

Three weeks ago, the Monday after Edgecombe came to the trailer, Nell sat down with Libby, Edgecombe, the Sasanoa superintendent, the principal, and the guidance counselor, and told them all what went on during her sophomore year and started up again this summer. Last week, Brad Ellis was suspended from his job at Hampden High School until further notice. The local news ran the story, keeping Nell's name out of it, but people are finding out anyway. One good thing that's come out of this is that Libby decided to let Nell ride the bus to school with me again. Guess she figures I'm a decent guard dog, if nothing else.

Nell's basically doing okay, considering. She's got Mags

and me. Mags bought her a little journal and some gel pens, and I see Nell writing in it all the time now, sitting with her legs tucked under her the way she used to when she played Matchmaker.

"They found Rhiannon yet?" Jesse says.

I shake my head. "At least her family knows she's alive. I hope that's what she wants. To be found."

"If she wanted to stay gone, all she had to do was keep her head down. Maybe she's ready to come back. Face everything."

I don't know how I feel about that. The idea of Rhiannon standing in front of me is like seeing somebody come back from the dead. I shake it off, put my hands in my back pockets, and wander in a figure eight around the rocks. "So why'd we need to come out here to talk?"

He doesn't answer right away, clearing his throat and looking down at the backpack. "'Cause. I been thinking about you a lot." He doesn't try to bury that in more words. I look back at him. He's got two flushed spots high on his cheekbones. "Missed you."

I stand there, feeling the rawness of his words.

He unzips the backpack. "Made you something."

I walk over to get a better look. He's takes out a metal tin. Inside is a circle of wood, a section cut from the trunk of a young birch. The bark's been stripped, and it's been sanded so smooth it almost looks like bone. On the face, he's carved

DP and JB. No heart, no plus sign, nothing like that. Just our initials together. The letters have been deeply, carefully worked in with a jackknife. The bottom of the tin is weighted with stones.

"Remember how you said it would be cool to put something in the quarry in case they ever drain the place, so people knew we were here?"

I take it and run my fingertips over the letters. "Like a time capsule."

"Yeah. I thought" —he shoves roughly at his hair, looking at the ledge—"I dunno, we could drop it down there." He laughs a little. "Make them wonder who we were someday."

I take the carving out and bring it close to my face, smelling the wood, blinking at the sting in my eyes.

"If you don't want to . . ."

"No. I do." I go to the ledge, taking a deep breath. I picture myself going over again, the dark water hurtling up to meet me, and vertigo makes me take a step back. Even though it's almost too nice to let go of, I seal the tin, hold out my hands, and let go, watching it fall all the way down to the splash.

We're quiet. His hand touches the back of my head, his fingers smoothing through my hair and holding it, loosely. I close my eyes.